Alfred H. Baumann
Free Public Library
7 Brophy Lane
Woodland Park, NJ 07424-2799

D1266306

CO-EDITED BY BARBARA RODEN

———

Acquainted with the Night
At Ease with the Dead
Midnight Never Comes
Shades of Darkness
Shadows and Silence

NORTHWEST PASSAGES

Barbara Roden

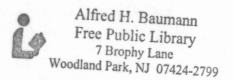

Alfred H. Baumann
Free Public Library
7 Brophy Lane
Woodland Park, NJ 07424-2799

PRIME BOOKS

NORTHWEST PASSAGES

—

Copyright © 2009 by Barbara Roden.
Introduction © 2009 by Michael Dirda.
Cover art by Elodie Bailly / Lizard / Rolffimages.
Cover design by Stephen H. Segal.

Prime Books
www.prime-books.com

Publisher's Note:
No portion of this book may be reproduced by any means, mechanical,
electronic, or otherwise, without first obtaining the permission of the
copyright holder.

For more information, contact Prime Books.

ISBN: 978-1-60701-205-4 (trade)
ISBN: 978-1-60701-206-5 (lettered)

CONTENTS

———

INTRODUCTION
Michael Dirda

THERE ARE THREE QUALITIES to Barbara Roden's *Northwest Passages* that any reader is sure to notice: the sheer variety of its ten stories, the clarity and assurance of the prose, and the theme of madness, of people gradually surrendering to a fever-dream that destroys, or justifies, their lives.

Roden most obviously reveals her mastery by setting her unsettling stories in a wide range of locales: a used bookstore, the Antarctic, a Vancouver hotel, a cabin in the Canadian woods, an abandoned amusement park, a modern hospital, a large Victorian household. There are, moreover, seemingly no limits to her imaginative sympathies, as these stories convincingly present elderly widows and widowers, abused children, contemporary young people, nineteenth century visionaries, serial killers, and even a world-weary vampire. Roden also possesses an accomplished talent for pastiche: she brilliantly mimics nineteenth century scientific tracts, the diary of an early Antarctic explorer, and the old-fashioned diction of the polite and diabolical Mr. Hobbes. When Roden cites passages from Kenneth Turnbull's *We Did Not All Come Back: Polar Explorers, 1818–1909,* both book and extracts sound absolutely authentic. She's that good.

Besides these gifts, one other aspect to Roden's imagination should be underscored. Along with a flair for creating atmosphere and feelings of increasing apprehension, her work is consistently pervaded by a quiet sadness about the human condition. Monsters and murderers, the innocent and the guilty, are all presented with real sympathy and understanding. There but for the grace of God, Roden would seem to say, go you or I.

Because all her stories, whatever their plots or backgrounds, are distinctly Rodenesque in that mix of pathos and uneasiness, they don't fit readily into any of the classic genre pigeonholes. Roden draws, as needed, on fantasy and horror, classic ghost story and dark psychological thriller. In this respect, she's in the tradition of the more subtle masters of the supernatural tale: Walter de la Mare, for instance, and Elizabeth Bowen. As the longtime editor of *All Hallows*, the journal of The Ghost Story Society, Roden has certainly read more dark fantasy and horror than most of us ever will, and you might expect her to produce tales in the manner of M. R. James. Yet her literary taste is far more extensive. She knows the corpus of Victorian fiction, especially Dickens (see, for instance, "The Appointed Time"), as well as the Sherlock Holmes canon (Roden is a member of the Baker Street Irregulars), the literature of Arctic and Antarctic exploration, a good deal of modern literature, and, seemingly, every film ever made.

In particular, Roden deeply admires *The Strange Last Voyage of Donald Crowhurst*, and that book may be a key to her imagination. In its pages, Nicholas Tomalin and Ron Hall re-create, from journals and other evidence, how Crowhurst, attempting to sail alone around the world, gradually loses his grip on reality and succumbs to madness, then suicide. Its influence— along with that of Poe—can be most strongly detected in "The Brink of Eternity". Still other Roden stories glancingly recall Arthur Conan Doyle's "The Captain of the *Pole-Star*", Algernon Blackwood's "The Wendigo", Ray Bradbury's tales of haunted or demonic carnivals, the urban horrors of Ramsey Campbell and the early Peter Straub. The last story in *Northwest Passages*, "After", is a double homage: to both the strange Constance Kent murder case and to James Hogg's chilling, and still underappreciated, *Memoirs and Confessions of a Justified Sinner*.

Of these ten stories, "Northwest Passage" is probably the best known, having been nominated for the World Fantasy Award. "The Palace", a real marvel, offers a highly original explanation for why its victim should be haunted by just these three revenants. Indeed, the psychology of her characters interests Roden as much

as the working out of a plot. The two stories about young girls—
"The Hiding Place" and "After"—frighten by the convincingness
of the girls' inner lives. A personal favourite, if only because of
its wintry melancholy, is "Endless Night"—a tale that blends
the mythology of undying vampires, the Wandering Jew, and
Frankenstein's abused monster. It also makes brilliant use of
that unnerving phenomenon mentioned by T. S. Eliot in one
of his notes for *The Waste Land*: "It was related that the party
of explorers, at the extremity of their strength, had the constant
delusion that there was *one more member* than could actually be
counted."

Northwest Passages is Barbara Roden's first collection, all but
one of the stories having been written during the last three or
four years. Yet, as I've emphasised, the collection avoids even the
least hint of sameyness. One looks forward to each successive
story with eagerness, never quite sure what to expect. Yet they all
fit unobtrusively together as ten facets of a single and singularly
elegant imagination.

Any reader of *Northwest Passages* will be eager for more
Barbara Roden. Happily, there are a number of as yet uncollected
stories out there—for instance, "Association Copy" in *Bound
for Evil*, edited by Tom English—and new ones should be
appearing soon in various anthologies. Lately, there have even
been rumors about a possible novel. Be that as it may, Barbara
Roden's *Northwest Passages* is an altogether masterly collection,
proof that a writer with truly scary talent is at work in Ashcroft,
British Columbia.

THE APPOINTED TIME

It is night in Lincoln's Inn—perplexed and troublous valley of the shadow of the law, where suitors generally find but little day—and fat candles are snuffed out in offices, and clerks have rattled down the crazy wooden stairs, and dispersed. The bell that rings at nine o'clock, has ceased its doleful clangor about nothing; the gates are shut; and the night-porter, a solemn warder with a mighty power of sleep, keeps guard in his lodge.

HENRY ANDERSON LOOKED UP from his book with a start. A noise had caught his ear; something outside the normal range of sounds that he had, after more than thirty years in the shop, come to know and expect and even, at times—especially lately—welcome. It was a thin, dusty sound, almost a sigh, and Henry glanced behind him, half-expecting to see a figure standing over his shoulder. Impossible; there had not been a customer in the shop for at least an hour, and he was all too aware that the apartment behind was painfully empty.

He kept his head up for another moment, listening. Around him stood row upon row of books, which seemed to be listening, too; holding their collective breath, watching, waiting, as if in anticipation of something which was hovering just outside Henry's vision. As indeed it was, had Henry but known; had he, as he gazed about him, been able to see beyond the front wall, into the street, where a figure stood, wrapped in evening shadows, its whole attention fixed on the dim light spilling out of the door of the shop.

In the ordinary course of things, Henry would have had the shop closed and locked now, the lights extinguished; but he had become engrossed in his book, and lost track of time. This was by no means unusual with Henry, and on most evenings no harm would have come of it. But this was an evening unlike any other in his life, although he did not yet know it. And so, after assuring himself that all was well inside the shop, his head dipped irresistibly back down towards his book, and the light continued to shine out into the damp streets, a lone beacon in an otherwise dark stretch of shops. And outside, the figure, after a moment of hesitation, drew nearer.

This was not the figure's usual habitat; it was used to more garish surroundings, louder streets. Chance had taken it further afield than usual, and in this unaccustomed environment it was cautious, wary. But cold and hunger and other, darker needs spurred it on, drawing it inexorably, inevitably closer to Henry and his quiet, tidy world.

It is a close night, though the damp cold is searching too; and there is a laggard mist a little way up in the air. It is a fine steaming night to turn the slaughter-houses, the unwholesome trades, the sewerage, bad water, and burial grounds to account, and give the Registrar of Deaths some extra business.

The noise again, louder this time. Henry's head jerked up, and he cocked it on one side, trying to determine what the sound was and where it came from. It had definitely sounded like a sigh; no mistaking it. It was followed by a silence which sounded expectant, as if awaiting some action on his part at which he could not guess.

Perhaps, thought Henry, it was time to start thinking about selling up and moving on. He *had* thought about it before; he and Mary had discussed it before she died, but lightly, as something that would not happen for a good many years yet. Then for some time he had not thought about very much of anything, selling the shop least of all. He had kept it going because *not* keeping it going had seemed unthinkable, another blow to the fabric of his life which would have been unbearable. Mary and the shop had been part of him for so long that to lose both would have been to lose every reason he had for getting up in the morning.

So he had clung to the shop, finding a kind of solace in the ordered ranks of books in their neatly labelled sections. It had not always been thus. When he had first bought the shop it had been little better than a junk-heap, a dispirited shambles of discarded, unwanted books, and he had had to spend a good deal of time patiently weeding out the multiple copies of battered paperbacks, their broken spines and chipped covers an affront to his notion of what books should be. Slowly he had built up a quietly successful bookstore, filled with the sorts of books he liked reading, all lovingly tended, neatly shelved, easily accessible. The shop itself attracted a loyal group of regular and semi-regular customers, who found a safe and companionable haven amongst the shelves and racks, a friendly and knowledgeable proprietor in Henry. "It's Mary's cookies people come for, really," he would say with a smile, and it was true that the plate of cookies put out every morning by the coffee machine had always been empty by day's end, the crushed cushions on the comfortable armchairs bearing silent witness to those who had found a home there. The cookies were from a box now, but the customers still came.

Outside the rain continued to drizzle, stretching damp fingers along the sidewalk. The figure in the shadows shivered, and gazed greedily at the light from the shop. It drew nearer still, eyes fixed on the door. The sound of a car in a nearby street caused it to hesitate, and draw back from the light momentarily; and that pause bought Henry Anderson a few more moments of life.

"It is a tainting sort of weather," says Mr Snagsby; "and I find it sinking to the spirits."

"By George! I find it gives me the horrors," returns Mr Weevle.

"Then, you see, you live in a lonesome way, and in a lonesome room, with a black circumstance hanging over it," says Mr Snagsby, looking in past the other's shoulder along the dark passage, and then falling back a step to look up at the house. "I couldn't live in that room alone, as you do, sir. I should get so fidgetty and worried of an

evening, sometimes, that I should be driven to come to the door, and stand here, sooner than sit there."

The sound had become louder, as if uttered by someone—or something—that was gaining strength, rallying for one supreme effort. The cry—for it *was* a cry, no doubt of it—startled Henry so much that he pulled himself out of his chair with a suddenness that made the bones and joints in his legs and back protest at the effort. He walked around the desk and peered into the depths of the shop, while his mind tried and failed to analyse and define the exact nature of the sound. He was forced back to his first, instinctive thought: a cry, and of pain, too. No; not pain, exactly: the *expectation* of pain, as of someone who cried out in anticipation of a cruel blow.

He shook his head. Definitely time to start thinking seriously about selling up, moving out, going somewhere warmer and drier. He was getting too old to manage the shop on his own, and the trade was changing too fast for him to keep up. Every day, it seemed, people asked him when he was going to take his stock on-line, and he would shake his head and say ruefully, "Ah, well, you can't teach an old dog new tricks." Now, standing in the familiar quiet of the shop, he shook his head again. "Old dog?" he muttered under his breath. "Old dinosaur, more like. Hearing things, too. What would Mary say?"

And yet the thought of leaving the shop, turning it over to another person, closing the door behind him forever, was one that he persisted in putting off. There were too many memories bound up within the four walls, jostling for space on the shelves, surrounding every bookcase, each piece of furniture. The armchairs, now; they were not the height of fashion, never had been—"But Mary, they're *comfortable*," he had said when he brought them back, and she had surveyed them with a look half-tolerant, half-exasperated. She had had the same look on her face every time Henry, faced with a need to create more space, had brought back another bookcase, discovered at a sale or in the dusty recesses of a used furniture shop. "If your goal was to not have any two bookcases in the shop matching, Henry," she had said once, "then you've certainly succeeded." But there was a smile on her face as she said it.

Henry smiled at the memory. Yes, the shop was full of memories, and he could laugh at most of them. "If these walls— no, if these *books* could speak," he thought, "they would certainly tell a tale or two!"

He glanced out the front window, vaguely surprised to see how dark it was. Time to close up for the night; more than time, in fact. Lock the doors, turn out the lights, then go and make some dinner, listen to the news, read for a time. A night like any other. But this was not to be a night like any other.

Had he gone to the door even then, he might have been in time, for the figure outside was still hesitating in the shadows, and the sight of Henry at the door, pulling down the blinds, turning the lock, would have been enough to send it scuttling back into the darkness. But he paused, and stretched, trying to relieve the ache in his back; and he was lost.

"Seems a Fate in it, don't there?" suggests the stationer.
"There does."
"Just so," observes the stationer, with his confirmatory cough.
"Quite a Fate in it. Quite a Fate."

At the sound of the door opening and shutting, Henry turned so quickly that his back gave a more violent spasm than before, causing him to draw his breath in sharply. A swift glance took in the—no, not customer, this was no customer come late, this was Trouble with a capital T, right here in his shop. Be calm, think, think, *think.* . . .

"Yes? What can I do for you?" He tried to make his voice sound curt, no-nonsense, but Henry was not used to being curt, and his voice wavered slightly. The figure moved forward, and Henry could see it more clearly. A youngish man, unruly dark hair framing a sullen face, a cheap imitation leather jacket zipped up to his chin, one hand visible, the other balled up in a pocket, clutching—what? Henry realised he did not want to know.

"What can you do for me? What can you do?" said the other, as if seriously pondering the question. "I'll tell you what you can do, old man—you can give me any money you've got, and quick, too, 'cause I don't like having to ask for things more than once."

Henry thought quickly, weighing his options. *What options?* said a voice in his head. *Don't try to be a hero. Give him what he wants and maybe he'll leave.* "All right, yes, money, by all means," he said, trying to keep the fear out of his voice. "I don't have much, but you can take it all, yes . . . " He moved to walk around the desk, and the other man stepped forward, closing the distance between them so suddenly that Henry pulled back.

"No tricks, old man," whispered the intruder. "See? I don't like tricks, and neither does my friend." He withdrew the hand that had been in his pocket, and Henry saw the gleam of a knife blade as it caught a ray of light from overhead. "Just move nice and slow."

Henry nodded. "The cash—I keep it there." He gestured towards the desk.

"Get it, then." The intruder's eyes left Henry for a moment and swept around the shop. "Anyone else here?"

"No. No one. I live by myself," said Henry, profoundly grateful—*I'm sorry, Mary*—that this was true.

"Great. Get the money, then."

"Yes." Henry moved behind the desk to the cash register and fumbled at the keys with fingers which seemed to have grown stiff and useless. *How does this thing open . . . please, please . . . let it be all right, oh, let it be all right . . .*

"Come on, old man, stop jerking me around. I don't have all day."

"No . . . yes, yes, I'm trying . . . just be a minute . . . "

"I don't *have* a minute!" the other exploded, thrusting himself across the desk so that he was inches away from Henry's trembling frame. "Aren't you listening?" He moved his hand so that the knife was between them. "I want that money *now*, old man, or I'll use this!" He grabbed Henry's shirt, pulling him halfway across the desk; and Henry, feeling himself losing his balance, flailed his arms, trying to stop himself from falling. One of his hands caught the intruder's arm; not a blow, not by any stretch, but unexpected, and feeling himself threatened the intruder lashed out, sending Henry reeling backwards, hands to his throat, staring uncomprehendingly at the redness which was covering them, covering his shirt, covering everything, even his eyes, which were straining into darkness, straining, trying to see, trying—and then there was silence, and Henry Anderson saw and heard no more.

Both sit silent, listening to the metal voices, near and distant, resounding from towers of various heights, in tones more various than their situations. When these at length cease, all seems more mysterious and quiet than before. One disagreeable result of whispering is, that it seems to evoke an atmosphere of silence, haunted by the ghosts of sound—strange cracks and tickings, the rustling of garments that have no substance in them, and the tread of dreadful feet, that would leave no mark on the sea-sand or the winter snow.

The intruder stood stock-still on his side of the desk, his chest heaving as with some great physical effort. He could see part of Henry's body, lying on its side where it had fallen, and he watched it for any movement, any sign of life. There was none. The job had been done well. The knife was still in his hand, and he gazed at it dispassionately. A box of tissues stood on a corner of the desk, and he took out a handful and wiped the blade off before placing the knife back in his pocket. He looked at the body again, his mind working as his breath came more easily and he found that he could think with something approaching clarity.

First he moved to the door, locking it and pulling down the blind, unconsciously carrying out the very actions which would have saved Henry's life. Then he returned to the desk and stood looking round the shop thoughtfully. Various bays formed by the arrangement of bookshelves stretched down both walls, all neatly labelled with signs hanging above them describing the books to be found therein. In the middle of the shop were a few armchairs, surrounding a small table which contained a coffee maker and a plate of cookies. The intruder helped himself to a handful of cookies and made a more thorough survey of the shop.

A door at the back caught his eye, and he made his way towards it, alert and cautious. The old man had said there was no one else there, but you never knew . . . He opened the door carefully, and saw a short hallway leading to what appeared to be a kitchen. A staircase, its upper reaches in darkness, led to the next floor.

He remembered Henry's words. *I live by myself.* The old man must have an apartment behind the shop, then! This was getting better and better. He'd be able to get the cash out of the register, have a good look round the apartment—there must be stuff worth taking from there, too—fix himself something to eat and drink, maybe even wait out the rain, before being on his way long before anyone discovered something wrong. What a stroke of luck!

A sound behind him in the shop made him jump, and he whirled around, knife at the ready.

Nothing.

He moved swiftly back towards the desk and looked at Henry. The body had not moved. The intruder turned his attention to the cash register, and in a matter of seconds had it open. He cleared out the contents, stuffing the money into his pockets, then looked to see if there was anything else worth having.

A book lay open on the desk. He flicked it shut and looked at the cover. *Bleak House* by Charles Dickens. The old man wouldn't be reading *that* again anytime soon.

Another noise disturbed him; this one came from the back of the shop, and for a moment he thought that someone had come through the door from the apartment, for a shadow seemed to pass lightly into one of the bays. He moved along the shop and peered between the shelves. There was no one there.

More sound; this time from the front of the shop. The intruder whirled around, and again thought he saw a shadow pass into one of the bays, this one near the window. He narrowed his eyes, peering through the gloomy shop. Was it his imagination, or were the lights getting dimmer?

"As to dead men, Tony," proceeds Mr Guppy, evading this proposal, "there have been dead men in most rooms."

"I know there have; but in most rooms you let them alone, and— and they let you alone," Tony answers.

Of course there was no one there when he reached the front of the shop. The door was locked tight, and no one could have come in through the door at the back without being seen. The intruder shrugged his shoulders and tried to laugh. Crazy. Imagining things. That's what it was. All these books, lined up, watching him, waiting . . .

Waiting! That was good. Waiting for what? He shook his head, then went back to the plate of cookies for another handful, as if to prove that he wasn't afraid, there was nothing to be afraid *of*, just a dead guy behind the desk and *he* wasn't going anywhere, wasn't going to be calling for any help, there wasn't even anyone to call except a load of books, and what help could they be? As if to prove his point he moved to the desk (although he was careful not to look too closely at Henry's body) and picked up the copy of *Bleak House*, gazing at it with contempt for a moment before flinging it to the back of the shop, where it fell with a flutter and crash.

And, mingled with these sounds, a cry, as of pain.

The intruder's head swivelled round, trying to locate the source of the cry. It sounded as if—*this was crazy*—as if it had come from the book. He moved through the shop towards the book, which was lying face up on the floor. He moved closer, almost against his will, looking to see if perhaps the book had hit something—*a pet of some kind, was there an animal in the shop?*—and touched the book gingerly, almost delicately, with his foot. It was just a book.

Mr Guppy takes the light. They go down, more dead than alive, and holding one another, push open the door of the back shop. The cat has retreated close to it, and stands snarling—not at them; at something on the ground, before the fire.

Another sound, behind him. He whirled around, eyes trying to adjust to the dimness—*there must be something wrong with the lights*—as a figure moved in front of the door and disappeared behind a bookshelf in a curious gliding motion. The intruder stared, heart pounding. *The old man had said he was alone.* How could anyone else be there? It wasn't possible. There was no one else in the shop; just him and a dead man, and a load of old books. No one else.

A murmur came from behind him, halfway along the shop, in a bay labelled—he could barely make out the sign, so dark had it become—*Literature*. There was an answering murmur—or so it seemed to the intruder—from a bay on the other side of the shop, this one labelled *Children's*. A dim memory stirred within him, and he was reminded of a time, impossibly long ago in what seemed another life, when he had played hide-and-seek, and had tried to track down those hiding by listening for the tell-tale signs of giggles and whispers. He could almost imagine people hiding behind the bookshelves, breath held, trying not to give themselves away, watching him to see what he would do.

"Who's there?" he called out roughly. "Come on out, where I can see you. Come on!"

No answer. But there was movement. He could sense it, rather than see it, as if shadows were massing behind the shelves, dark clouds of movement, full of purpose. His head swivelled from side to side, trying to pin down the danger, define it, attack it. His hand clenched the knife, poised in front of him, ready to strike.

A small sigh behind him, at the back of the shop. He twisted round, every nerve alert, ready to face whoever—*whatever*—had come in.

They advance slowly, looking at all these things. The cat remains where they found her, still snarling at the something on the ground, before the fire and between the two chairs. What is it? Hold up the light?

It was a boy. The intruder could see little of him, apart from the fact that he looked thin and pale. He was holding something; a funny sort of broom. *The old man's grandkid, come downstairs to see what's up.* A wave of relief washed over him. A kid with a broom: pathetic. He could deal with this, no problem. He put the hand with the knife behind his back and adopted a sickly, wheedling tone.

"Hey, kid, sorry you were bothered, okay? Me and your granddad were just talking about business; you know, business—nothing for you to worry about, so why don't you just . . . "

The boy wasn't listening to him; wasn't even looking at him. He was looking at something else, something behind him. The intruder turned around, and stared in disbelief at the figures moving towards him. *It couldn't be . . . it wasn't possible . . . it was just him and a dead man and a load of old books, for Christ's sake . . . nothing else . . .*

There was something wrong with them; something which his brain tried to comprehend even as he moved backwards, unaware of the figures advancing towards him from the rear of the shop, led by the child with the broom. The clothing—they looked like figures from old movies, or from pictures in books.

Help, help, help! Come into this house, for Heaven's sake!
Plenty will come in, but none can help.

ENDLESS NIGHT

"Thank you so much for speaking with me. And for these journals, which have never seen the light of day. I'm honoured that you'd entrust them to me."

"That's quite all right." Emily Edwards smiled; a delighted smile, like a child surveying an unexpected and particularly wonderful present. "I don't receive very many visitors; and old people do like speaking about the past. No"—she held up a hand to stop him—"I *am* old; not elderly, not 'getting on', nor any of the other euphemisms people use these days. When one has passed one's centenary, 'old' is the only word which applies."

"Well, your stories were fascinating, Miss Edwards. As I said, there are so few people alive now who remember these men."

Another smile, gentle this time. "One of the unfortunate things about living to my age is that all the people one knew in any meaningful or intimate way have died; there is no one left with whom I can share these things. Perhaps that is why I have so enjoyed this talk. It brings them all back to me. Sir Ernest; such a charismatic man, even when he was obviously in ill-health and worried about money. I used to thrill to his stories; to hear him talk of that desperate crossing of South Georgia Island to Stromness, of how they heard the whistle at the whaling station and knew that they were so very close to being saved, and then deciding to take a treacherous route down the slope to save themselves a five-mile hike when they were near exhaustion. He would drop his voice then, and say to me 'Miss Emily'—he always called me Miss Emily, which was the name of his wife, as you know; it made me feel very grown-up, even though I was only eleven—'Miss Emily, I do not know how we did it.

Yet afterwards we all said the same thing, those three of us who made that crossing: that there had been another with us, a secret one, who guided our steps and brought us to safety.' I used to think it a very comforting story, when I was a child, but now—I am not as sure."

"Why not?"

For a moment he thought that she had not heard. Her eyes, which until that moment had been sharp and blue as Antarctic ice, dimmed, reflecting each of her hundred-and-one years as she gazed at her father's photograph on the wall opposite. He had an idea that she was not even with him in her comfortable room, that she was instead back in the parlour of her parents' home in north London ninety years earlier, listening to Ernest Shackleton talk of his miraculous escape after the sinking of the *Endurance*, or her father's no less amazing tales of his own Antarctic travels. He was about to get up and start putting away his recording equipment when she spoke.

"As I told you, my father would gladly speak about his time in Antarctica with the Mawson and Shackleton expeditions, but of the James Wentworth expedition aboard the *Fortitude* in 1910 he rarely talked. He used to become quite angry with me if I mentioned it, and I learned not to raise the subject. I will always remember one thing he *did* say of it: 'It was hard to know how many people were there. I sometimes felt that there were too many of us.' And it would be frightening to think, in that place where so few people are, that there was another with you who should not be."

The statement did not appear to require an answer, for which the thin man in jeans and rumpled sweater was glad. Instead he said, "If you remember anything else, or if, by chance, you should come across those journals from the 1910 expedition, please do contact me, Miss Edwards."

"Yes, I have your card." Emily nodded towards the table beside her, where a crisp white card lay beside a small ceramic tabby cat, crouched as if eyeing a mouse in its hole. Her gaze rested on it for a moment before she picked it up.

"I had this when I was a child; I carried it with me everywhere.

It's really a wonder that it has survived this long." She gazed at it for a moment, a half-smile on her lips. "Sir Ernest said that it put him in mind of Mrs. Chippy, the ship's cat." Her smile faded. "He was always very sorry, you know, about what he had to do, and sorry that it caused an estrangement between him and Mr. McNish; he felt that the carpenter never forgave him for having Mrs. Chippy and the pups shot before they embarked on their journey in the boats."

"It was rather cruel, though, wasn't it? A cat, after all; what harm could there have been in taking it with them?"

"Ah, well." Emily set it carefully back down on the table. "I thought that, too, when I was young; but now I see that Sir Ernest was quite right. There was no room for sentimentality, or personal feeling; his task was to ensure that his men survived. Sometimes, to achieve that, hard decisions must be made. One must put one's own feelings and inclinations aside, and act for the greater good."

He sensed a closing, as of something else she might have said but had decided against. No matter; it had been a most productive afternoon. At the door Emily smiled as she shook his hand.

"I look forward to reading your book when it comes out."

"Well"—he paused, somewhat embarrassed—"it won't be out for a couple of years yet. These things take time, and I'm still at an early stage in my researches."

Emily laughed; a lovely sound, like bells chiming. "Oh, I do not plan on going anywhere just yet. You must bring me a copy when it is published, and let me read again about those long ago days. The past, where everything has already happened and there can be no surprises, can be a very comforting place when one is old."

It was past six o'clock when the writer left, but Emily was not hungry. She made a pot of tea, then took her cup and saucer into the main room and placed it on the table by her chair, beside the ceramic cat. She looked at it for a moment, and ran a finger down its back as if stroking it; then she picked up the card and considered it for a few moments.

"I think that I was right not to show him," she said, as if speaking to someone else present in the room. "I doubt that he would have understood. It is for the best."

Thus reminded, however, she could not easily forget. She crossed the room to a small rosewood writing desk in one corner, unlocked it, and pulled down the front panel, revealing tidily arranged cubbyholes and drawers of various sizes. With another key she unlocked the largest of the drawers, and withdrew from it a notebook bound in leather, much battered and weathered, as with long use in difficult conditions. She returned with it to her armchair, but it was some minutes before she opened it, and when she did it was with an air almost of sadness. She ran her fingers over the faded ink of the words on the first page.

Robert James Edwards
Science Officer
H.M.S. *Fortitude*
1910–11

"No," she said aloud, as if continuing her last conversation, "there can be no surprises about the past; everything there has happened. One would like to think it happened for the best; but we can never be sure. And *that* is not comforting at all." Then she opened the journal and began to read from it, even though the story was an old one which she knew by heart.

ဆ ၷ

20 November 1910: A relief to be here in Hobart, on the brink of starting the final leg of our sea voyage. The endless days of fundraising, organisation, and meetings in London are well behind us, and the Guvnor is in high spirits, and as usual has infected everyone with his enthusiasm. He called us all together this morning, and said that of the hundreds upon hundreds of men who had applied to take part in the expedition when it was announced in England, we had been hand-picked, and that everything he has seen on the journey thus far has reinforced the rightness of his choices; but that the true test is still to come—in the journey across the great Southern Ocean and along the uncharted coast of Antarctica. We shall be seeing sights that no human has yet viewed and will, if all goes to plan, be in a position to furnish exact information which will be of inestimable value to those who come after us. Chief among this information will be noting locations where future parties can establish camps, so that they might use these as bases for exploring the great heart of this unknown land, and perhaps even establishing a preliminary base for Mawson's push, rumoured to be taking place in a year's time. We are not tasked with doing much in the way of exploring ourselves, save in the vicinity of any base we do establish, but we have the dogs and sledges to enable us at least to make brief sorties into that mysterious continent, and I think that all the men are as eager as I to set foot where no man has ever trodden.

Of course, we all realise the dangers inherent in this voyage; none more so than the Guvnor, who today enjoined anyone who had the least doubt to say so now, while there was still an opportunity to leave. Needless to say, no one spoke, until Richards gave a cry of "Three cheers for the *Fortitude*, and all who sail in her!"; a cheer which echoed to the very skies, and set the dogs barking on the deck, so furiously that the Guvnor singled out Castleton and called good-naturedly, "Castleton, quiet your dogs down, there's a good chap, or we shall have the neighbours complaining!", which elicited a hearty laugh from all.

22 November: Such a tumultuous forty-eight hours we have not seen on this voyage, and I earnestly hope that the worst is now behind us. Two days ago the Guvnor was praising his hand-picked crew, and I, too, was thinking how our party had pulled together on the trip from Plymouth, which boded well, I thought, for the trials which surely face us; and now we have said farewell to one of our number, and made room for another. Chadwick, whose excellent meals brightened the early part of our voyage, is to be left in Hobart following a freakish accident which none could have foreseen, he having been knocked down in the street by a runaway horse and cart. His injuries are not, thank Heaven, life threatening, but are sufficient to make it impossible for him to continue as part of the expedition.

It is undoubtedly a very serious blow to the fabric of our party; but help has arrived in the form of Charles De Vere, who was actually present when the accident occurred, and was apparently instrumental in removing the injured man to a place of safety following the incident. He came by the ship the next day, to enquire after Chadwick, and was invited aboard; upon meeting with the Guvnor he disclosed that he has, himself, worked as a ship's cook, having reached Hobart in that capacity. The long and the short of it is that after much discussion, the Guvnor has offered him Chadwick's place on the expedition, and De Vere has accepted.

"Needs must when the devil drives," the Guvnor said to me, somewhat ruefully, when De Vere had left to collect his things. "We can't do without a cook. Ah well, we have a few days more here in Hobart, and shall see how this De Vere works out."

What the Guvnor did not add—but was, I know, uppermost in his mind—is that a few days on board a ship at dockside is a very different proposition to what we shall be facing once we depart. We must all hope for the best.

28 November: We are set to leave tomorrow; the last of the supplies have been loaded, the last visiting dignitary has toured the ship and departed—glad, no doubt, to be going home safe to down pillows and a comfortable bed—and the men have written their last letters home, to be posted when the *Fortitude* has left. They are the final words we shall be able to send our loved ones before our return, whenever that will be, and a thin thread of melancholy pervades the ship tonight. I have written to Mary, and enclosed a message for sweet little Emily; by the time I return home she will have changed greatly from the little girl—scarcely more than a babe in arms—whom I left. She will not remember her father; but she and Mary are never far from my mind, and their photographs gaze down at me from the tiny shelf in my cabin, keeping watch over me as I sleep.

I said that the men had written their last letters home; but there was one exception. De Vere had no letters to give me, and while I made no comment he obviously noted my surprise, for he gave a wintry smile. "I said my goodbyes long ago," was all he said, and I did not press him, for there is something about his manner that discourages chatter. Not that he is standoffish, or unfriendly; rather, there is an air about him, as of a person who has spent a good deal of time alone, and has thus become a solitude unto himself. The Guvnor is pleased with him, though, and I must say that the man's cooking is superb. He spends most of his time in the tiny galley; to acquaint himself with his new domain, he told me. The results coming from it indicate that he is putting his time to good use, although I hope he will not have many occasions to favour us with seal consommé or Penguin *à la* Emperor.

Castleton had the largest batch of letters to send. I found him on the deck as usual, near the kennels of his charges. He is as protective of his dogs as a mother is of her children, and with good cause, for on these half-wild creatures the sledge teams shall depend. His control over them is quite wonderful. Some of the men are inclined to distrust the animals, which seem as akin to the domesticated dogs we all know as tigers are to tabby cats; none more so than De Vere who, I notice, gives them a wide berth on the rare occasions when he is on the deck. This wariness appears to be mutual; Castleton says that it is because the dogs scent food on De Vere's clothing.

29 November: At last we are under way, and all crowded to the ship's rail as the *Fortitude* departed from Hobart, to take a last look at civilisation. Even De Vere emerged into the sunlight, sheltering his sage eyes with his hand as we watched the shore recede and then vanish. I think it fair to say that despite the mingled wonder and excitement we all share about the expedition, the feelings of the men at thus seeing the known world slip away from us were mixed; all save De Vere, whose expression was one of relief before he retreated once more to his sanctum. I know that the Guvnor—whose judgement of character is second to none—is satisfied with the man, and with what he was able to find out about him at such short notice, but I cannot help but wonder if there is something which makes De Vere anxious to be away from Hobart.

20 December: The Southern Ocean has not been kind to us; the storms of the last three weeks have left us longing for the occasional glimpse of blue sky. We had some idea of what to expect, but as the Guvnor reminds us, we are charting new territory every day, and must be prepared for any eventuality. We have repaired most of the damage done to the bridge and superstructure by the heavy seas of a fortnight ago, taking advantage of a rare spell of relative calm yesterday to accomplish the task and working well into the night, so as to be ready should the wind and water resume their attack.

The strain is showing on all the men, and I am thankful that the cessation of the tumultuous seas has enabled De Vere to provide hot food once more; the days of cold rations, when the pitching of the ship made the galley unusable, told on all of us. The cook's complexion, which has always been pale, has assumed a truly startling pallor, and his face looks lined and haggard. He spent most of yesterday supplying hot food and a seemingly endless stream of strong coffee for all of us, and then came and helped with the work on deck, which continued well into the long Antarctic summer night. I had wondered if he was in a fit state to do such heavy labour, but he set to with a will, and proved he was the equal of any aboard.

22 December: Yet another accident has claimed one of our party; but this one with graver consequences than the one which injured Chadwick. The spell of calmer weather which enabled us to carry out the much-needed repairs to the ship was all too short, and it was not long after we had completed our work that the storm resumed with even more fury than before, and there was a very real possibility that the sea waves would breach our supply of fresh water, which would very seriously endanger the fate of the expedition. As it was, those of us who had managed to drop off into some kind of sleep awoke to find several inches of icy water around our feet; and the dogs were in a general state of uproar, having been deluged by waves. I stumbled on to the deck and began helping Castleton and one or two others who were removing the dogs to a more sheltered location—a difficult task given the rolling of the ship and the state of the frantic animals. I was busy concentrating on the task at hand, and thus did not see one of the kennels come loose from its moorings on the deck; but we all heard the terrible cry of agony which followed.

When we rushed to investigate we found young Walker crushed between the heavy wooden kennel and the rail. De Vere had reached the spot before us and, in a fit of energy which can only be described as superhuman, managed single-handedly to shift the kennel out of the way and free Walker, who was writhing and moaning in pain. Beddoes was instantly summoned, and a quick look at the doctor's face showed the gravity of the situation. Walker was taken below, and it was some time before Beddoes emerged, looking graver than before, an equally grim-faced Guvnor with him. The report is that Walker's leg is badly broken, and there is a possibility of internal injuries. The best that can be done is to make the injured man as comfortable as possible, and hope that the injuries are not as severe as they appear.

25 December: A sombre Christmas Day. De Vere, in an attempt to lighten the mood, produced a truly sumptuous Christmas dinner for us all, which did go some way towards brightening our spirits, and afterwards the Guvnor conducted a short but moving Christmas Day service for all the men save Walker, who cannot be moved, and De Vere, who volunteered to sit with the injured man. One thing for which we give thanks is that the storms which have dogged our journey thus far seem to have abated; we have had no further blasts such as the one which did so much damage, and the Guvnor is hopeful that it will not be very much longer before we may hope to see the coast of Antarctica.

28 December: De Vere has been spending a great deal of time with Walker, who is, alas, no better; Beddoes's worried face tells us all that we need know on that score. He has sunk into a restless, feverish sleep which does nothing to refresh him, and seems to have wasted away to a mere shell of his former self in a shockingly brief period of time. De Vere, conversely, appears to have shaken off the adverse effects which the rough weather had on him; I had occasion to visit the galley earlier in the day, and was pleased to see that our cook's visage has assumed a ruddy hue, and the haggard look has disappeared.

De Vere's attendance on the injured man has gone some way to mitigating his standing as the expedition's "odd man out". Several of the men have worked with others here on various voyages, and are old Antarctic hands, while the others were all selected by the Guvnor after careful consideration: not only of their own qualities, but with an eye to how they would work as part of the larger group. He did not, of course, have this luxury with De Vere, whose air of solitude has had the effect of making others keep their distance. Add to this the fact that he spends most of his time in the galley, and is thus excused from taking part in much of the daily routine of the ship, and it is perhaps not surprising that he remains something of a cipher.

31 December: A melancholy farewell to the old year. Walker is no better, and Beddoes merely shakes his head when asked about him. Our progress is slower than we anticipated, for we are plagued with a never-dissipating fog which wreathes the ship, reducing visibility to almost nothing. Brash ice chokes the sea: millions of pieces of it, which grind against the ship in a never-ceasing cacophony. We are making little more than three knots, for we dare not go any faster, and risk running the *Fortitude* against a larger piece which could pierce the hull; on the other hand, we must maintain speed, lest we become mired in a fast-freezing mass. It is delicate work, and Mr. Andrews is maintaining a near-constant watch, for as captain he bears ultimate responsibility for the ship and her crew, and is determined to keep us safe.

I hope that 1911 begins more happily than 1910 looks set to end.

3 January 1911: Sad news today. Walker succumbed to his injuries in the middle of last night. The Guvnor gathered us all together this morning to inform us. De Vere was with Walker at the end, so the man did not die alone, a fact for which we are all grateful. I think we all knew that there was little hope of recovery; I was with him briefly only yesterday, and was shocked by how pale and gaunt he looked.

There was a brief discussion as to whether or not we should bury Walker at sea, or wait until we made land and bury him ashore. However, we do not know when—or even if—we shall make landfall, and it was decided by us all to wait until the water around the ship is sufficiently clear of ice and bury him at sea.

5 January: A welcome break in the fog today, enabling us to obtain a clear view of our surroundings for the first time in many days. We all knew that we were sailing into these waters at the most treacherous time of the southern summer, when the ice breaking up in the Ross Sea would be swept across our path, but we could not wait until later when the way would be clearer, or we would risk being frozen in the ice before we completed our work. As it is, the prospect which greeted us was not heartening; the way south is choked, as far as the eye can see, with vast bergs of ice; one, which was directly in front of us, stretched more than a mile in length, and was pitted along its base by caves, in which the water boomed and echoed.

Though the icebergs separate us from our goal, it must be

admitted that they are beautiful. When I tell people at home of them, they are always surprised to hear that the bergs and massive floes are not pure white, but rather contain a multitude of colours: shades of lilac and mauve and blue and green, while pieces which have turned over display the brilliant hues of the algae which live in these waters. Their majesty, however, is every bit as awesome as has been depicted, in words and in art; Coleridge's inspired vision in his "Ancient Mariner" being a case in point.

I was standing at the rail this evening, listening to the ice as it prowled restlessly about the hull, gazing out upon the larger floes and bergs surrounding us and thinking along these lines, when I became aware of someone standing at my elbow. It was De Vere, who had come up beside me as soundlessly as a cat. We stood in not uncompanionable silence for some moments; then, as if he were reading my thoughts, he said quietly, "Coleridge was correct, was he not? How does he put it:

> 'The ice was here, the ice was there
> The ice was all around:
> It cracked and growled, and roared and howled,
> Like noises in a swound!'

"Quite extraordinary, for a man who was never here. And Doré's illustrations for the work are likewise inspired. Of course, he made a rather dreadful *faux pas* with his polar bears climbing up the floes, although it does make a fine illustration. He was not at all apologetic when his mistake was pointed out to him. 'If I wish to place polar bears on the southern ice I shall.' Well, we must allow as great an artist as Doré some licence."

I admitted that I had been thinking much the same thing, at least about Coleridge. De Vere smiled.

"Truly one of our greatest and most inspired poets. We must forever deplore that visitor from Porlock who disturbed him in the midst of 'Kubla Khan'. And 'Christabel'; what might that poem have become had Coleridge finished it? That is the common cry; yet Coleridge's fate was always to have a vision so vast that in writing of it he could never truly 'finish', in the conventional sense. In that he must surely echo life. Nothing is ever 'finished', not really, save in death, and it is this last point which plays such a central role in 'Christabel'. Is the Lady Geraldine truly alive, or is she undead? He would never confirm it, but I always suspected that Coleridge was inspired, in part, to write 'Christabel' because of his earlier creation, the Nightmare Life-in-Death, who 'thicks men's blood with cold'. When she wins the Mariner in her game of dice with Death, does he join her in a deathless state, to roam the world forever? It is a terrible fate to contemplate."

"Surely not," I replied; "only imagine all that one could see and do were one given eternal life. More than one man has sought it."

De Vere, whose eyes had focussed on the ice around us, turned and fixed me with a steady gaze. The summer night was upon us, and it was sufficiently dark that I could not see his face distinctly; yet his grey eyes were dark pools, which displayed a grief without a pang, one so old that the original sting had turned to dull, unvarying sorrow.

"Eternal life," he repeated, and I heard bitterness underlying his words. "I do not think that those who seek it have truly considered it in all its consequences."

I did not know how to respond to this statement. Instead I remarked on his apparent familiarity with the works of Doré and Coleridge. De Vere nodded.

"I have made something of a study of the literature of the undead, if literature it is. *Varney the Vampyre*; certainly not literature, yet possessed of a crude power, although not to be mentioned in the same breath as works such as Mr. Poe's 'Berenice' or the Irishman Le Fanu's sublime 'Carmilla'."

I consider myself to be a well-read man, but not in this field, as I have never had an inclination for bogey stories. I made a reference to the only work with which I was familiar that seemed relevant, and my companion shook his head.

"Stoker's novel is certainly powerful; but he makes of the central character too romantic a figure. Lord Byron has much for which to answer. And such a jumble of legends and traditions and lore, picked up here and there and then adapted to suit the needs of the novelist! Stoker never seems to consider the logical results of the depredations of the Count; if he were as bloodthirsty as depicted, and leaving behind such a trail of victims who become, in time, like him, then our world would be overrun." He shook his head. "One thing that the author depicted well was the essential isolation of his creation. Stoker does not tell us how long it was before the Count realised how alone he was, even in the midst of bustling London. Not long, I suspect."

It was an odd conversation to be having at such a time, and in such a place. De Vere must have realised this, for he gave an apologetic smile.

"I am sorry for leading the conversation in such melancholy channels, especially in light of what has happened. Did you know Walker very well?"

"No," I replied; "I did not meet him until shortly before we sailed from England. This was his first Antarctic voyage. He hoped, if the Guvnor gave him a good report at the end of it, to sign on with Mawson's next expedition, or even with Shackleton or Scott. Good Antarctic hands are in short supply. I know that the Guvnor, who has never lost a man on any of his expeditions, appreciates the time that you spent with Walker, so that he did not die alone. We all do."

"Being alone is a terrible thing," said De Vere, in so soft a voice that I could scarce hear him. "I only wish that . . . " He stopped. "I wish that it could have been avoided, that I could have prevented it. I had hoped . . . " He stopped once more.

"But what could you have done?" I asked in some surprise, when he showed no sign, this time, of breaking the silence. "You did more than enough. As I said, we are all grateful."

He appeared not to hear my last words. "More than enough," he repeated, in a voice of such emptiness that I could make no reply; and before long the cook excused himself to tend his duties before retiring for the night. I stayed on deck for a little time after, smoking a pipe and reflecting on our strange conversation. That De Vere is a man of education and intelligence I had already guessed, from his voice and manner and speech; he is clearly not a common sailor or sea-cook. What had brought him to Australia, however, and in such a capacity, I do not know. Perhaps he is one of those men, ill-suited to the rank and expectations of his birth, who seeks to test himself in places and situations which he would not otherwise encounter; or one of the restless souls who finds himself constrained by the demands of society.

It was, by this time, quite late; the only souls stirring on deck were the men of the watch, whom it was easy to identify: Richards with his yellow scarf, about which he has taken some good-natured ribbing; Wellington, the shortest man in our crew but with the strength and tenacity of a bulldog; and McAllister, with his ferocious red beard. All eyes would, I knew, be on the ice, for an accident here would mean the end.

The dogs were agitated; I could hear whining and a few low growls from their kennels. I glanced in that direction, and was startled to see a man, or so I thought, standing in the shadows beside them. There was no one on the watch near that spot, I knew, and while it was not unthinkable that some insomniac had come up on deck, what startled me was the resemblance the figure bore to Walker: the thin, eager face, the manner in which he held himself, even the clothing called to mind our fallen comrade. I shook my head, to clear it, and when I looked again the figure was gone.

This is, I fear, what comes of talks such as the one which I had with De Vere earlier. I must banish these thoughts from my head, as having no place on this voyage.

7 January: There was a sufficient clearing of the ice around the ship today to enable us to commit Walker's body to the deep. The service was brief, but very moving, and the faces of the men were solemn; none more so than De Vere, who still seems somewhat distraught, and who lingered at the rail's edge for some time, watching the spot where Walker's remains slipped beneath the water.

The ice which is keeping us from the coastline is as thick as ever; yet we are noting that many of the massive chunks around us are embedded with rocky debris, which would seem to indicate the presence of land nearby. We all hope this is a sign that, before long, we will sight that elusive coastline which hovers just outside our view.

17 January: We have reached our El Dorado at last! Early this morning the watch wakened the Guvnor and Mr. Andrews to announce that they had sighted a rocky beach which looked suitable for a base camp. This news, coming as it does on the heels of all that we have seen and charted in the last few days, has inspired a celebration amongst the expedition members that equals that which we displayed when leaving Plymouth to begin our voyage. The glad news spread quickly, and within minutes everyone was on deck—some of the men only half-dressed—to catch a glimpse of the spot, on a sheltered bay where the *Fortitude* will be able to anchor safely. There was an excited babble of voices, and even some impromptu dancing, as the prospect of setting foot in this unknown land took hold; I suspect that we will be broaching some of the twenty or so cases of champagne which we have brought with us.

And yet I found myself scanning the faces on deck, and counting, for ever since the evening of that conversation with De Vere I have half-convinced myself that there are more men on board the ship than there should be. Quite how and why this idea has taken hold I cannot say, and it is not something which I can discuss with anyone else aboard; but I cannot shake the conviction that this shadowy other is Walker. If I believed in ghosts I could think that our late crewmate has returned to haunt the scene of his hopes and dreams; but I do not believe, and even to mention the idea would lead to serious concerns regarding my sanity. De Vere's talk has obviously played on my mind. Bogeys indeed!

The man himself seems to have regretted his speech that night. He spends most of his time in the galley, only venturing out on deck in the late evening, but he has restricted his comments to commonplaces about the weather, or the day's discoveries. The dogs are as uncomfortable with him as ever, but De Vere appears to be trying to accustom them to his presence, for he is often near them, speaking with Castleton. The dog master spends most of his time when not on watch, or asleep, with his charges, ensuring that they are kept healthy for when we need them for the sledging parties, a task which we are all well content to leave him to. "If he doesn't stop spending so much time alone with those brutes he'll soon forget how to talk, and start barking instead," said Richards one evening.

The dogs may be robust, but Castleton himself is not looking well; he appears pale, and more tired than usual. It cannot be attributed to anything lacking in our diet, for the Guvnor has ensured that our provisions are excellent, and should the need arise we can augment our supplies with seal meat, which has proven such an excellent staple for travellers in the north polar regions. It could be that some illness is doing the rounds, for De Vere was once again looking pale some days ago, but seems to have improved. I saw him only a few minutes ago on the deck, looking the picture of health. While the rest of us have focussed our gazes landward, the cook was looking back the way we had come, as if keeping watch for something he expected to see behind us.

20 January: It has been a Herculean task, landing all the supplies, but at last it is finished. The men who have remained on the beach, constructing the hut, have done yeomans' work and, when the *Fortitude* departs tomorrow to continue along the coast on its charting mission, we shall have a secure roof over our heads. That it shall also be warm is thanks to the work of De Vere. When we went to assemble the stove we found that a box of vital parts was missing. McAllister recalled seeing a box fall from the motor launch during one of its landings, and when we crowded to the water's edge we did indeed see the box lying approximately seven feet down, in a bed of the kelp which grows along the coast. As we debated how best to grapple it to the surface, De Vere quietly and calmly removed his outer clothing and boots and plunged into the icy water. He had to surface three times for great gulps of air before diving down once more to tear the remaining kelp away from the box and then carry it to the surface. It was a heroic act, but he deflected all attempts at praise. "It needed to be done," he said simply.

I have erected a small shed for my scientific equipment, at a little distance from the main hut. The dogs are tethered at about the same distance in the other direction, and we are anticipating making some sledging runs soon, although Castleton advises that the animals will be difficult to handle at first, which means that only those with some previous skill in that area will go on the initial journeys. It is debatable whether Castleton himself will be in a fit state to be one of these men, for he is still suffering from some illness which is leaving him in a weakened state; it is all he can do to manage his tasks with the dogs, and De Vere has had to help him.

And still—I hesitate to confess it—I cannot shake myself of this feeling of someone with us who should not be here. With all the bustle of transferring the supplies and erecting the camp it has been impossible for me to keep track of everyone, but I am sure that I have seen movement beyond the science hut when there should be no one there. If these delusions—for such they must be—continue, then I shall have to consider treatment when we return to England, or risk being unable to take part in future expeditions. I am conscious it is hallucination, but it is a phantasm frozen in place, at once too fixed to dislodge and too damaging to confess to another. We have but seven weeks—eight at most—before the ship returns to take us back to Hobart, in advance of the Antarctic winter; I pray that all will be well until then.

24 January: Our first sledging mission has been a success; two parties of three men each ascended the pathway that we have carved from the beach to the plateau above and behind us, and from there we travelled about four miles inland, attaining an altitude of 1500 feet. The feelings of us all as we topped the final rise and saw inland across that vast featureless plateau are indescribable. We were all conscious that we were gazing upon land that no human eye has ever seen, as we gazed southwards to where the ice seemed to dissolve into a white, impenetrable haze. The enormity of the landscape, and our own insignificance within it, struck us all, for it was a subdued party that made its way back to the camp before the night began to draw in to make travel impossible; there are crevasses—some hidden, some not— all about, which will make travel in anything other than daylight impossible. We were prepared to spend the night on the plateau should the need arise, but we were all glad to be back in the icicled hut with our fellows.

The mood there was subdued also. Castleton assisted, this morning, in harnessing the dogs to the sledges, but a task of which he would have made short work only a month ago seemed almost beyond him; and the look in his eyes as he watched us leave, on a mission of which he was to have been a part, tore at the soul. De Vere's health contrasted starkly with the wan face of the man beside him, yet the cook had looked almost as stricken as the dog master as we left the camp.

1 February: I did not think that I would find myself writing these words, but the *Fortitude* cannot return too quickly. It is not only Castleton's health that is worrisome; it is the growing conviction that there is something wrong with *me*. The fancy that someone else abides here grows stronger by the day and, despite my best efforts, I cannot rid myself of it. I have tried, as delicately as possible, to raise the question with some of the others, but their laughter indicates that no one else is suffering. "Get better snow goggles, old man," was Richards's response. The only person who did not laugh was De Vere, whose look of concern told me that he senses my anxiety.

6 February: The end has come, and while it is difficult to write this, I feel I must; as if setting it down on paper will go some way to exorcising it from my mind. I know, however, that the scenes of the last two days will be with me until the grave.

Two nights ago I saw Walker again, as plainly as could be. It was shortly before dark, and I was returning from the hut which shelters my scientific equipment. The wind, which howls down from the icy plateau above us, had ceased for a time, and I took advantage of the relative calm to light my pipe.

All was quiet, save for a subdued noise from the men in the hut, and the growling of one or two of the dogs. I stood for a moment, gazing about me, marvelling at the sheer immensity of where I was. Save for the *Fortitude* and her crew, and Scott's party—wherever they may be—there are no people within 1200 miles of us, and we are as isolated from the rest of the world and her bustle as if we were on the moon. Once again the notion of our own insignificance in this uninhabited land struck me, and I shivered, knocked the ashes out of my pipe, and prepared to go to the main hut.

A movement caught my eye, behind the shed containing my equipment; it appeared to be the figure of a man, thrown into relief against the backdrop of ice. I called out sharply "Who's there?" and, not receiving an answer, took a few steps in the direction of the movement; but moments later stopped short when the other figure in turn took a step towards me, and I saw that it was Walker.

And yet that does not convey the extra horror of what I saw. It was not Walker as I remembered him, either from the early part of the voyage or in the period just before his death; then he had looked ghastly enough, but it was nothing as to how he appeared before me now. He was painfully thin, the colour of the ice and snow behind him, and in his eyes was a terrible light; they seemed to glow like twin lucifers. His nose was eaten away, and his lips, purple and swollen, were drawn back from his gleaming teeth in a terrible parody of a smile; yet there was nothing of mirth in the look which was directed towards me. I felt that I was frozen where I stood, unable to move, and I wondered what I would do if the figure advanced any further.

It was De Vere who saved me. A cry must have escaped my lips, and the cook heard it, for I was aware that he was standing beside me. He said something in a low voice, words that I was unable to distinguish, and then he was helping me—not towards the main hut, thank God, for I was in no state to present myself before the others, but to the science hut. He pulled open the door and we stumbled inside, and De Vere lit the lantern which was hanging from the ceiling. For a moment, as the match flared, his own eyes seemed to glow; then the lamp was sending its comforting light, and all was as it should be.

He was obviously concerned; I could see that in his drawn brow, in the anxious expression of his eyes. I found myself telling him what I had seen, but if I thought that he would immediately laugh and tell me I was imagining things I was much mistaken. He again said some words in a low voice; guttural and harsh, in a language I did not understand. When he looked at me his grey eyes were filled with such pain that I recoiled slightly. He shook his head.

"I am sorry," he said in a quiet voice. "Sorry that you have seen what you did, and . . . for other things. I had hoped . . . "

His voice trailed off. When he spoke again it was more to himself than to me; he seemed almost to have forgotten my presence.

"I have lived a long time, Mr. Edwards, and travelled a great deal; all my years, in fact, from place to place, never staying long in one location. At length I arrived in Australia, travelling ever further south, away from civilisation, until I found myself in Hobart, and believed it was the end. Then the *Fortitude* arrived, bound on its mission even further south, to a land where for several months of the year it is always night. Paradise indeed, I thought." His smile was twisted. "I should have remembered the words of Blake: 'Some are born to sweet delight / Some are born to endless night.' It is not a Paradise at all."

I tried to speak, but he silenced me with a gesture of his hand and a look from those haunted eyes. "If I needed something from you, would you help me?" he asked abruptly. I nodded, and he thought for a moment. "There are no sledge trips tomorrow; am I correct?"

"Yes," I replied, somewhat bewildered by the sudden change

in the direction of the conversation. "The Guvnor feels that the men need a day of rest, so no trips are planned. Why?"

"Can you arrange that a single trip should be made, and that it shall be only you and I who travel?"

"It would be highly irregular; usually there are three men to a sledge, because of the difficulty of . . . "

"Yes, yes, I understand that. But it is important that it should be just the two of us. Can it be managed?"

"If it is important enough, then yes, I should think so."

"It is more important than you know." He gave a small smile, and some of the pain seemed gone from his eyes. "Far more important. Tomorrow night this will be over. I promise you."

I had little sleep that night, and next day was up far earlier than necessary, preparing the sled and ensuring that all was in order. There had been some surprise when I announced that De Vere and I would be off, taking one of the sledges ourselves, but I explained it by saying that the cook merely wanted an opportunity to obtain a glimpse of that vast land for himself, and that we would not be travelling far. When De Vere came out to the sledge he was carrying a small bag. It was surprisingly heavy, but I found a place for it, and moments later the dogs strained into their harnesses, and we were away.

The journey up to the plateau passed uneventfully under the leaden sun, and we made good time on the trail, which was by now well established. When we topped the final rise I stopped the sledge, so that we could both look out across that vast wasteland of ice and snow, stretching away to the South Pole hundreds and hundreds of miles distant. De Vere meditated upon it for some minutes, then turned to me.

"Thank you for bringing me here," he said in his quiet voice. "We are about four miles from camp, I think you said?" When I concurred, he continued, "That is a distance which you can travel by yourself, is it not?"

"Yes, of course," I replied, somewhat puzzled.

"I thought as much, or I would not have brought you all this way. And I did want to see this"—he gestured at the silent heart of the continent behind us—"just once. Such a terrible beauty on the surface, and underneath, treachery. You say here there are crevasses?"

"Yes," I said. "We must be careful when breaking new trails, lest a snow bridge collapse under us. Three days ago a large crevasse opened up to our right"—I pointed—"and there was a very real fear that one of the sledges was going to be carried down into it. It was only some quick work on the part of McAllister that kept it from plunging through."

"Could you find the spot again?"

"Easily. We are not far."

"Good." He turned to the sledge, ignoring the movement and barking of the dogs; they had not been much trouble when there had been work to do, but now, stopped, they appeared restless, even nervous. De Vere rustled around among the items stowed on the sledge, and pulled out the bag he had given me. He hesitated for a moment; then he walked to where I stood waiting and passed it to me.

"I would like you to open that," he said, and when I did so I found a small, ornate box made of mahogany, secured with a stout brass hasp. "Open the box, and remove what is inside."

I had no idea what to expect; but any words I might have said failed me when I undid the hasp, opened the lid, and found inside the box a revolver. I looked up at De Vere, who wore a mirthless smile.

"It belonged to a man who thought to use it on me, some years ago," he said simply. "That man died. I think you will find, if you look, that it is loaded."

I opened the chamber, and saw that it was so. I am by no means an expert with firearms, but the bullets seemed to be almost tarnished, as with great age. I closed the chamber, and glanced at De Vere.

"Now we are going to go over to the edge of the crevasse, and you are going to shoot me." The words were said matter-of-factly, and what followed was in the same dispassionate tone, as if he were speaking of the weather, or what he planned to serve for dinner that evening. "Stand close, so as not to miss. When you return to camp you will tell them that we came too near to the edge of the crevasse, that a mass of snow collapsed under me, and that there was nothing you could do. I doubt that any blame or stigma will attach to you—not with your reputation—and while it may be difficult for you for a time, you will perhaps take solace in the fact that you will not see Walker again, and that Castleton's health will soon improve." He paused. "I am sorry about them both; more than I can say." Then he added some words in an undertone, which I did not quite catch; one word sounded like "hungry", and another like "tired", but in truth I was so overwhelmed that I was barely in a position to make sense of anything. One monstrous fact alone stood out hard and clear, and I struggled to accept it.

"Are you . . . are you ill, then?" I asked at last, trying to find some explanation at which my mind did not rebel. "Some disease that will claim you?"

"If you want to put it that way, yes; a disease. If that makes it easier for you." He reached out and put a hand on my arm. "You have been friendly, and I have not had many that I could call a friend. I thank you, and ask you to do this one thing for me; and, in the end, for all of you."

I looked into his eyes, dark as thunderclouds, and recalled our conversation on board the ship following Walker's death, and for a moment had a vision of something dark and terrible. I thought of the look on Walker's face—or the thing that I had thought was Walker—when I had seen it the night before. "Will you end up like him?" I asked suddenly, and De Vere seemed to know to what I referred, for he shook his head.

"No, but if you do not do this then others will," he said simply. I knew then how I must act. He obviously saw the look of resolution in my face, for he said again, quietly, "Thank you," then turned and began walking towards the crevasse in the ice.

I cannot write in detail of what followed in the next few minutes. I remained beside the crevasse, staring blankly down into the

depths which now held him, and it was only with considerable
effort that I finally roused myself enough to stumble back to the
dogs, which had at last quietened. The trip back to camp was a
blur of white, and I have no doubt that, when I stumbled down
the final stretch of the path, I appeared sufficiently wild-eyed and
distraught that my story was accepted without question.

The Guvnor had a long talk with me this morning when I woke,
unrefreshed, from a troubled sleep. He appears satisfied with my
answers, and while he did upbraid me slightly for failing to take
a third person with us—as is standard on these trips—he agreed
that the presence of another would probably have done nothing
to help save De Vere.

Pray God he never finds out the truth.

15 February: More than a week since De Vere's death, and I have
not seen Walker in that time. Castleton, too, is much improved,
and appears well on the way to regaining his full health.

Subsequent sledge parties have inspected the crevasse, and
agree that it was a terrible accident, but one that could not have
been avoided. I have not been up on the plateau since my trip
with De Vere. My thoughts continually turn to the man whom I
left there, and I recall what Cook wrote more than one hundred
years ago. He was speaking of this place; but the words could, I
think, equally be applied to De Vere: "Doomed by nature never
once to feel the warmth of the sun's rays, but to be buried in
everlasting snow and ice."

                                               ℘　♋

A soft flutter of leaves whispered like a sigh as Emily finished
reading. The last traces of day had vanished, leaving behind
shadows which pooled at the corners of the room. She sat in
silence for some time, her eyes far away; then she closed the
journal gently, almost with reverence, and placed it on the table

beside her. The writer's card stared up at her, and she considered it.

"He would not understand," she said at last. "And they are all dead; they can neither explain nor defend themselves or their actions." She looked at her father's photograph, now blurred in the gathering darkness. "Yet you did not destroy this." She touched the journal with fingers delicate as a snowflake. "You left it for me to decide, keeping this a secret even from my mother. You must have thought that I would know what to do."

Pray God he never finds out the truth.

She remained in her chair for some moments longer. Then, with an effort, Emily rose from her chair and, picking up the journal, crossed once more to the rosewood desk and its shadows. She placed the journal in its drawer, where it rested beside a pipe which had lain unsmoked for decades. The ceramic cat watched with blank eyes as she turned out the light. In so doing she knocked the card to the floor, where it lay undisturbed.

THE PALACE

I

"WHAT DOES THE NIGHT WIND SAY?"

The voice came from what looked like a pile of rags, half-concealed in a recessed doorway behind him, and Mark almost dropped his cigarette. He had nipped out of the hotel for a quick smoke, and had thought he had the street outside The Palace Hotel to himself. It was past one o'clock, the pubs and hotel bars had disgorged their patrons a half-hour ago, and he had been enjoying the quiet Vancouver night, mild despite the fact that October had set in. He had walked fifty yards or so from the hotel's main entrance, leaving behind the gleaming stone and glass of the hotel's frontage, exchanging it for the dirty, shabby row of shops which occupied the rest of the block. That, Mark reflected, was downtown Vancouver for you; it didn't take long to go from splendour to squalor. All the world in a city block.

The figure in the doorway moved slightly, and Mark saw that it was Jane, one of the permanent residents of the downtown Vancouver streets. Her lined and weathered face gave no secrets away as to her age, or history, or the circumstances which had brought her here; she simply *was*, in the same way as the Woodwards building or the Ovaltine Café. He had seen her several times, shuffling along the sidewalk or hunched in a doorway, but it was the first time she had spoken to him, although Mark wondered if she actually *was* speaking to him, or merely talking to herself. But her eyes, incongruously bright in her dark face, were looking directly at him, as if in expectation of an answer, and she asked again, "What does the night wind say?"

"I don't know," Mark replied. He glanced at the trees planted

49

along the sidewalk of Hastings Street, their leaves still green and, tonight, undisturbed by even a hint of breeze. "I don't think it's saying much of anything. Perfect Vancouver night."

"Perfect?" Jane moved forward so that she could look round the edge of the doorway, and her glance moved down the street to where the lights from The Palace's lobby gleamed softly onto the sidewalk. "No. Not perfect. Not here." She tapped the side of her head, near her eyes. "I see. Too much." She shook her head. "Beautiful place. I come here long ago because someone say this city so beautiful. But ugly, too. The night wind knows. Sees beautiful city, with ugly people, sometimes."

Mark had moved closer to her, to hear her words better. She was a Native woman—he could see that now—and her voice had a softness, a musicality to it which had not been ground out of her by the life she led, so far from where she must have grown up. He wondered for a moment where that place was, and if she could go back to it.

As if she had read his thoughts, she said, "No go back. Past is dead place; bad place. Ugly people there too. Ugly people everywhere." She looked at Mark sadly. "Everywhere," she emphasised. "Ugly people do ugly things, and cannot fix."

"Do they try?" She was like the Ancient Mariner, fixing him with her eye, and he found he wanted to stay and listen.

"Sometimes." Jane was silent then, and Mark thought the conversation, such as it was, had ended; but as he started to say he had to get back to work, she said "Some bad things, cannot be fixed. Some things too bad, too hard. Night wind knows, says these things, but people not hear."

"I see." Mark did not know if he saw or not, but his answer satisfied Jane, who was still looking towards the front doors of The Palace. Mark looked that way too, and remembered that he had a job to be doing. "Well, I've got to go," he said somewhat awkwardly, and Jane looked at him for a moment, then nodded.

"Yes. You go. But watch for ugly people. You watch."

"Yes, yes I will." He hesitated for a moment, then pulled his wallet from his pocket and took out a two-dollar bill. "Here. Have this." He stretched out his arm, and her hand snaked out to take the money. For a moment her fingers brushed his, and then money and hand had disappeared within the folds of clothing around her, and Mark had turned and started towards the hotel. When he got to the door he looked back, but could see nothing of Jane. He glanced once more at the trees and sky, and shivered slightly as an errant breeze, harbinger of the coming winter, blew down the street. Then he was inside the warmth and radiance of The Palace, and the night wind was forgotten.

II

"Do you believe in ghosts?"

"What is this, quiz night?"

"What do you mean?"

"Nothing." Mark shook his head. "No, I don't."

"Do you believe in vampires?"

"No." Relieved at something that put his encounter with Jane out of his mind, he smiled. Sylvia, looking down, didn't notice.

"Do you believe in werewolves, mummies, or zombies?"

"No, no, and yes."

"Yes?" Sylvia looked up, startled. Mark's smile had broadened into a grin, and she grinned back. "Now you're being silly."

"Silly? Me? I'm not the one who started with the Twenty Questions. Anyway, I have seen zombies. So have you; in the morning, when the guests start to check out." He leaned over the front desk. "What is this, some sort of magazine quiz you're doing? 'Are you open to the paranormal', that kind of thing? Don't you have work to do?"

"No, it's not a quiz, and I am working, actually, in case you hadn't noticed." Sylvia held up a stack of registration cards, then resumed sorting through them. "It's just something I saw on the news the other night; there was this special series they're doing before Halloween, and they were going around Vancouver and showing all these places that're supposed to be haunted, and there was this one place in Burnaby that's an art gallery now but the people who work there keep hearing things, like footsteps in the hallway when no one else is there, and one time this workman put down his hammer or something and walked away, and when he came back it had been moved to the other side of the workbench, but there he was all alone in the building, so no one else *could* have moved it, and I just thought, you know, I'm glad I work here, because wouldn't it be creepy to work somewhere like that?"

Sylvia finished off in a rush, the way she often did, like a car running out of gas. Mark laughed.

"Some people would say it was really creepy to work graveyard shift."

Sylvia frowned. "Well, yeah, I suppose it's not for everyone. But you like it, don't you, Raymond?"

This was directed down the length of the front desk towards where a tall, thin man in hotel uniform—standard male employee issue of light brown suit, white shirt, and cheap burgundy tie—stood, entering figures on a sheet of paper. He looked up and blinked at Mark and Sylvia. "What's that?"

"I said, you like working the graveyard shift, don't you?"

Raymond considered her thoughtfully for a moment, then shrugged. "It's a job," he said finally. "You get used to it after a while."

"Not me." Sylvia shook her head. "Soon as I get enough seniority, wham! I'm outta here, onto afternoons. No more graveyard shift, thanks very much. Let someone else have the fun. What about you, Mark?"

He shook his head. "I don't know. It's not too bad; like Raymond says, you get used to it after a while. I guess you can get used to anything, if you try. But it's not up to me. I'm just a Duty Manager; I don't have seniority like you union guys. I'm here until someone decides it's time for me to move on to bigger and better things."

"Aw, listen to this, 'I'm just a Duty Manager.' Poor guy." Sylvia shuffled the reg cards some more, made a note on one, continued shuffling. "I don't know how you do it, Raymond," she said in the night auditor's direction. "How long have you been doing this? Five years?" She shook her head. "No way I could work graveyard that long. No way."

Raymond gave a small polite smile which almost reached his eyes before flickering out. He shrugged again. "You get used to it," he repeated. "I have, anyway. It's quiet. Usually." He bent back down to his sheet of figures.

Where some people would have taken his final word as an insult, Sylvia picked up on the fact that it was just Raymond's way, and that no insult had been intended. She was quick, and bright; wasted, really, on the graveyard shift, Mark thought. If she'd started at the beginning of the summer she'd have soon moved on to better hours, but she had been hired after the busy season had ended, when several of the temporary summer staff—students, mostly—had left, and would now be stuck on graveyards until someone higher up the pecking order moved on. She would have most of her work done by the time update started at around 3.30, and would then settle in by the switchboard, reading, until early morning checkouts began. The job itself wasn't bad; just the hours. Unless you were a bat, or a vampire.

"So what was the verdict on this haunted art gallery? Any idea who's doing the haunting? Or is it just some story the news guys worked up to give people a scare?"

"Well, they're not sure; I mean, I don't think anyone's really seen anything, but then I guess that isn't surprising, 'cause if you could *see* ghosts—if they're real—then I guess they'd be all misty and everything and half the time you wouldn't even know you'd seen one, but they think it's the woman who used to own the place, who's angry because her husband didn't leave the house to the right people when she died, or something like that, and now she's not happy."

"So she moves hammers around?"

"I guess there's not much else she *can* do, when you think about it. I mean, if she wanted something, and her husband didn't do it for her after she died, then I guess she'd be kinda upset, but since he's dead it wouldn't really be fair to go after other people, innocent people, I mean, who didn't have anything to do with it; she'd want to get back at him, and so now all she can really do is scare folks a bit, remind them of what happened so she won't be forgotten. And isn't that all ghosts can do to you? Scare you? It's not like they can shoot you or attack you or anything, just kind of stand around and moan."

There was a muttered curse from the other end of the desk, and Mark and Sylvia both turned. Raymond was tearing a strip of paper from the adding machine he had been working on, and they watched him ball it up and throw it in the garbage can beside him. Mark could tell, from Raymond's posture, that he knew he had attracted their attention but was determined not to look at them, and when he glanced at Sylvia he saw that she realised it as well. She shrugged slightly, as if to say "Takes all kinds," but before she could say anything they heard the switchboard ring, and she went to answer the phone. The graveyard shift was a lean machine, as Danny, the night bellman, said: apart from him and the three behind the desk, the only other staff member was Bob, the elderly security guard who was probably out prowling the parking garage, making sure no drunks were bedding down in the stairwells.

Mark continued to watch Raymond, who was now punching—somewhat ostentatiously, Mark thought—the buttons on the adding machine, in an "I don't know about you but *someone* around here has got to work" kind of way. Raymond was a nice guy, and a hard worker, and certainly knew his job—five years doing the same thing in the same place tended to do that to you—but on the serious side, which was what five years of graveyard shift would *certainly* do to you. Their paycheques reminded them every two weeks that "Ours is a service industry", but Mark was sometimes thankful that night audit involved little direct contact with the guests.

The sound of heavy doors closing echoed through the lobby, and moments later Giovanni appeared round the corner from the direction of the hotel's lobby bar, a dark, wood-panelled space which looked out onto Hastings Street. It had been a fixture in the hotel for years, a place where people went to do some serious drinking; anyone who wanted drinks with mildly salacious names, or with paper umbrellas stuck in them, usually ended up in the lounge on the top floor, with its views over downtown, and live jazz on weekends. The King's Arms, with its doors onto the street, attracted a somewhat rougher clientele, but Giovanni—known to all as Joe—had presided over it for more than two decades, and was known to run a tight ship. More than one unruly drunk, mistaking Joe's affable manner for weakness, had found himself quickly, and effectively, disabused of this notion.

On this night Joe was all smiles as he tossed a packet of credit card slips and bills onto the counter in front of Raymond. "Here you go," he said. "All finished and closed up."

"Any trouble tonight?" Mark asked.

"No, everyone was pretty quiet. Slow night."

"So I can go clear the machine, then?" said Raymond.

"Go right ahead, my friend."

Mark passed Raymond the keys, and the auditor put down his pen and hurried out from behind the desk. Mark and Joe watched him as he crossed the lobby and went round the corner. Joe shook his head.

"Weird guy," he said. "Harmless, I guess, but weird."

Mark was about to ask what he meant when Sylvia came back out from the switchboard.

"Some people from England, asking about reserving a room for Expo," she said, shaking her head. "Second call like that I've had this week. And Expo's not until 1986!"

Mark smiled. "Some people like to plan ahead," he said. "Besides, two years'll go faster than you know it. They're probably smart to book this far ahead; I think a lot of people are going to want to come to Expo, and Vancouver's pretty short on hotel space for a big city."

Sylvia rolled her eyes. "Yeah, maybe. But if I plan a vacation two *weeks* ahead I think I'm taking a long-term view."

"Remind me not to plan any vacations with you."

Sylvia winked at him. "Ah, c'mon, could be fun."

"I'll think about it."

Joe, who had been listening to the conversation, nodded his head thoughtfully. "Lots of people will come for Expo. Vancouver is a beautiful place. All my family back in Italy wants to come over in two years, to see this beautiful place I tell them about."

Sylvia still looked doubtful. "Yeah, Vancouver's beautiful, in

the right places. Not down here, though. There's too much . . . "
She paused, looking for the right word.

"Ugliness?" Mark supplied, remembering Jane's words.

"Yeah. There's so much ugliness down here."

"Look." Joe gestured towards the main doors, where a group
of well-dressed people had just alighted from a taxi. Laughing
and chatting, they clattered towards the elevators, their voices
echoing around the empty lobby. Outside, the taxi pulled away,
and they watched as the flags hanging above the door stirred
in the wind. They looked soft and golden in the light from the
lobby, and it was hard to remember that only steps away there
was desolation and suffering and the darkness of people ground
down by life.

"You see?" said Joe. "Beautiful people in a beautiful city. In
two years we will show the world what it is like here, and many
more people will come after that."

The flags continued to flow gently in the night wind. Mark
wondered what it was saying.

III

Mark stood on the sidewalk outside The King's Arms, watching
as the woman made her way down the street. A few scattered
curses could still be heard, growing fainter as the figure moved
away. A cold breeze brought more leaves off the trees, and they
skittered along the road, making dry, rasping noises. He shivered
and turned to Bob. "Think we're okay now?"

"Yeah." The security guard nodded. "That should do it
for the night. I'll keep an eye open and make sure she doesn't
come back." He shook his head. "The drunks I can handle;
what gets to me are the women. Maybe it's 'cause I have two
daughters."

Mark watched as the retreating figure turned a corner and
disappeared from sight. "I don't know how they can live like
that."

Bob shrugged. "No place else to go, most of 'em. At least
it's warmer here than in Toronto. That's what brings 'em to
Vancouver. It's what brought me here when I retired."

"You were a cop, weren't you? Toronto City?"

"Yep. Thirty years. Saw some things, I can tell you. Still, it was a piece of cake in comparison, from what I can see. We had problems downtown, but nothing like you see here." He shook his head again. "More drugs here; port city and all that. Stuff goes down here that you just don't get in Toronto. The Sutton case—never had anything like that in Toronto."

"The Sutton case." Mark nodded. "Yeah, I remember that. Seven women?"

"Eight. Jeez, that was bad. Bring back the death penalty, I say. Fucker like that—excuse my French—doesn't deserve to be alive, even if he is rotting in a jail cell in Kingston. Waste of taxpayers' money. Never should have got to eight, either. Wouldn't have, if it had been in North Van or Kerrisdale or anywhere except down here, Skid Row. One woman disappears from some middle-class neighbourhood, her body turns up in a dumpster a few miles away, people are going to be screaming for the police to do something about it, but women disappear from down here, and who cares? Who even notices? Didn't look good for the Vancouver cops; black eye for the city. Especially when they found out they had the right guy after five murders, and let him go."

"Yeah, I'd forgotten that." Mark frowned, recalling. "Something about some other person making crank calls to the police, led them in the wrong direction."

"That's it. Police had Sutton in the frame, main suspect, and then they got calls from someone claiming to be the murderer, along with a letter from—where was it?—the interior somewhere, Kelowna or Vernon, same place as the calls, anyway. Seemed legit, police took it seriously, and since they knew Sutton hadn't been there they let him go. He killed three more women before he got caught. Figured the calls and letter were from some wannabe copycat, or someone's idea of a sick joke gone wrong." Bob shook his head. "Some twisted, sad people out there. You'd've thought something like that would keep women off the streets down here, but they're still around, worse than ever. Now the city's talking about trying to do something about them and the drunks and the drug dealers, get 'em outta sight before Expo comes along; looks bad for the tourists, seeing junkies and prostitutes all over the place. They'll just end up moving them along somewhere else, let someone else deal with them. Cosmetics, that's all it is; like putting a bandaid on a broken leg. And nothing's really changed since the Sutton case, that's the really sad thing. Whole fucking mess could happen all over again any time, and get to more than eight, for all the notice anyone'd take. There's a few people trying to help, but not many." He jerked his thumb over his shoulder in the direction of the lobby. "Raymond in there, for instance."

"Raymond?" Mark exclaimed. "What does *he* do?"

"Helps out at a shelter on Cambie, near the cenotaph. Didn't you know? Yeah, I've seen him there a couple of times. Asked him about it once, but he didn't want to talk about it."

"Yeah, he's not the talkative type, Raymond. Keeps to himself."

Bob laughed. "I noticed. Just goes to show, you never can tell about people." He looked at his watch. "Gotta go check the parking lot and back entrance; found a couple of winos behind the dumpster there two nights ago, want to make sure they haven't come back. It's getting colder now, they're looking for somewhere more sheltered. Page me if our friend comes back."

"Will do."

Mark watched the burly figure of the security guard walk away down the sidewalk and turn the corner towards the entrance to the hotel parking lot. He fumbled in his pocket and lit a cigarette, taking a deep drag. Further down the street a movement caught his eye, and he saw a figure stagger out of a doorway and turn away, weaving down the street. A car that was driving along Hastings slowed, then stopped as another figure moved out from the shadows close to the buildings and leaned in the open passenger window. Mark could see that it was a woman, dressed, despite the weather, in a short skirt and short-sleeved, clingy top. He wondered if it was the same woman Bob had seen off the premises a few minutes earlier. It could have been; it was hard to tell at that distance. The thought flitted through Mark's head that all the women down here looked the same anyway, and he shook himself angrily. Wasn't that part of the problem that Bob had been talking about?

He heard the sound of a door slamming, and realised that the woman had disappeared into the car which had stopped for her. It pulled away and drove off down Hastings. *They don't call it the world's oldest profession for nothing*, Mark thought. *Nothing'll ever change.*

There was a flare of light behind him, and he turned to see that someone had entered The King's Arms. Mark moved closer to one of the windows, peered through the glass, and saw that it was Raymond, obviously going to clear the cash register where the bartender and servers rang up the orders. He watched as the tall man disappeared behind the bar and walked to the machine at the far end. It was darker down there, and Mark wondered how he could see what he was doing. *Five years he's been doing it*, he thought. *He could probably manage it blindfolded.*

He watched as Raymond set the machine clearing, and then was surprised to see the auditor turn away from the register and look into the corner of the bar furthest from where Mark stood. He had his back to Mark, but it looked as if he was speaking with, or to, someone: his head bobbed up and down, and his hands moved in a gesture which made it look as if he were trying to explain something. Mark squinted through the glass, trying to see who he was talking to, but it was dark in the corner, and all he could make out were shadows. If there was someone else there, the person was keeping well out of view.

Mark was even more surprised when, a moment later, Raymond reached up and turned on the television set which was mounted in the corner over the bar. The glow from the screen illuminated that section of the room, but only faintly. The shadows were still thick, but . . . yes! There *was* someone there, he thought. There, in the corner, a figure, surely. . . .

He leaned closer to the window, and inadvertently struck it with his forehead. He pulled back in surprise, but not before he saw the auditor turn with a visible start. Mark thought that

Raymond said something, but he could not hear it through the glass. He saw the man reach up and turn off the television set, and the corner retreated into shadows.

A moment later Mark was back inside the hotel, and had pulled open the doors leading into the bar. He reached to his right and flicked on the bank of switches there, and immediately the room was flooded with light. Raymond was behind the bar, his attention focused on the cash register as if his life depended on it. Mark scanned the room, but there was no sign of anyone else, and no way that anyone could have left without being seen. Unless that person was behind the bar with Raymond . . . but that was ridiculous. Mark cleared his throat.

"Uh, Raymond . . . sorry if I startled you. I was just . . . I thought that . . . hey, if you want the TV on when you're in here that's fine, not a problem . . . " He trailed off, aware that he was babbling and obscurely angry about the fact. He took a breath. "If there's something you want to talk about . . . " *Why had he said that?* "Okay. I'll just leave you to it." He turned and left the bar before Raymond could say anything.

IV

For the rest of the night Mark found himself thinking, at odd moments, about what he had seen in the bar. On the surface, there seemed little that was troubling. What had actually happened? Raymond had been talking to himself; well, that wasn't exactly uncommon. He had turned on the television in the bar; not a hanging offence. He had seemed startled when Mark banged the window; who wouldn't be, well after midnight, in a dark bar, alone?

But *had* he been alone? Mark realised that was the aspect of the whole business that was niggling at him. He could have sworn there had been someone else present, in the shadows in the corner. Thinking about it, he saw that the presence of another person made the whole scenario perfectly simple. Raymond *had* been talking to someone, had turned on the TV for that person, and had been startled when he had been spotted.

Only there hadn't been anyone else there. Raymond had

come out almost immediately after Mark, and had locked the doors behind him. Later, feeling slightly embarrassed, Mark took advantage of the auditor's absence behind the desk to go and check the bar. Both sets of doors—the one into the lobby and the one that opened onto Hastings—were firmly locked, and there was no one in the room. Mark stood by the doorway for a few moments, shaking his head. With the lights on the room looked commonplace, resolutely ordinary, stools lined in orderly fashion against the bar, chairs and tables empty, waiting for the next day's custom. The brass footrail against the bar gleamed softly; glasses sparkled; bottles of liquor glowed dully, amber and red and gold, full of promise. Yet in spite of this, Mark shivered. The King's Arms was not, he thought, somewhere he would care to drink, or spend any more time in than he had to. If Raymond wanted to sneak in and put the television on to pass some time, he was welcome to the place.

Mark snapped the lights off and took one more almost involuntary glance backward. The movement in the shadowy corner furthest from him he put down to the reflections from the street light outside. He pulled the doors to, made sure they were securely locked, and headed into the brightly lit lobby.

Behind the desk Raymond had his head down, and seemed to be studiously avoiding catching Mark's eye. Sylvia was busy posting bar charges to guest accounts, and Mark didn't want to say anything in front of her. Besides, what was there to say? The graveyard shift was a funny place; the normal rules didn't apply. Everyone knew that. Probably Raymond had been caught doing the same thing by another Duty Manager, and been hauled over the coals for it, and now feared a repetition. Mark decided that the best thing to do was forget about it.

Later that night he was in the kitchen, rustling up a sandwich. Sylvia was already at one of the tables in the empty restaurant, eating a piece of pie and reading a thick paperback. Mark took his sandwich and a glass of milk over to the table and slid onto the bench opposite. He glanced at the title of the book.

"*Tales of Mystery and Imagination*, huh? What're you trying to do, impress someone?"

Sylvia grinned. "I like to surprise people. My mom actually got me onto Poe; read me 'A Cask of Amontillado' when I was about eight. Scared the crap out of me; I had nightmares about being bricked up alive for days afterward. I loved it, though. It's brilliant stuff. Listen to this." She opened the book and began to read aloud, rather self-consciously:

> "During the whole of a dull, dark, and soundless day in the autumn of the year, when the clouds hung oppressively low in the heavens, I had been passing alone, on horseback, through a singularly dreary tract of country; and at length found myself, as the shades of the evening drew on, within view of the melancholy House of Usher."

She looked up. "Great stuff, isn't it? Here's another favourite." She flipped forward a few pages, cleared her throat, and read:

> "And travellers now within that valley,
> Through the red-litten windows, see
> Vast forms that move fantastically
> To a discordant melody;
> While, like a ghastly rapid river,
> Through the pale door
> A hideous throng rush out forever
> And laugh—but smile no more."

"That explains why you watch stuff about ghosts on TV."

Sylvia slid a bookmark between the pages and laid the book down on the table. "I guess. I've just always liked things like that: Bigfoot, Loch Ness Monster, Ogopogo. Bring it on, I say."

"I'm surprised you can work graveyard shift. Doesn't it spook you?"

Sylvia took a bite of pie and considered the question for a moment. "Nah, not really." She met Mark's gaze and added, "Well, sometimes." There was a pause. "Front desk isn't so bad. Night audit's kind of creepy sometimes, wandering around the hotel when it's dark, clearing the machines. Glad I only do it two nights a week. Don't know how Raymond stands it the rest of the time."

"Funny how he never joins us for some food. Doesn't the guy get hungry?"

Sylvia swallowed another mouthful of pie. "Yeah, 'course he does. He's not *that* weird."

Mark remembered Joe's words of a few weeks ago. "You think Raymond's weird, then?"

"Kind of. Not that there's anything wrong with him; I've worked with worse, believe me. It's just that . . . " She paused. "I guess I'm just not used to working with people I don't know much about. I mean, you work with someone, especially on graveyard shift, you talk, right? Like we do. Just stupid stuff, everyday stuff, not trying to solve all the problems in the world, just shooting the breeze. But Raymond—he never talks about himself. I asked him once where he was from, and he just said he was from the Interior, and I said "Gee, must be kind of different, living here in Vancouver, then", thinking maybe he'd open up a bit, but he just said yes, it was, and that was it. Every time I try to talk with him it's like that; not unfriendly, just . . . It's like trying to play tennis with someone who never hits the ball back to you, so I've pretty much given it up. Some people just don't like talking about themselves."

"He ever mention a family, anything like that?"

"Nope. I asked Kathie on the morning shift about him once— she's been here forever, knows everything about everyone—and she said he's never mentioned anyone else. Came here five years ago from another hotel in the chain—Victoria, I think—and been here ever since. They tried to get him to go up to the accounting department a couple of years back, she said—figured he'd had enough of the graveyard shift, and he's not the greatest person in the world with customers anyway—but he said no, he was fine where he was." Sylvia took another bite of pie. "Oh yeah, another thing she said was that there was some fuss a couple of years ago—kind of thing you wouldn't remember about anyone else, but Raymond's so . . . what's the word . . . "

"Weird?"

"Yeah, weird about sums it up. Anyway, Kathie said that they found out he hadn't taken any vacation in the three years he'd been here. I dunno how they missed it, but he just kept coming in to work, week in and week out, and no one noticed he hadn't taken any holidays. I guess it's easy in a hotel, everyone working shifts, not like in an office nine to five. There was a fuss about it, I guess, and they tried to make him take a big whack of holidays all at once, but he just said no way." Sylvia shook her head. "Crazy, huh? It's not like he would have lost pay or anything, but he just refused, said he didn't need a holiday, didn't want to go anywhere, he didn't care if he lost the time or the pay or anything."

"So what happened?"

Sylvia shrugged. "Kathie says they came to some kind of arrangement; he got back pay for the time he'd accrued, but he was told he had to take his holidays in future, it was in the contract and there'd be hell with the union otherwise. Apparently Raymond wasn't very happy. Guy never gets sick, either; Kathie figures he must have weeks of sick time stored up."

Mark thought this over. "Do you think . . . do you think he's got a problem of some kind?"

"What kind of problem?"

"I don't know." Mark paused, thinking of the scene in the bar earlier. "Could he . . . could he have a drink problem, maybe?"

"Drink problem? Raymond?" To Mark's surprise she looked thoughtful, almost concerned. "What makes you think that?"

Mark sighed. It all seemed so stupid, really, and yet he found he wanted to talk about it. So he told Sylvia about the scene in the bar earlier, expecting that she'd laugh and tell him he needed to get moved off the graveyard shift before he started seeing pink elephants in the elevator, but instead she just looked at him silently for a few moments and then said slowly, "That's weird."

"There's that word again."

"Yeah, it kind of comes up naturally where Raymond's concerned." She was silent, as if trying to decide what to say.

"You know I do night audit two nights a week? Well, the three nights when Raymond's on audit and I'm on desk, I can't help noticing that he . . . well, he seems to spend a lot of time in The King's Arms. Now hang on"—seeing the expression on Mark's face—"I don't say he's got a drink problem, but I kind of think that . . . well, that maybe he did, once."

The silence stretched out for what seemed a long time. Finally Sylvia continued, although now her eyes did not meet Mark's; instead, her fingers played over the edges of her book and her gaze was fixed on the bird on the cover. "My dad had a drinking problem," she said finally, in a low voice. "It got worse as the years went on, and when I was about—oh, eleven or twelve— things *really* got bad. I don't know what happened in the end—my mom's never talked about it—but she walked out and took my sister and me with her. We lived with my grandparents for a few weeks, and I remember my dad coming round to see my mom, and them talking for a long time while my grandma took us for a walk or something. I guess they finally reached an agreement, and Dad went on the wagon. He was out two or three nights a week; afterwards I realised it was AA meetings. It worked; I mean, things weren't brilliant, but it was okay. Better than it had been, at least." She took a deep breath. "Anyway, what I'm getting at is that I see the signs in Raymond. My dad hasn't taken a drink since then—far as I know—but sometimes we'll be at a restaurant or a family gathering or something, and there's some booze there, and Dad'll just get this look on his face, kind of half-scared, half-longing." Sylvia shrugged. "It's hard to describe; I guess you have to live through it. But I see that—or think I see it—in Raymond. When he was training me on audit I saw him standing there in The King's Arms, looking at the bar and all the bottles, and I saw that same look on his face that Dad has sometimes."

"I see." Mark was silent for a moment. "So you think Raymond spends too much time in the bar?"

"Yeah. No . . . I mean, what's 'too much'? All I know is that it takes me about five minutes, tops, to clear the machine in there, and he's in there for twenty at least. And if you're wondering why I've never said anything, it's 'cause it doesn't seem to matter. He gets the job done, right? So he likes to hang out in the bar; well, we hang out here, so what's the difference? Except I can't see why anyone'd want to hang out in there, especially after it's closed. Place gives me the creeps."

"Why?"

"I don't know. I just don't like it in there after it's closed. The cleaners don't, either."

"Don't they?"

"Nah. That's why they're always there soon as it closes, to give it the once over while Joe's still in there cashing out and getting things put away. I talked to Sunita about it one night."

"What did she say?"

Sylvia shrugged. "Just that they don't like it in there. Too many shadows."

"What on earth does that mean?"

"Just what she says. C'mon, you say you saw it yourself tonight. That corner, over in the back, near the machine. It's like there's someone there, just out of sight. Sometimes I think that if I look out of the corner of my eye I'll actually see whoever it is."

"Have you?"

"No. I've never tried."

There was silence then. Sylvia looked at her watch, sighed, and picked up her book.

"C'mon, Mr. Duty Manager, time to get back to work, or we're gonna be in trouble. Danny'll be sending out a search party. We've got us a hotel to run."

V

The truth was, the hotel pretty much ran itself at night, something that the graveyard shift workers never really admitted to anyone else. Yes, the hours were crap; but apart from that it was a great job, as Mark had to admit.

As November turned into December and the countdown to Christmas began, he found himself watching Raymond with—curiosity was too strong a word, more a mild interest. There was nothing in the man's demeanour or behaviour to excite such curiosity; he seemed the same as always, quiet, hard-working, and competent. Still, Mark found himself mentally keeping tabs on what the auditor did during his shift, and realised quickly that Sylvia was right: he did seem to spend more time in The King's Arms than the work demanded. He refrained from saying anything, however. The man did his job, and gave no cause for complaint. Whatever he did in there wasn't hurting anyone.

Mark also tried to draw the other man out about himself, but quickly found that Raymond was not forthcoming. He answered questions politely, yet with a bare minimum of information that almost verged on curtness but stayed just the right side of the line. It was if he felt that any information he volunteered about himself came with a price, and that he had spent many years ensuring that he kept the books balanced.

One evening in mid-December they were in their usual places: Raymond at the far end of the desk working on the Sales and Labour report, Danny off collecting menu cards, Bob on his rounds, and Sylvia sorting keys from the drop box into the wooden slots in the drawers in the desk. It was nearly 3.00 am, and somewhere far off Mark could hear the dim buzz of a vacuum cleaner as the night cleaners went about their business. A car drove slowly past on Hastings, headlights causing shadows to skitter across the lobby floor. Mark watched it disappear from view.

"Wonder what they're doing here this time of night," he said, more to break the silence than anything else.

Sylvia looked up. "That's what they call a rhetorical question, isn't it?" Mark looked puzzled. "C'mon, you're not *that* innocent. There's only one thing people come down here for at this time of night. Well, two things, really."

"Oh, I know that." Mark looked back out at the now quiet street and shook his head. "You can't really imagine it, though, can you? That kind of life. It's like another world out there. You walk out there in the daytime, it's all—I don't know—*normal* people, shopping, catching buses, going to work, all that everyday stuff we all do. But when you go out there at night. . . . Jesus, you wonder where these people are all day. Hidden away, like vampires, waiting for the night."

"They're not that hidden in the day," Sylvia pointed out. "You just have to know where to look; or where not to. But yeah, it's a lot worse at night. On Thursday I got propositioned twice walking here from the bus stop. Never happens during the day. And if you even *think* about making a joke about that comment I'll throw a tray of keys at you."

Mark stared at her. "You get propositioned?"

Sylvia put on an air of mock anger. "Don't sound so surprised. And I did say it only happened at night. Seriously, yeah, happens all the time."

"What do you say?"

"Depends. If they ask how much I charge I tell them they can't afford it, and if they ask me if I'm available I tell them that I will be at 8.00, when my shift at the police station is over. Usually does the trick, no pun intended."

Mark shook his head. "I can't believe it." Seeing Sylvia's look, he added hastily, "I don't mean it that way, I mean that . . . you don't look like a prostitute, that's all."

"What's a prostitute look like?" Sylvia countered. "I mean, they're women, same as me. They don't all wear skirts up to here and tops down to here and fishnet stockings. Anyway, I get the feeling that the guys who proposition me don't even see *me*, if you get what I mean. They just see a woman, and figure if a woman's down here at this time of night, on her own, there's only one reason for that. Far as they're concerned, we're all interchangeable. I bet that five—no, two—minutes after a guy propositions me, he couldn't tell you what colour my hair was, what I was wearing, or anything. I'm just a piece of meat to them. You're shopping for dinner, looking at steaks in a grocery store, they all look pretty much the same. That's why stuff can happen to these women and no one makes a fuss. They're interchangeable. One of them disappears, who knows? Who cares? There'll be another one to take her place. That's how that guy—what's-his-face, Sutton—could get away with it. No one cared."

"Bob said pretty much the same thing to me once."

Sylvia nodded. "Well, he's right. There's Sutton, killing all these women, and no one even noticed they were gone until some of the families began kicking up a fuss, wouldn't take no for an answer. Even then no one suspected there was a serial killer on the loose." She dropped a key into its slot, checked the inside of the key drop box, and closed the drawer. "Anyway, there's no reason you'd ever have to think about things like getting hit up on the street; you're a guy, you'll never have to worry about someone rolling down their car window and asking you how much you charge. Unless you're on the asking end," she added, "and I can't picture that, somehow, unless you were plastered. No telling what stupid things otherwise nice guys'll do when they're drunk."

There was a clatter and a muffled curse from the far end of the desk, and Sylvia and Mark turned to look. Raymond was scrabbling with a bottle of white-out which had dropped to the counter; as they watched, a small pool of milky white spread out across the half-completed report he had been working on. Sylvia grabbed a box of Kleenex from under the desk and hurried down, but Raymond almost pushed her away.

"It's fine. I'll clean it up. I don't need any help."

"Are you sure? Here's some Kleenex, let me . . . "

"No! Leave me alone!" This time he did push out, and Sylvia backed away, holding up the Kleenex box like a shield. It would almost have been funny in other circumstances, but there was not a trace of humour in the situation. Raymond drew himself upright with a hissed intake of breath and seemed about to say something; then he turned away from Sylvia, carefully picked up the report, and deposited it in the garbage can by his side before pulling a handkerchief out of his pocket and dabbing at the small puddle of white left on the counter. Then he began gathering together papers with hands which, Mark saw, trembled slightly.

"I'm going to take this into the back office," he said in a voice that sounded strained. Before Mark could say anything, Raymond had opened the door beside him and disappeared.

"Well." Sylvia watched the door swing back into place.

"There's something you don't see every day." She moved back to her station and put the box of Kleenex back under the desk. "Was it something I said?"

"Maybe. You were talking about getting drunk."

"Yeah." She looked at Mark, eyes wide. "Jeez, I didn't even think, it just sort of came out."

"I don't think that's what got him upset. I was watching him while you were talking about Sutton; he was looking kind of . . . " Mark stopped, trying to think of the right word to describe the look on Raymond's face, and it came unbidden. "Haunted."

Sylvia stared, puzzled. "But why would that bother him? It's ancient history; the guy's in prison. Raymond couldn't possibly . . . "

"I don't know." A fragment of conversation came back to Mark. "Bob says that Raymond works—volunteers—at some shelter down on Cambie. Maybe—I don't know, it's a long shot, but maybe he knew one of the women who was killed."

"Jesus." Sylvia looked pale. "Maybe I should go and say something, apologise."

"For what? 'Sorry for making conversation'? Besides, he's the one who should be apologising to you. Let it go."

It was easy advice to give, but Mark found it hard to take. For the rest of the night Raymond stayed in the back office, head down, working at his reports. To say he was ignoring the others would not have been accurate, as outwardly he seemed the same as always. Twice, however, when Mark went through the office, he saw the auditor sitting, staring at the desk, only resuming work when he realised that Mark was there. Raymond's hands, Mark noticed, were still shaking slightly.

"I think maybe Raymond's coming down with something," he said later to Sylvia, as the first of the morning team began coming on shift. "He doesn't look well. Thank God he's only got one night to go before the weekend; with luck he'll get it out of his system over the next few days. Even if he's not getting sick, it'll give him a chance to cool down, and things can go back to normal."

Mark was to remember those words, with something like regret, less than twenty-four hours later.

VI

Saturday was never Mark's favourite night of the week; the prospect of dealing with rowdy drunks coming out of The King's Arms always depressed him. But he had little time to think about that the next night, for within half an hour of arriving he received a phone call which put all other thoughts out of his mind.

"Just had a call from Air Canada at the airport," he informed the night shift. "They're shut down out there; bad fog. They had hoped it would clear, but no luck; nothing's taking off. All the hotels in Richmond are full, and they're sending a bunch of people our way. About a hundred, from what I gather, but it could be more. Too bad we didn't know about this half an hour ago, we could have kept some of the evening shift on." He thought for a moment. "Sylvia, I need you to set up a group name, start blocking off some rooms, get reg cards made up. Danny, keep an ear out for the switchboard and give Sylvia a hand with keys; I want them in envelopes with all the reg cards for when the guests get here. Raymond, I need you to start getting meal vouchers ready. They're too late for dinner, but they get $8.50 a person for breakfast. Here." Mark fished a couple of pads of vouchers out of a desk drawer. "Start writing. When you get finished you can help Sylvia with the reg cards."

Raymond stared at Mark as if he had started speaking in Greek. "But what about the night audit?"

Mark shook his head. "Forget night audit right now; we need to get as much sorted out as possible before the buses arrive. We're going to have a hundred tired and pissed-off people here inside of"—he looked at his watch—"twenty minutes. When they get here, they're going to want to get checked in and get to their rooms. The easier we make that process, the easier our lives will be. Get busy."

The first bus arrived at 12.30, with another hard on its heels, and a third one arrived soon after. The stream of people seemed never-ending, and although Mark, Sylvia, and Raymond worked as fast as they could, the line-ups didn't seem to get any less long, while tempers, in contrast, got shorter as the minutes ticked by. Sylvia kept a cheery smile on her face, but Raymond checked his watch every other minute, or so it seemed to Mark, until he wanted to shake him. Joe had long since closed up The King's Arms by the time the last of the guests were checked in, and Raymond had been ordered to go and sit by the switchboard to take the steady stream of wake-up call requests while Sylvia got the check-ins processed. This he did with a bad grace that pushed Mark's already frayed temper almost to the breaking point; when he emerged from the switchboard just after 2.00 and headed for the door, Mark snapped.

"Where do you think you're going?"

"The bar." Raymond nodded his head in the direction of the pub. "I have to go and clear the machine in there."

"No. There's still work to do here. We need to get all these charges posted so we can start update, otherwise there'll be hell to pay when people start checking out. You can help Sylvia."

"But . . . but we need to clear the machines!"

"Yes; after we get the charges posted."

"But you don't understand . . . "

"I understand, Raymond, that I've asked you to do something. Just do it. Sylvia, hand me those bar bills, I'll give you a hand."

Sylvia handed Mark a stack of bills, and he walked to a computer midway down the desk. For a time there was silence as the three of them worked, but it was a strained, uncomfortable silence, and Mark was relieved when the last of the charges had been posted. He stretched, looked at his watch, and turned to Raymond, who looked nervous and twitchy.

"Right. Machines. You can go and do the restaurant and the lounge. Sylvia can do the bar."

"What?" Raymond and Sylvia's words echoed each other; only whereas Sylvia looked puzzled, Raymond looked almost panicked.

"You heard me. Go and get those machines cleared; Sylvia, take the key and go clear the machine in The King's Arms.

We're way behind; we don't need anyone lingering in the pub tonight."

Raymond's head jerked back as if he had been hit; then, without a word, he turned and headed out from behind the desk, in the direction of the restaurant. Sylvia started to say something, but took one look at Mark's face and thought better of it.

She was back quickly, trailing a roll of machine tape behind her. Mark thought she looked pale. *Not surprising*, he told himself, and thought no more of it.

The rest of the night—or what was left of it—went by in a blur. There was no time even to go and get a cup of coffee; Danny brought them sandwiches around 4.00, but they were left largely untouched. It was well past 8.00 by the time they had finished everything, and by then the morning shift and senior management had arrived, a steady stream of guests was checking out, The Palace had shrugged off its night-time air of darkness and silence, and become once more a bustling downtown hotel.

Mark and Sylvia went for a bite of breakfast in the hotel restaurant; one of the perks of the graveyard shift. They ate in silence for the most part; a not uncomfortable silence, thought Mark, who was happy enough to let his mind wander. He was brought back to his surroundings by a sudden question.

"Why did you make me go and clear the machine in the bar?"

"Why . . . what?" He shook his head. "I don't know, I just wanted it done fast. If Raymond'd disappeared in there we wouldn't have seen him for ages. And to be honest, he was pissing me off, looking at the time every few seconds, like we were keeping him from something important."

"I wish you'd sent him, though."

Mark remembered Sylvia's pale face. "Hey, is something wrong?" he asked in concern. "Did something happen?"

"I don't know." Mark waited. "Remember what I said about shadows in there? Maybe it's just me, maybe I was tired and stressed, but . . . it just seemed like there were an awful lot of them." She gave a weak laugh. "I could've sworn, though, there was someone in there, in that dark corner, moving around, like

they were . . . I don't know . . . impatient? No, that's not it."
She thought. "Angry," she said finally. "There was a real feeling
of anger in there." She looked at Mark's face. "I know, I know,
overactive imagination. Still, I didn't like it." Sylvia took a last
gulp of coffee. "At least I don't have to go in there tonight,
with the bar being closed on a Sunday. And you're right, I think
Raymond *is* coming down with something. At least he gets a
couple of days off now. As long as we don't get any more delayed
flights, we'll be okay. Things couldn't really get any worse."

She was wrong, Mark realised later. Things could get *much*
worse.

ഔ   ങ

The calm before the storm, Mark thought, long after; two quiet
nights, where the only untoward event was Sylvia's nervousness
about going into The King's Arms on Monday to clear the
machine. Mark noticed that she made sure to go in to the bar
even before Joe had closed up, but he refrained from making
any comments, even as a joke. Somehow it didn't seem a joking
matter.

By unspoken common consent, neither Sylvia nor Mark spoke
about what had happened on Saturday. When Mark came in on
Tuesday he found himself hoping that Raymond had shaken off
whatever was bothering him. The auditor still looked pale, but
apart from that seemed more or less his usual self, and Mark
hoped this signalled that normal service—normal for Raymond,
anyway—was now being resumed.

The phone call came in not long after midnight, when the
night shift had gone and Sylvia was responsible for answering the
telephone. Mark only half-noticed as she went to answer, and
when, a minute or so later, she came back behind the desk he
didn't even look up until he heard her whisper "Mark."

He turned to her. "Yes, what is . . . " he started to say; but
one look at her face cut the words off in mid-flow. "Jesus, what's
wrong? Are you okay?"

Sylvia, wide-eyed, her face white, shook her head. "I'm fine;
but Mark, that was a bomb threat."

"What!?"

Sylvia nodded. "Someone—a guy—just phoned, said there was a bomb in the hotel, in The King's Arms, and it was going to go off sometime tonight. What do we do?"

"Keep calm, that's what we do." Mark grabbed the walkie-talkie off the counter. "Bob, Mark here. Come to the front desk immediately; we have a security alert." He turned back to Sylvia. "Keep calm. Raymond, go and find Danny, tell him to come here right away. I'll phone the police."

By the time he was off the phone Bob had arrived. Mark was only too happy to let the older man take charge.

"Sylvia, don't answer the phone if it rings; let Mark do that. Go in the back office, get a piece of paper, and write down everything you can remember about the phone call: what the caller said, anything about his voice, if you could hear any sounds in the background. Do it now while it's fresh in your head. He said the bomb was in The King's Arms?"

"Yes."

"And did he say exactly when it would go off?"

"Just that it would be tonight."

"Should we go and evacuate the bar, tell everyone they have to leave?" asked Mark.

Bob shook his head. "You wanna be the one to go in and tell a bunch of serious drinkers they have to leave before closing time? Believe me, they won't care about a bomb threat, but they will care about being cut off before the bar shuts. The police'll be here any minute; let them take care of that."

Four police cars arrived within two minutes, and a no-nonsense sergeant took charge of the situation immediately. He listened to Sylvia's account of the phone call she had taken, and nodded in approval when Bob told him what he had advised.

"That's right; we need you"—he looked at Sylvia—"to write down all you can remember." He turned to Mark. "We're going to have to evacuate the hotel as well as the bar, sir. Bomb goes off in there"—he jerked his head in the direction of The King's Arms—"this whole building is compromised. How many rooms are occupied?"

"About fifty. We're nowhere near full."

"That's good. I'll need printouts showing all the occupied rooms. Two of my men will go and get everyone out of the bar; anywhere else open?"

"The lounge on the top floor."

"Right, we'll need to get them out too. I'll get some of my men knocking on room doors. It would be helpful if you and another staff member could come with us, reassure people."

"Couldn't we just ring the fire alarm?"

The sergeant shook his head decisively. "We don't want to panic people; the last thing we want is people stampeding out of here. And in my experience you always get people who ignore fire alarms. No; we need to go door to door, tell people they have to get dressed and leave immediately, and send them to a designated spot clear of the building. We'll need another staff member there with an occupancy list, so we can make sure everyone's accounted for. I'd suggest the parking lot down the block. We'll have some more men out there to make sure everyone gets clear of the hotel, and in the meantime the bomb squad will check out the bar. How many staff do you have on?"

Mark gestured down the length of the desk, where Sylvia, Raymond, Bob, and Danny were standing. "This is it, except for the cleaners, and the staff in the bar and lounge."

"Right." The sergeant eyed them up, then nodded at Bob. "You round up the cleaners and then go up to the lounge, get everyone out. I'll send someone with you. You and you"—he gestured to Mark and Raymond—"go with my men and start knocking on doors. You"—this to Danny—"can take a list and start checking people's names off when they get to the parking lot. And you can help him," he said to Sylvia, "as soon as you've written down everything about the call while it's fresh in your mind. Now let's go; we don't know how much time we have, if there is a bomb."

Mark went with the sergeant and another policeman, and began knocking on doors. *Thank God this didn't happen last Saturday, with an almost full hotel* he thought, as they knocked on yet another door, and politely but firmly told the startled occupant that there was a police matter under investigation, could you please get dressed as quickly as possible, leave your belongings, and proceed outside. There were no real difficulties—the presence of two policemen seemed to stifle any urge guests might have had to get angry or ask questions—and Mark was glad when they had finished and were outside.

A chill wind blew down the street, and Mark wished he'd put on his coat. The parking lot was full of anxious people, milling about in some confusion, and the police were dealing with two drunk bar customers who had objected to being cut off early. Looking around in between stints of reassuring anxious guests, Mark saw that they had attracted—not a crowd, for it was nothing that conspicuous, but certainly a group of interested onlookers, who were, however, keeping well back in the shadows: perhaps out of deference to the police presence, or perhaps, Mark thought, because their lives were naturally lived out of plain sight, and they were more comfortable seeing without being clearly seen. He shivered again.

"Cold?" Sylvia asked. She had finished writing down her statement and was standing beside Mark, stamping her feet up and down.

"Yes. Sort of. You okay?"

"Yeah." She shook her head in disbelief. "Just when you thought things couldn't get any worse. Everyone accounted for?"

"Yes, everyone's here. Plus a few extras. Could have sold tickets."

"Or coffee. Mmm, what I wouldn't give for a cup of coffee right now. This wind is freezing."

"'What does the night wind say?'" asked Mark.

"What?"

"It's something someone said to me a while back. An old street woman, Jane. You've probably seen her."

"Yeah, I know who you mean." Sylvia scanned the faces around the parking lot. "Isn't that her over there, near Raymond?"

Mark looked in the direction Sylvia was pointing. There *was* someone standing near Raymond, at the edge of the crowd, but before he could be certain the figure had slipped away into the shadows. He turned back to Sylvia. "Could have been; hard to tell."

"What did she say about the night wind?"

Mark tried to remember. "Something about it seeing a beautiful city with ugly people in it; people who look nice, but do bad things, and sometimes try to fix them, but can't."

Sylvia stared at him. "What a weird thing to say. What did she mean?"

Mark shrugged. "I have no idea; I didn't really want to get into a philosophical debate with her. But she's been around here a long time, seen some things herself, so I guess she knows what she's talking about."

Their conversation was interrupted by the sergeant, who came to report that the bomb squad had finished searching The King's Arms and found nothing suspicious. "A false alarm, sir; most of them are, but you can't be too safe. You can start moving the guests back in; we'll keep a couple of men here for the rest of the night, just in case."

"Thanks, sergeant. Okay, troops." He turned to Sylvia, Raymond, and Danny; the rest of the evening staff had been sent home long ago. "Let's get these good people back inside. Danny, head to the restaurant and get some coffee going for anyone who wants it. Raymond, you're really going to have to hustle on the audit so we can get into update. Sylvia, I'll give you a hand with the posting as soon as I get everyone settled. Let's go."

Back in the hotel, it did not take long for the lobby to empty, most guests preferring the warmth of their beds to a cup of hotel coffee. Raymond came to ask Mark for the key to the bar.

"Don't think you need it; the door's open. Couple of policemen still there."

Raymond stared at him. "What do you mean? What are they doing there? How long will they be?"

Mark frowned. "I have no idea; why don't you ask them? Anyway, what's it matter? I'd think you'd be glad of some company in there for a change."

They were idle words, meaning nothing, and Mark was unprepared for the alteration that came over Raymond's face. He went white—Mark thought he was going to faint—and when he spoke his voice was hoarse.

"Why did you say that?"

"I don't know. Hey, are you all right?"

"Yes, yes, I'm fine." He looked far from fine, however.

"Look, Raymond, I don't mean this to sound harsh, and I know we've all been through a lot, but we really do need to get a move on. We've got less than an hour to get ready for update. Do you want Sylvia to . . . "

"No." Raymond pulled himself together with a visible effort. "I'll go. I'll do it."

Mark watched him walk round the desk and head towards the bar, and the thought flashed through his mind that this was what someone walking to his own execution would look like. He shook his head. It had been a long night.

He and Sylvia worked at getting bills posted to guest accounts, and Mark barely noticed as Raymond walked past on his way to the restaurant. He only looked up when, a moment later, a policeman arrived at the desk.

"Excuse me, you Mr. Johnson, the night manager?"

"Yes."

"Found this in the parking lot." The policeman held up a man's wallet. "It might belong to someone here. There's a B.C. driver's licence inside, name of Raymond Young. He a guest?"

"No, he's my night auditor. He'll be back in a few minutes."

"Perhaps you could give it to him then, sir. Must've fallen out of his pocket when he was outside. Ask him to check it; if there's anything missing he can report it to one of the officers."

"Yes, I'll do that." Mark watched as the policeman walked away across the lobby, then opened the wallet. A driver's licence showed Raymond's unsmiling face; there was one credit card tucked in another slot, and some paper money. Apart from that the wallet appeared to be empty.

"His wallet's about as forthcoming as he is," said Mark.

"They say you can tell a lot about someone from something

he carries around with him all the time. Guess it's true." Sylvia watched as Mark began investigating the various slots inside the wallet. "Hey, what're you doing?"

"Just looking," he said. "I want to see what else . . . ah, what's this?"

He had opened a small flap that was fastened with a snap, and pulled out a yellowed piece of paper. It was newsprint, and from the creases and wear on it had obviously been in the wallet for some time. Mark opened it carefully.

"'Andrew Sutton, who was charged with the murder of eight prostitutes from Vancouver's Skid Row area, has been found guilty of eight counts of first degree murder.'" Mark looked up, frowning. "Why on earth has he got this?" He looked more closely at the piece of paper. "It's from the *Vancouver Sun*, June 1975." He scanned the article. "It's a summary of the case and a report on the verdict."

"I don't get it." Sylvia looked puzzled. "Why on earth does he carry that around with him? It's ancient history."

"I don't know." Mark carefully folded the piece of paper and returned it to its place inside the wallet. "But I know one thing: I don't want to be the person who asks him about it. Remember how he got last week, when you were talking about it? Once was enough. He's acting oddly enough as it is."

"Maybe he *did* know someone involved in the case. Maybe he carries it around to remember."

"Maybe. Most people'd carry a picture, though. Look out, here he comes. Hey, Raymond, you lost your wallet."

Raymond looked at Mark, eyes dull. *Like an animal in a trap*, thought Mark automatically.

"Did I?" He reached into his back pocket, and for a moment a flare of panic welled up in his eyes.

"Don't worry, here it is. Police found it in the parking lot. Said you should check it, make sure nothing's missing."

"Yes. Yes, I will." He took the wallet and placed it in his pocket; then, like an automaton, he took his place at the end of the desk without another word, and was silent for the rest of the night.

ဆ ၺ

The next night should have been the start of Mark's weekend, but shortly after getting home he had a phone call from the hotel. Peter, who did graveyard Duty Manager shift two nights a week, was ill; it was a lot to ask, given what he'd gone through, but they were short on people who could do the job, and there was sure to be catching up to do, and would Mark mind. . . .

Mark did mind, but he knew better than to say so. "Duty Manager," he muttered to himself, burying his head in the pillow to try to block out the wan December sunlight that found its way through the curtains. "Glorified dogsbody. Wonder what I'll get tonight?"

But all was blessedly quiet when he got to the hotel just after eleven. Sylvia was off, doubtless enjoying the first of her two days of freedom, her place taken by Shelley, a gum-chewing blonde Mark didn't care for. Raymond was down at the far end of the desk, and one glance showed that he was seriously unwell. At first Mark thought he had come down with the same bug that was currently laying other employees low, but a closer look disabused him of the notion. He looked like a . . . like a whipped dog approaching its master, anticipating another blow and yet unable to stay away. Mark took a deep breath and was about to say something, but the look in the auditor's eye stopped him. There was nothing he could say in the face of such obvious despair.

He did a round of the hotel with Bob, then went back to the desk and retreated into the front desk manager's office near the switchboard, intent on catching up on the paperwork he hadn't got to the night before. He barely noticed when Raymond came in for the key to the bar shortly after 1.00; he found the man's presence disquieting, and was glad when he took the key silently, with a hand that was shaking, and left the office without a word.

Some time later Mark was roused by a tap on the door. Shelley poked her head round the edge.

"Hey, any idea what's happened to Raymond?"

"Why? Is he ill?"

"I dunno." Shelley shrugged. "He went off to clear the machines and I haven't seen him since."

"Jesus!" Mark looked at his watch. "That was forty minutes ago! And you've only just noticed?"

Shelley looked hurt. "Hey, I'm not his mother. I thought you might have had him doing something. And he's so quiet, most of the time you don't see him even when he's there."

"Shit. Okay, Shelly, I'll deal with it. Get back to the desk."

Mark went out the door that connected the office to the main lobby and headed for The King's Arms, sure that was where he would find the auditor. He swung round the corner and was confronted by the closed doors of the bar; when he tried the handles he found they were locked. Perhaps he was wrong—if so, where on earth could . . .

He heard a sound, small and stifled, from inside. He put his ear to the door. Silence. No, there it was again. Was it words? It was hard to tell. Then he heard what sounded like laughter, only it was a humourless, mirthless laughter that sent shivers down Mark's spine.

There was a spare set of keys in the manager's office, and Mark hurried back to the desk. Shelley looked up.

"Find him?"

"Yeah; yeah, everything's fine," Mark said. But he was lying, and he knew it. He did not know what lay behind the door, but whatever it was it was not fine, it was light years from being fine, and although he did not want to go in there he knew that he had no choice.

Back at the doors of the bar, Mark inserted the key and felt the heavy bolt slide back. He pulled one of the doors open as quietly as possible and slipped into the gloom inside. He was on the wrong side of the door for the lights, and had to cross to the other side of the entrance to reach them, and in that brief moment his eyes swept the bar and saw Raymond in the far corner, amongst the darkest shadows, huddled on the floor. He was turned away from the door, looking up, his arms reaching out as if in supplication, a stream of words Mark could not make out issuing from his lips. A moment later the room was flooded with light and Raymond screamed; but not before Mark saw what was surrounding him, the three figures with pale faces and burning eyes and an air of terrible anger mixed with profound sadness.

He hurried over to Raymond—it took all the courage he could summon to force his feet across the intervening distance—and knelt down beside him. The auditor turned to Mark and grasped at the lapels of his jacket.

"Did you see them? Did you?" he begged. His eyes were huge and staring, and looked over Mark's shoulder rather than directly at him. Mark moved so that his own back was against the wall, and there could be nothing behind him.

"What's going on, Raymond?" he asked, as quietly as he could. Raymond had twisted so he could look up into the corner. Mark refused to follow his gaze.

"You saw them, didn't you? Didn't you?" he demanded. Then, more quietly, as if exhausted, "I can tell that you did. I can see it in your eyes. And you only saw them for a moment. I used to see them all the time. Then I found a way for them to leave me, so I could have some peace. They like it here; it's dark and quiet, and near where they used to live. So now they stay here, but when I don't come and see them they . . . they get angry. So angry. I try to tell them if I won't be here . . . warn them . . . but I couldn't this time. . . . "

"Raymond, I . . . I don't know what I saw. I don't know if I saw anything."

"You did. I can tell." Raymond's head sank down on his chest, and Mark thought that he had fainted. Then he heard the auditor say, in a voice that was barely audible, "I was young and stupid . . . drunk . . . thought it was just a joke. I don't know why I . . . " Raymond stopped, and took a deep breath. "It was so long ago. I thought I could make them happy, but I can't. No matter what I do. And I try so hard." Then he began to cry, low, choked, rasping sobs, and Mark could think of nothing to say.

℘ ℘

Mark was not surprised, when he returned to work two days later, to find that Raymond was off on sick leave for an indeterminate period. The doctor's note was vague, merely stating that Mr. Young would be unable to return to work for some weeks due to illness; at Mark's urging the matter was not pressed. Three weeks later Raymond sent in a letter of resignation; his two weeks' notice would be taken as sick leave. He asked that his final paycheque be mailed to his home address. It was highly irregular, but after Mark had a quiet word with the personnel manager, the matter was dropped.

While he was in the personnel office, he took the opportunity of looking through Raymond's file. He had worked at another hotel in the chain, in Victoria, and previous to that had worked at a hotel in Kelowna. Both gave good, although not glowing, references, commending him for his work habits but indicating that his inter-personal skills were, perhaps, lacking. A note on his application form, presumably scribbled by whoever had interviewed him for the job at The Palace, read, in a section titled "Comments on applicant", "Steady, quiet, polite, good with numbers. Has worked graveyard shift; says he likes the hours, wants to work in downtown Vancouver." Beside this, a small notation in the margin read "Drink problem (?)".

With Raymond gone, Sylvia took over as night auditor five nights a week. She reported to Mark that the shadows in The King's Arms were gone, a change which she attributed to new light fixtures. She still does not like going in there, however; she can't say why, precisely.

Mark has never tried to explain. Occasionally, though, when he goes outside to smoke a quiet cigarette in the middle of the night, he finds himself looking in through the window of The King's Arms, searching the far corner where the shadows are darkest. Sometimes he thinks, just for a moment, that he sees movement there, and hears laughter which does not contain the faintest trace of warmth or humour. He shivers then, and tells himself it is only the night wind, and hurries back inside The Palace, and tries not to think about what the wind is saying.

OUT AND BACK

"Keep your eyes open. I don't want to miss it."

"How hard can it be to miss?" Linda asked, pushing a strand of hair behind her ear. "It's not the sort of thing you're going to drive past and not see."

"It's been abandoned for a long time," said Allan patiently. "It's not like there are going to be signs. Besides"—he waved one hand at the dispirited housing development they were driving through—"the place has grown up a lot. Back when it was built it was a long way from anywhere; nothing but scrub and fields."

"So why'd anyone build an amusement park miles from where people lived?" Linda wasn't particularly interested in the answer, but it had been a long drive, and she was tired of the silence; tired, full stop.

Allan shrugged. "I dunno. Guess land was cheap. And there's a lake; that's what it was named after. Must've been a popular spot for people to come with their families."

"What are you expecting to see?"

"I'm not sure. I haven't been able to find out much. It's kind of off the beaten track"—Linda gave a hollow laugh, as if to say *You're kidding me*—"and not too many people seem to have been here. I'm hoping to get some good pictures; put them up on my website."

"Great." Linda stared out the window. "We take a day out of our vacation just so you can maybe get some pictures of you're not sure what—*if* it's still there, and *if* we find it—and then you'll spend hours putting them up on a website for three people to see. Hooray."

Allan glanced sideways at her. "Hey, it's just one day. I didn't think you'd mind."

"Well, you got it wrong then. It's one day out of the vacation I've been looking forward to for months, thinking—stupid me— that we'd have a nice relaxing time, no chasing around like we do every weekend, me being dragged off to some abandoned place or weird site that you just *have* to see. All I want is a *rest*, Allan."

"You didn't have to come, you know. You could have stayed back at the hotel."

"Yeah, I guess I could. While you took the car, I could've stayed in the hotel room, and then when I got bored I could've gone down to the pool, and then I could've gone back to the room. Thrilling. Holidays are supposed to be about doing things together."

Allan shook his head. There was no point arguing with her when she got like this. When he'd realised their trip would take them so close—well, a hundred miles or so—to White Lake Park he'd planned to visit it; he just hadn't mentioned it to Linda until that morning. He'd honestly thought that the idea of visiting another abandoned amusement park would appeal to her as much as it did to him; it wasn't every day you got a chance to see something like this. He was trying to figure out a way to say this without provoking her further when he glanced to his left and saw something that made him start, so that the car swerved and Linda uttered a startled "Hey!"

"Look! Over there! Do you see it?" Allan slowed the car to a crawl. "There!"

Linda craned her neck and peered through the driver's window. Behind the tired, sagging houses that lined the road she could see the tops of trees, an unbroken line stretching in both directions and apparently away from the houses as well. For a few moments that was all she could see, and she was about to ask what he was looking at when she saw it too.

It came into focus so suddenly that she almost jerked her head back in surprise. One moment she was looking at an innocuous treescape, leafy green boughs of maples and oaks and buckeyes fluttering in the breeze, and the next she could see, twisting its way through the branches, the unmistakable silhouette of a roller coaster track, wooden supports criss-crossing beneath. Her

eye followed the track and she saw it dip out of sight behind
the houses; then, further ahead, it rose again, and she had an
impression as of some huge beast crouched behind the houses,
watching, waiting. She shook her head and blinked, and despite
the heat of the day she shivered.

Allan had pulled onto the shoulder and stopped the car. "There
must be a way in," he muttered. "Some sort of entrance . . . "

"Long gone, I'll bet," said Linda. "Place is probably locked
up tighter than a drum. Can you imagine the lawsuits?"

Allan didn't hear; or at least pretended not to. "There's got
to be access from behind these houses. They back right onto it."

"What are you going to do? Walk through someone's back
yard, climb their fence? Honestly, Allan. . . . "

"There." He pointed to a house that stood slightly apart
from its neighbours. It was a good deal older than most of the
other houses in the area, sitting in the middle of an unkempt
lawn choked with dandelions, a battered wooden fence which
had once been white standing guard in front like a mouthful of
broken teeth. To one side was a dusty laneway with a half-dozen
cars parked in it, and Allan looked at them with suspicion.

"Typical," he muttered. "Bet all these people are here to
look at the park. Won't be able to move for tripping over them,
gawking, taking pictures."

"And that makes them different to you—how, exactly?"

Allan said nothing as he pulled in beside the last one in
the row, a dirty Ford Focus with a baby seat in the back. He
reached into the back of their own car and fished around for
the bag containing his camera and notebook. When he got out,
he slammed the door with more force than Linda thought was
strictly necessary, although she refrained from commenting.

The late morning heat was oppressive, like a wet woollen
blanket. Linda pushed a limp strand of brown hair behind one
ear, then smoothed out her skirt, which felt damp and clammy.
Allan glanced at her.

"Don't know why you wore that," he muttered. "Not very
practical."

"Yeah, well, maybe if you'd told me we'd be climbing over

fences and forcing our way through undergrowth I'd've worn something more suitable, like Army fatigues and steel-toed boots. Silly me, I thought when you said 'amusement park' it meant some place civilised, with a midway and something to eat. My own stupid fault; after all this time I should've known better."

Allan said nothing. They were here now, and he was determined to make the most of it. Nothing Linda said would get him down. He'd deal with it later, like he always did; try to smooth things over. The main thing at the moment was to figure out a way into the park.

"Looks as if there might be a door in that fence." He glanced at the house. "Wouldn't be surprised if this was built when the park was."

"Maybe." Linda shrugged. She had been looking at the row of cars. "Don't think you have to worry too much about anyone else beating you to your scoop." When Allan looked puzzled, she pointed. "Most of these are pretty old; don't look like they've gone anywhere in years. Someone probably has a spare parts business on the side."

Allan looked more closely at the cars, and had to admit that Linda was probably right. They all looked old and battered; at least two of them had flat tires, and the oldest one—a mid-1970s station wagon at the far end of the row—was so rusted that the car would likely fall to pieces if anyone tried to move it. *No competition*, he thought with satisfaction.

Linda's voice broke in on his thoughts. "So, what're we going to do? Stand here all day? C'mon, Allan, let's get this over with."

"All right, all right." He slung the bag over his shoulder. Part of him wanted to head straight to the fence and go in, not bother with anything like permission in case someone tried to stop him, but another part of him knew from experience that it was best to get acknowledgement from someone—anyone—of what he was doing, to save awkwardness later on. Not that something like lack of permission would stop him; he'd just find another way in. He always did. He jerked his head in the direction of the house. "I'm just going to go and make sure it's okay," he said, and began walking towards what looked like the main door, at the back of the house facing the park. After a moment Linda followed him.

There was no doorbell, so Allan rapped on the wooden door, the sound harsh in the still morning air. After a few moments there was a noise from inside, as of footsteps hurrying; a woman's voice called out anxiously "Bill?", and the door opened so suddenly that both of them stepped back a pace.

The woman who stood framed in the peeling paint of the door frame was probably in her early thirties, but looked considerably older: her hair had obviously not been cut for some time, and was streaked with grey, and she wore no make-up on her pale face. She was dressed in a faded T-shirt and skirt, the latter with its hem trailing down at one side and two or three rips, inexpertly mended, threatening to unravel further. A small child—a boy, no more than three or so—was peering from behind her legs, looking half-fearfully, half-hopefully at Allan and Linda. There was a suggestion of more people further down the hallway— a muffled murmur, as of voices whispering—but no one else appeared.

Allan cleared his throat. "Uh, hi. We were—we were hoping to be able to get into the park, have a look around. Do you think that would be a problem?"

The woman looked them both up and down. A look almost of disappointment had appeared on her face when she had opened the door and seen them; it was now replaced by one of resignation, and Allan had a sinking feeling that she was going to tell them they couldn't go in. *Some sort of caretaker*, he thought; *there's bound to be one.* He was taken aback when she said, in a flat voice, "There's nothing to stop you going in, if you want to."

"Really? Wow, that's—that's great. Thanks."

"Don't thank me. It's got nothing to do with me. Anyone who wants to go in there is free to do so."

"Ah. Well, that's good to know. Are you the caretaker or something?"

"No. This used to be the caretaker's house, a long time ago. You can get into the park through there." She pointed to the door in the fence at the bottom of the yard.

"I see." Allan nodded towards the parked cars. "Guess you get a lot of people coming here, wanting to have a look."

The woman followed his gaze. "A few. Not many. Those cars are all ours."

" 'Ours'?" Allan queried.

"Yes. The people in this house."

"Have you lived here long?"

"I've been here for . . . " The woman paused and her brow furrowed, as if the effort of calculating were a difficult one. "Two years. Maybe. Not as long as some."

"I see." There was a pause, and when it looked set to continue indefinitely Allan said, "So it's okay if we go in, then? We won't disturb anything, cause any damage. We'll let you know when we're done, if you want, tell you when we're leaving."

"Oh, that's fine. We'll know when you're done."

"Ah. Well, that's—that's great, then. We'll see you later."

The woman said nothing, merely looked at them as they turned and headed towards the door in the fence. They were both conscious of her gaze on them as they made their way through the long grass, although when Linda turned and looked while Allan wrestled with the door in the fence she saw that the woman had gone and the house door was shut. She thought she saw a curtain twitch on one of the lower windows, and there was a suggestion of a figure standing at one of the upstairs windows, but she could not be sure.

Allan grunted and swore as he struggled with the door, which was jammed shut. "One good thing; it means no one else has been this way for a while," he said, giving the door a shove. With a creak and a groan it swung open, and Allan almost fell through, recovering his balance at the last moment. He peered through the opening and took a deep breath. She couldn't see his face, but Linda knew that his eyes were shining and that he had a goofy smile on his face, like a kid getting his first look at the tree on Christmas morning. *How can I compete with that?* she thought; and before she could block it out came the answer: *You can't.*

She watched as he disappeared through the door, and for a moment she thought about not following him, of heading back to the car—she had a spare set of keys in her bag, after all, she could just get in and drive away, leave him here to his precious park, go do something interesting, something *she* wanted to do, instead of trailing after him as she had so many times, pretending to be interested. He probably wouldn't even notice she wasn't there. Then, as she saw him receding into the undergrowth that choked the other side of the fence, she took a deep breath of her own and followed him in.

If she hadn't known she was in a former amusement park, she would never have guessed. Trees crowded round on all sides and weeds ran rampant; there was the suggestion of a trail, but nothing to indicate what the site had once been, until she was brought up short by Allan stopping suddenly in front of her and muttering "Holy shit, that's brilliant." A moment later he was fumbling inside his bag for his camera, and Linda moved around him so that she could see.

A white shape loomed out of a thicket of buckeyes ahead and to their right. It looked as though the vegetation were trying to seize the building and pull it back in amongst the trees, and it took Linda a moment to realise what it was: a small booth with an overhanging roof and windows on three of the four sides, one of them half covered with a wooden shutter. The building had once been painted in gay shades of red and yellow, but the paint had faded and peeled, and one side showed signs of scorching. Linda was trying to figure out what it was when Allan spoke.

"Ticket booth," he flung over his shoulder. "Great, isn't it?"

"Brilliant." Linda took a step closer. "Why's it burned?"

"I dunno. I think there's a lot of fire damage in the park. People get in, start fires just for the fun of it."

"Whatever turns you on, I guess." Linda tried to picture what the booth would have looked like with children lined up in front, jostling each other as they waited impatiently to buy tickets, coins and crumpled dollar bills clutched in sticky hands, the sounds and smells of the midway assailing and enticing them from all sides, but failed utterly. Nothing of that past remained: instead of the music and clatter of the rides there was the soft, sad sound of wind through branches; instead of the smell of corn dogs and fried onions and cotton candy there was the scent of grass and dirt and dead leaves. She shivered and moved closer to Allan.

"Can we go now?" she asked, and he turned to her, startled.

"What do you mean, go? We only just got here. There's tons more to see."

"I just meant can we move on? How many pictures of a ticket booth do you really need?"

"Yeah, okay, I see what you mean." He dug around inside his bag for a moment and pulled out a crumpled piece of paper. He studied it, twisting it and glancing round him as if trying to orientate himself. "Okay, we came in about here," he muttered, looking at the paper, "which means that if we head in that direction"—he pointed—"we should hit the midway. C'mon, let's go."

They skirted round the empty booth, Linda casting a backward glance at it as they moved away. The one shutter still in place moved slightly, as if waving at her, and she quickly turned and headed after Allan, who was following a rough path which led deeper into the trees.

"So, are we headed anywhere in particular, or are we just wandering aimlessly?" Linda's voice sounded harsh in the silence.

"Well, I really want to see some of the midway rides; what's left of them, anyway. That's where the real interest is."

"Interest? You're kidding me." Linda waved one hand at the desolation around them. "If there was any interest in this place it wouldn't be left here to rot. What happened to it, anyway?"

Allan shrugged. "I don't know. There're different stories. A big fire in the grand ballroom; that happened when the park was still going, and they had to shut it down for a while, and I think people started drifting away, forgot it was here. And there's supposed to have been someone who died on one of the rides."

Linda stopped in her tracks. "Tell me you're joking."

"No, of course not." Allan stared at her. "What's wrong?"

"Are we here on another one of your ghost hunts?"

"No, we're not here on a 'ghost hunt'. Honestly, what do you take me for?"

"It wouldn't be the first time. Remember that house you just *had* to go to on a certain date, and that place—where was it—where that ghost ship was supposed to appear? Took me two days to get warm again, all so you could think that maybe you saw something. That I *didn't* see, in case you forgot."

Allan shook his head. "Jeez, Linda, would you stop twisting things? All I said was there's a story about someone dying here on one of the rides. I don't even know if it's true. It's hard to pin down that kind of thing; these places always try to hush it up if they can. If it did happen, it was a long time ago."

Linda looked around. Trees whispered in the faint breeze; somewhere far off a bird chirped. "Everything here happened a long time ago," she said flatly. "I've never been anywhere so empty."

"Yeah, well, it's not that empty." Allan pointed to their left, and Linda saw a faint glimmer of white. "Lots to see, for those who are interested. Who *care*."

"I care," Linda muttered. "I care about getting the hell out of here and getting on with our holiday."

"I know. You've made that clear. Only—well, we're here now. Let's just look around a bit more, okay? Please."

"Fine. But you owe me, big time."

Allan, having gained his point, said nothing, but hurried off in the direction of the blur of white they had seen. Linda, after a moment's hesitation, followed.

As they got closer the shape revealed itself as a large building which had once, no doubt, been impressive, but was now in danger of collapsing in on itself. Two blank windows, like eyes, stared out from under a high roof, and what had once been an overhang running the length of the building's front had had its supports give way and was now hanging limp against the wall. Beside it was another building in even more desperate shape, a tangle of trees and vines choking collapsed timbers, threatening to drag the whole structure into the ground. Allan whistled.

"This is great." The camera was out again and he was snapping away. "I'm going to get some brilliant pictures."

"Of what?"

Allan spared her a quick glance. "What d'you mean?"

"I mean what is it we're looking at, exactly?"

"Oh. I see." Allan considered the buildings, then looked at his plan of the park. "I *think* this one"—he pointed to the more intact of the two buildings—"was the Bumper Car ride, and the other one was the Fun House."

"Some fun." Linda looked at the battered building and shivered. "Looks like a good stiff breeze would knock it over."

"Yeah, I'm lucky I got here before that happened." Allan headed towards the Bumper Car ride. "I'm gonna take a look inside."

"Are you sure that's safe?" Linda didn't really want to get any closer to it, but she followed anyway, picking her way through the weeds pushing way up through the cracked ground.

"Only one way to find out," said Allan, his voice muffled as he pushed his way through an opening where several boards had fallen, in to a section that was leaning—dangerously, Linda thought—to one side. "Oh, man, look at this!"

It took a few moments before Linda's eyes adjusted to the gloom of the building, which was in stark contrast to the brassy brightness outside. The openings along the sides, which would once have been thronged with onlookers watching the happy mayhem within, were boarded up in places, and in others choked with trees, which stifled the sunlight trying to filter in from without. The floor was covered in dirt and leaves and splintered pieces of wood, and in one corner lay a heap of what looked like broken chairs. Running along the back, across from where they stood, was what had obviously once been a covered gallery: a few shafts of sunlight punched their way through holes in the roof, and cables dangled limp from overhead, the lights they had once supported long gone.

Allan was picking his way carefully across the floor, pausing every now and then to take a picture. "Jeez, I'd love to find some of the cars," Linda heard him say. "Wonder what happened to them. Oh, hey, look at this!"

"What?" Linda had only moved a couple of feet away from where they had entered, and was reluctant to advance any further; the building looked anything but stable.

"There's a hole in the floor here; looks like someone cut through with a chainsaw. I can't really see much . . . hang on a sec." He fished around inside his bag and pulled out a flashlight, then shone it through the hole. "Nothing but a load of junk," he said, disappointed. "Hey, what the . . . " He moved suddenly to his left, trying to angle the flashlight as if to see better, and there was a cracking sound from beneath his feet. He scrambled backward as Linda retreated to the side of the building.

"Allan, for heaven's sake, come away from there. That floor's probably rotted through. If you fall in there you could kill yourself."

"No, it's okay, just something shifting. All right, all right"— as Linda opened her mouth to protest—"I'm coming back. Nothing much more to see in here anyway."

"What was down there?"

"I told you; just a load of junk, dead leaves, that sort of thing."

"I thought you saw something else."

"No, just shadows, that's all." They were back outside, and Linda breathed a bit more freely now that they were on safe ground. "C'mon, I want to check out the Fun House."

"You've got to be kidding." Linda glanced at the dilapidated building beside them. "It makes that last one look like a prize home exhibit."

Allan said nothing, but walked away around the front of the Fun House, past a rusting, peeling iron rail that led up a concrete slope to where the entrance had apparently been. There was a wire cage beside it half-obscured by trees, and Allan pointed to it.

"That would have been where the ticket guy sat, probably; look, you can see the exit sign on the other side of it. Looks like they had another fire here." Out came the camera. "I'm just going to walk round, see if I can get a better shot." Before Linda could say anything, Allan disappeared around the corner.

Linda ran her eyes over the front of the building. The entrance looked almost passable, but the exit was covered with boards clumsily stacked against it. One was slightly askew, as if someone had tried to get in that way, and all showed signs of scorching.

Too bad the whole thing didn't go up, thought Linda. *Would've been an improvement.*

There was a sound behind her, off in the trees, as of a branch snapping. She whirled round, peering into the undergrowth. Nothing moved. "Allan?" she called, rather faintly; then, more loudly, "Allan? Where are you?"

No answer. Damn, she hoped he hadn't found a way in. The place was ready to collapse. "Allan!" she called, anger giving an edge to her voice. "Allan, come back here!"

Still nothing. She turned and looked again at the undergrowth, and as she did so caught, out of the corner of her eye, movement inside the wire cage by the Fun House entrance. She swung her head back towards it and could see, between the trees, a figure inside it, half-crouched down as if looking for something. *Or trying to hide.*

"Allan! Allan, this isn't funny. It may have been a Fun House once, but that's no reason to . . . "

"Who're you talking to?"

Linda spun round. Allan had come up behind her, from the passage between the Fun House and the Bumper Car building. "Is there someone here?"

"No, I . . . " Linda looked back at the wire cage. The trees shifted in the wind, almost as if obliging her, and she could see that it was empty. "I thought there was someone in there, that you were playing a joke."

"Not me. The only way to get in there is from inside the building, and I can't find any way in that looks safe." He sounded regretful. "Got some good pictures, though."

"Oh, well, as long as you've got some good pictures then everything's okay, isn't it?"

"What's wrong?" Allan sounded genuinely puzzled.

"Nothing. Nothing at all. I'm just getting tired of poking around old buildings that should've been pulled down years ago, that's all. Like that abandoned factory two months ago, where I got that gash on my knee. Thought I was going to need stitches."

"Well, you didn't, did you?" pointed out Allan, in a reasonable tone that set Linda's teeth on edge. "Okay, c'mon, let's see what else we can find."

"More abandoned buildings, probably. Thrilling. Let's face it: you've seen one, you've pretty much seen them all."

"I guess." Allan didn't sound convinced. "But there's more here than just empty buildings; there's lots of rides still on the site. One site I found said that there's a Tumble Bug ride somewhere; there are only four in existence still."

Linda stared at him. "You know, I've been trailing after you to places like this for three years now, but you never cease to amaze me. You're thirty-two, for God's sake. Shouldn't you have grown out of this sort of thing? Going around looking at all this shit that no one except you and a handful of other people care about? Children's rides! Why?"

"Because—well, because I like it, that's why!" He shook his head. "What's not to like? It's all a part of our past, and it's disappearing, and unless people like me find it, see it, photograph it, it'll be as if it never existed; it'll just be pictures in books that no one looks at." He gestured at the expanse of greenery around them, the forlorn buildings behind them. "This used to be an amusement park; and not just that, it was the midway, the heart of the whole place. Can't you picture it the way it would have been fifty years ago, with kids, families, music playing, the smell of fried onions, the sound of the rides? All those children, almost sick with excitement at the thought of a day at White Lake Park? All the happiness that was here once? *Someone* has to remember it, otherwise it might as well never have been."

Linda started to say something, but was stopped by the look on Allan's face. He looked like a big kid himself; in the car, on the drive out to the park, his face had worn the expression of a child anticipating a major treat. She sighed instead, and made a *You win* gesture with her hands. "I don't want to be here all day, Allan, okay? It's too hot, and this place gives me the creeps."

"Yeah, what was it that spooked you so much back there?" Allan gestured at the Fun House.

"I told you; I thought I saw someone in that wire cage thing." She recalled something else. "And before that I thought I heard someone in the bushes over there." She pointed.

"Really?" Glad to be back on neutral territory, Allan took a few steps in that direction. "Over here?"

"Yeah. Look, it was probably just the wind or a squirrel or something. Forget it."

"No, hang on a minute. . . . " Allan moved away through the trees, and it did not take many steps before he appeared to be swallowed up. Linda waited for a moment, staring intently at where he had vanished. Suddenly she heard a choked cry, followed by a short laugh. "Hey, Linda, come here. I found your intruder."

"What? Allan, this isn't funny."

"No, honest." He reappeared between the trees. "Come look."

She followed him into the undergrowth, peering nervously around her. Allan motioned to a dense clump of maple saplings. "Come and see." Gingerly she stepped forward, and parted the lower branches; then jumped backward with a screech.

A face was leering at her: livid and fierce, vivid reds and too-pale whites. It took a moment for her to register what it was, and when she did she turned on Allan in anger.

"You bastard! You knew I'd jump, that it'd scare me half to death. Jerk."

It was a wooden sign, in the shape of a clown. Out of the garish red mouth came a speech balloon, inside which were the words YOU MUST BE THIS TALL TO RIDE THIS RIDE. One of the clown's arms had obviously indicated the height requirement, but it had vanished; only a jagged stump bleeding splinters remained.

Allan raised his arms in a would-be placating gesture. "Hey,

I'm sorry, I didn't realise it would make you jump like that. Startled me, too; but look." He pointed further into the trees, and Linda unwillingly looked in that direction, her heart still pounding. She could vaguely make out, in the undergrowth, metal shapes, trees growing through and around them.

"What is it?"

Allan had set off in the direction of the shapes. "I think it's the—yeah, it's the Flying Cages!" he called over his shoulder. "Man, I've never seen one of these rides; read about them, though. Used to be in the touring carnivals that went round the county fairs and things, but you don't see them anymore."

When she got closer, Linda wondered why anyone had bothered in the first place. The ride seemed to consist of four large metal cages, each one originally a different colour, although the paintwork had faded and chipped away, leaving only a few traces on the metalwork. One of the cars still had remnants of pale blue cloth trailing from the sides, and Allan nodded.

"That would have been where the cages were padded," he said. He went up to the nearest one and gave it a push. There was a harsh squealing noise and the cage began to move slightly, and Allan gave it another, harder push. It rocked back and forth for a few moments, the framework which supported it groaning in protest at the unexpected movement. After a few moments its movements stilled and it came to rest once more, and there was silence.

"Wow, it still works. This one, anyway."

"Is that all it did? Swung back and forth?"

"I think so. Like I said, I've never actually seen one before."

"Guess those really were simpler times."

"Oh, c'mon, Linda. A lot of rides look pretty tame from the ground, but when you're in 'em they're terrifying. That whole loss of control thing. I mean, imagine being in one of these, it's swinging back and forth, higher and higher, faster and faster, and there's music playing, and you're bouncing from side to side, trying not to lose your balance, watching the ground come at you, people screaming, yelling . . . it's a real rush."

"I'll take your word for it. That kind of thing never appealed much to me. I like to keep my feet on the ground. Even when I was a kid I didn't like to . . . hey, are you listening?"

Allan had turned his head suddenly, and was gazing back the way they had come. When Linda repeated her question he turned back to her with a start, as if only just remembering she were there.

"Did you hear that?" he asked, puzzled.

"What? I didn't hear anything."

"I heard—well, I thought I heard music."

"Music?" Linda stared at him. "No, I didn't hear any music. Maybe someone's car stereo turned up, or music from a nearby house."

"No." Allan shook his head. "It almost sounded like . . . I don't know, like old-fashioned calliope music." When Linda looked puzzled, he said impatiently, "You know, like on a carousel. A merry-go-round."

"Nope. Didn't hear anything like that." She gave a short laugh. "What a pair; I see things, you hear things. Maybe it's time to leave."

"No. Not yet. There's too much more I want to see."

Linda glanced at her watch, then at the sun overhead. "Okay, Allan. But not too much longer. And no more scares, right?"

"Right."

They headed back the way they'd come, Linda carefully not looking at where she knew the clown stood. Once back in front of the Fun House they stopped, and Allan looked at his plan.

"This way, I think," he said.

"You *think*? Where're we going now?"

"Further along the midway."

"Looking for your Stumble Bugs?"

"Tumble Bugs," he said impatiently. "No; well, yes. I mean, I want to see them, obviously——"

"Obviously."

"But there's lots of stuff here I want to see. I just want to wander down the midway, see what we find." And he set off, leaving Linda to trail behind.

They walked for thirty yards or so, Linda looking behind her now and then to see where they'd come from; she wanted to be sure they knew how to get out again when Allan finally got tired and called it a day. She also couldn't quite shake off a feeling that they were being followed, and she wondered if the woman at the house had tipped someone off that they were in there. She was glancing over her shoulder again—was that someone moving back behind a tree, just out of sight?—when Allan stopped dead and she stumbled against him. She was about to say something when he shushed her and pointed to their right.

"What is it?" she asked, any urge she might have had to say "Sorry" gone, but he merely made another shushing noise and pointed again. She looked in that direction, but even then it was a few moments before she realised what she was looking at.

"Ferris Wheel," Allan whispered. "Wonderful!" And he was off, camera raised, leaving Linda to stand and stare.

It had been a Ferris Wheel, once, but now it was a shell of its former self. They were sideways on to it and she could see the outer rings which had once supported the cars, which were gone. Trees grew up and through the Wheel's structure, and it looked like a giant child's toy suspended in the branches, ready to break free and roll away in a heavy wind. She would not even have seen it had Allan not pointed it out, and Linda shivered, wondering what else was in the trees, then hurried to catch up to Allan, who was at the base of the Wheel, staring at it in admiration.

"This is incredible," he said, turning to her, eyes aglow. "I had no idea there was so much of it left. Amazing."

"Wonderful." She gazed up through the branches to where the Wheel sat silently above them. "This place is like a graveyard. No, it's like a morgue, full of dead bodies. Couldn't someone have given them a decent burial, at least?"

Allan shrugged. "Probably cost too much. Cheaper to leave it here than break it up and haul it out." He raised the camera again. "Just a few more shots."

"I've heard that song before," Linda muttered, but stood while he took more pictures, stopping every now and then to throw out some comment that she only half-heard. She glanced back the way they had come, and there it was again; that faint trace of movement at the corner of her eye, as of someone ducking out of sight. She shook her head. If someone had tipped off the police then the cops wouldn't be hiding behind trees.

"Okay, let's go." Allan was beside her, his eyes sparkling, his face happier than she had seen it in some time. "I've got a real treat for you now. No"—he raised a finger to his lips—"I'm not going to tell you. You'll see for yourself. We're almost there; it wasn't too far from the Ferris Wheel."

They walked back to the cracked surface of what Linda supposed had been the main course of the midway, and had not gone far before Allan stopped. "There," he said proudly, as if he had conjured it up out of mid-air in a spectacular piece of magic, and Linda saw the Coaster.

It had looked impressive and faintly menacing from the road, but now, close to, it was even more startling. They were standing near one end—the turnaround, Linda knew it was called—and could just make out the rest of the structure stretching out through the trees, dipping and twisting. Allan, of course, had his camera up, and Linda gazed at him for a moment, wondering how a person could be so enthusiastic about something like this. She had been wondering for three years now, and was beginning to think the question would never be answered; at least not in a way she would ever understand.

Her gaze fell to the uneven surface in front of them. The sun was at their back and she could see her own shadow, clear and sharp, on the ground in front of her. Her eyes flicked to the ground in front of Allan, and she noted that his own shadow was much less distinct. *Some trick of the light; or the ground* she thought, and was about to say something when she caught her breath with a hiss.

There was a third shadow stretched out in front of them.

It was clearly the head and shoulders of someone—a man, she thought—who appeared to be standing roughly equidistant between her and Allan, and slightly behind them. She turned her head so suddenly that she felt something pop between her shoulders.

There was no one there.

When she looked forward again, the shadow was gone.

She blinked and shook her head, her eyes darting from side to side. She had seen it, as clearly as she had seen their own shadows; but it couldn't have been there. She told herself that, firmly, as she followed Allan towards the Coaster, which seemed to emerge from the trees the closer they got to it, as if shaking itself off like a dog coming out of water. Allan was in a fever of excitement; Linda was surprised he could keep the camera steady as he darted about, taking pictures from every angle.

"Oh, man, this is incredible. I had no idea it was in this good a state!" He looked up at the wooden struts which now rose above them, criss-crossing, supporting the track which looked to be intact. "Amazing. Almost looks operational. Wouldn't be surprised to see a car coming along the tracks."

Linda knew that he was seeing a different Coaster to the one she was looking at; one without maples choking the tracks, or dead trees leaning drunkenly against the supports of the first turnaround, one where guard rails weren't missing and footings weren't rotting and sinking into the muddy earth. To Allan, she knew, it looked as it had in its heyday, a place of happiness and excitement and laughter, and for a moment she wished she could see it through his eyes. Before she could say anything, however, he was off again, heading towards a long, low building with an arched roof at the far end of the track, calling "Loading station!" over his shoulder as he went.

Linda picked her way through the trees, cursing as something caught at her skirt. It took her a few moments to work it free, and when she looked up Allan was gone. On the archway over the entrance she could make out the word COASTER, or at least what remained of it; some of the letters had fallen off, and what was left was the word COST, with only shadows of the other letters marking where they had once stood.

She dropped her eyes, trying to see into the station, but all she could make out was a suggestion of railings, with a bench at one side. It was full of shadows, and she wished again that she could see it as Allan did.

She was suddenly aware of how exposed she must look,

alone and vulnerable, and her eyes automatically raked the undergrowth around her, which seemed full of movement, although when her eyes fell directly on a spot there was nothing to be seen. She thought she saw someone move quickly behind a small outbuilding on the far side of the track, by the dips, and remembered her earlier impression of being followed. If there was someone else in the park, she definitely didn't want to be there by herself, so even though she had no desire to go inside the station she trudged towards it and climbed the cracked ramp leading up from ground level.

Within it was cooler, and she could smell rotted leaves and damp earth and something else, something more pungent, less wholesome. She did not want to think about what it was. From outside came the sound of a voice, and her immediate thought was Allan, calling her; but after a moment she realised that it didn't sound like Allan at all, certainly not him calling her, more like someone having a conversation. The contrast between the dimness inside and the sunshine outside meant she could see little beyond the station, and she made her way down the platform towards the sound of the voice, noting the rails still standing primly alongside the track, the faded yellow line on the concrete indicating where those waiting had had to stand, the brake levers standing at odd angles like thin tombstones.

Something skittered under one of the benches. *A leaf, or maybe a mouse,* she told herself, and hurried forward.

There was movement from outside the station, but when she emerged there was no one in sight. She stared, wondering where Allan could have got to. She looked down what she knew was the brake run, and could see more maples and buckeyes poking between the rails, but there was no sign of Allan. She was about to call out when she heard his voice behind her, down at the other end of the platform.

"What're you doing down there? Come here! You've got to see this; it's great!"

Linda had turned in the direction of his voice, and now whipped her head back round, gazing down the brake run once more. No one was there, of course, and yet . . . She shook her head, surprised to find herself on the verge of tears. She didn't understand what was going on, and she wanted to run, bolt like an animal, back to the car, get the hell out of Dodge. . . .

Allan called again. "You coming? I want to show you something. Hurry!"

She was on the verge of asking why; it wasn't as if anything in the park was going anywhere. Instead she took a deep breath, set her shoulders, and marched determinedly down the centre of the platform, looking neither to left nor right, ignoring the whispers which started up outside the station as soon as she turned her back. *Only trees, Linda; it's only the trees.*

Allan was standing in the stretch of track which left the station heading towards the lift hill; she had somehow missed him on her initial walk past. The track curved sharply to the right and she could see, beyond Allan, what looked like a shed built across the track, curving with it. The open entranceway was choked with undergrowth and blocked by a fallen tree; she could make out blackness beyond, but nothing more.

"Look at that!" Allan gestured to the shed. "This is really something special. The track is pretty basic—your ordinary out and back layout—but you don't often see this."

"What's 'this'?" asked Linda. "Why did someone build a shed over the track?"

"It's not a shed, it's a tunnel. Look"—Allan pointed back towards the station—"the train would have left the station, started into the curve towards the lift hill, and then—wham! into a tunnel." He peered at the opening. "Hard to tell what sort of doors there would have been; maybe crash doors, like in a dark ride." He shook his head. "Can't tell from here. Maybe the other side is better." And without another word he was off, heading around the inside of the curve, leaving Linda trailing in his wake.

She caught up to him at the other end of the tunnel. To her right the lift hill ascended, a dead tree suspended across it; to her left she could see the tunnel exit. A corrugated iron door stood across one side; the other gaped open, and for a moment Linda thought that something darted back into the shadows. *This is crazy*, she thought, *you're seeing things*. Yet when Allan moved towards the opening she heard an edge of panic in her voice as she called out "Where are you going?"

"I want to see inside the tunnel; see how clear it is." Linda cast her eyes along the structure, which looked more or less intact at either end but appeared badly damaged in the middle, where a tree had come down on the roof.

"I don't think that's a very good idea, Allan." She didn't move, couldn't, from where she stood. "C'mon"—this as he approached the entrance, shining his flashlight through the door—"let's go. We still have to find your Tumble Bugs, or whatever they're called."

"I don't care about those." Allan pushed through the open door, and she saw his figure swallowed up by the tunnel. She wanted to scream, but bit her lip and called out again "Allan! Please!"

"Oh, Linda, you've got to see this," she heard him say. His voice sounded as if it was coming from far away. "Man, this is better than I could have imagined. There's an old coaster car in here, in pretty good shape. This is just amaz——"

His voice stopped suddenly, as if someone had hit a mute button. Linda waited for a moment, then called "Allan?" in a voice she barely recognised as her own; when there was no reply she called again, louder, but there was nothing except the sound of branches clattering against each other and, somewhere, a faint snatch of music that was snuffed out almost instantly.

She knew she had to look, go up to the tunnel entrance and see what had happened—he'd fallen, something had hit him, he'd collapsed—but the mouth of the tunnel seemed—*busy*, somehow, as if there were too many shadows there. She gave a thin scream, like an animal in a trap; then, as the shadows seemed to thicken and grow darker she turned, turned and ran, like a frightened child, heedless, uncaring, back the way they had come, her bag banging against her side with each step, her breath coming in ragged gasps, her ears filled with sounds she did not want to identify, shadows running alongside her, thin shapes clutching at her legs, until she was somehow—miraculously—back at the door in the fence, shouldering her way through, careless of how she might look to anyone watching, running up to the house, pounding on the door, and only then, it seemed, pausing for a moment to think about what had happened, what had to be done. . . .

The door swung inward and the woman they had spoken with earlier stood framed inside the opening. She looked at Linda; then her eyes travelled past her, and Linda, even in her confusion, saw a look of pain mixed with sadness settle in her face. She looked back at Linda.

"My boyfriend," Linda gasped, trying to form her thoughts into something coherent, something that would make sense. "My boyfriend—he's in there, in the park, something's happened to him. . . ."

"I know." The voice was quiet, but there was sorrow contained within it.

"What do you mean, you know? How can you know?"

"I do. We all do."

Linda took a deep breath, tried to calm herself. "I need to use your phone, call the police, the ambulance, someone. I think he might be hurt."

"No, he's not hurt."

"How do you *know*?" Linda almost screamed. "You weren't there. He was inside that tunnel, by the Coaster; some of it had collapsed, he might be lying there injured, I need to get *help*."

"No one can help." The woman's eyes flicked over Linda's shoulder again, towards the park. "There's nothing anyone can do. Believe me."

"But you don't *understand*," begged Linda, her voice harsh. "He's in there, he could be hurt, I need to *do* something."

"There's nothing you can do. He'll come out if he wants to. Some of them do. You can wait here with us, if you like."

Linda tried to make sense of what she was hearing. "What do you mean, some of them do? Some of who? And who do you mean by 'us'?"

The woman half-turned her head, towards the hallway behind her. "Us," she said simply.

Linda looked over the woman's shoulder, and saw that there were others behind her; women, all, half-a-dozen or so. One or two looked to be the same age as the woman in the doorway; the others were older, middle-aged at least, or perhaps they only looked so. It was difficult to tell. All were plainly dressed, in clothing that ranged from threadbare to out-of-date; apart from that, their only commonality was a look that Linda could only think of as resigned sadness. She turned back to the woman in the doorway.

"Who are you?" she asked, in a voice that sounded as if it came from many miles away. "Why are you here?"

"We're waiting," the woman said simply. "Some of us have been waiting a long time." She nodded towards the cars parked in the lane beside the house. "Some of us can't leave. So we wait. What else can we do?"

Linda shivered. Her mind seemed to be retreating from her body, but she heard herself say "So they come back—sometimes?"

"Yes. But it can be a long time; if it happens." The woman looked at Linda, her gaze steady. "You have to be prepared to wait. Are you?"

Linda took a deep breath and drew herself upright. As she did so her bag shifted against her hip, and she heard the rattle of the car keys from deep inside it. An image of Allan's face as she had seen it at the Coaster flashed before her; excited, eager, happy, in a way that she had seldom seen it.

"I don't know," she replied finally. "Can I think about it for a minute?"

"Yes, of course. We have all the time in the world."

There was nothing more to be said. The door closed.

All the time in the world.

But it would not take her that long to decide.

THE WIDE, WIDE SEA

BLUE SKY AND WHITE CLOUDS ABOVE, yellow and green plains below, stretching as far as the eye could see and brushed by the wind which never seemed to rest: no relief, no respite, no indication that either sky or plains had an end. Rolling hills tantalised with hints of what could be just over, just beyond them; false hints. Eliza, raising a weary, weathered hand to brush a limp strand of brown hair from her face, knew that if she were to make her way to the top of one of the hills, she would only see more of the same. The same sky, the same endless plains, perhaps a few trees or low bushes to indicate where water was to be found, a few brave wildflowers—harebells, anemones, prairie roses—striving to bring some colour to the landscape, but none of the landmarks with which she was familiar, that had marked her world in the small village in which she had spent all her life until a few short months ago. That had been a landscape defined by man, with roads and walls and fences, fields still called by the names of people who had lived generations earlier, houses and barns that had stood for hundreds of years and might stand for hundreds more. Here there was nothing old except the land itself, and it had no names, no landmarks to which someone might point, nothing to guide the unwary or the lost.

Peter was out there, breaking more of the land—their land, the 160 acres which the government of Canada had promised to anyone who was prepared to come and start a new life in a new country. He had been mesmerised by the railway car which had appeared at the country fair near Devizes two years earlier, garlanded with wheat sheafs and promises: of land, opportunity, prosperity in a place which was, to Eliza, as remote as the mountains of the moon. Canada was a large mass of red on the map which Mr. Jenkins, the schoolmaster, had hung on the wall of the schoolhouse with his thin white hands, part of the great British Empire on which the sun never set. When Eliza thought about Canada at all—which was seldom—she had a vague idea of mountains and snow, of trappers and hunters and explorers, of brave priests bringing the word of God to Red Indians. It had never occurred to her that people—ordinary people—might choose to live there, and when she saw the railway car she was unable to muster more than a cursory interest. She and Peter had only been officially walking out together for a few days, and she was anxious that they be seen and noted, and hopeful that Peter would comment on her new bonnet. Not that it was, strictly speaking, new—merely an old bonnet which she had turned and adorned with fresh ribbon—but she had still hoped for a compliment, or a comment about how the blue of the ribbon set off her eyes.

Peter's own brown eyes, however, were fixed on the wagon. A cheerful agent, his ruddy complexion and clear eyes a testimony to the healthful Canadian air, his accent strikingly at odds with what Eliza was used to, was busy handing out leaflets to all who were interested. Peter stood, listening intently in a way that he had never managed in the schoolroom, where he had always seemed constrained, hemmed in, his clear eyes and strong body wanting to be out of doors, working, doing. He even overcame his habit of silence enough to ask the occasional question, referring often to the papers clutched in his hand. Eventually Eliza, bored, moved away towards the tea tent, where Peter found her a few minutes later.

"Look at this!" he exclaimed, holding up one of the leaflets. "Free Land!" it cried, and "Cash Bonuses!" Peter's eyes gleamed with an excitement Eliza had never before seen. "It says here"— he fumbled open the slender leaflet with his large, rough farmer's hands and found the passage he wanted—"that the government of Canada will give 160 acres of land to any man as wants to claim it!" His face filled with wonder. "Can you imagine that, Eliza? One hundred and sixty acres of land, free for the taking?" He shook his head. "And they say it's a grand land for growing;

all you need is seed and a bit of water, and any man can have as fine a crop of wheat as you can imagine, and ready markets for it too. Look." He shuffled through the assortment of papers until he found the one he wanted, and held it out to Eliza, who hesitated a moment before stretching out one of her small, delicate-looking hands—of which she was inordinately proud—to take it. Emblazoned across the front were the words "The Last Best West", and a hand-tinted image of a field of wheat, stretching out endlessly under a clear blue sky until both were halted by the white border around the picture.

She thought of that image now as she gazed out at the reality before her. It had looked so safe, so placid, neatly contained by the leaflet's cover: manageable, knowable. Eliza had been here for three months, but already she realised how wrong she had been. It had been presented to her as a Promised Land, but she saw now that it was more akin to Egypt under the Pharaohs, a place where fire and hail, drought and insects could wipe out the work of a summer, a year, a lifetime in an instant. She would never know this land, never feel content here the way Peter did. He did not feel the pressure of the sky bearing down upon him until he wanted to scream; he saw only the clear blue immensity of it, felt the life-giving sun. He did not feel as if he were drowning when he gazed out across the land, lost in its immensity; he only realised the opportunity it afforded, a rare chance for a man to make a new life. He did not hear the ever-present wind calling his name; he only raised his face to it, welcoming its cooling breath.

And he never saw Mrs. Oleson.

Eliza turned sharply, suddenly, in a gesture that had become so habitual she scarcely noticed it anymore, and looked back at the house which was her entire world. It stood alone and unprotected, its unweathered wood harsh against the backdrop of prairie. It might have fallen from the sky, dropped by some god's careless, uncaring child who had tired of a plaything. For a moment a vision came to her of the low stone farmhouse in which she had spent her whole life; in which the lives of generations of her family had been spent, so that every room, every piece of furniture, even the stones themselves were as familiar to her as her own name, were infused—or so it seemed to her now—with the unseen presences of many people, of births and deaths, the commonplace, the everyday, the normal. Here, in this alien landscape, there was nothing familiar, no landmarks, nothing to guide her, nowhere to hide.

She shivered, feeling exposed, naked. Nothing had prepared her for this. She had spent most of the long sea voyage in the tiny cabin which she had shared with three other girls—strangers, all—and had seldom ventured up on deck. The first time she had done so the vastness of the ocean had made her hang back from the railings, afraid that she would fall into those endless depths and be lost forever. A fragment of a poem that Mr. Jenkins had read to them came, unbidden, to her mind:

> Alone, alone, all, all alone,
> Alone on a wide wide sea!
> And never a saint took pity on
> My soul in agony.

She had almost hoped that she would be seasick, so that she would have an excuse to stay safely in her cabin, a reason for avoiding the deck; but her body was as robust as always, and she had not felt the slightest twinge of sickness. She knew that this was one of the reasons Peter had asked her to marry him; he had said as much, the evening of the country fair, when he had walked her home. It was their first chance to be alone and, while he had still said nothing about her bonnet, she had wondered if he would hold her hand, or at least take her arm when they skirted the field where Mr. Miller's bull glared out at the world from angry eyes and pawed the ground in fierce jabs. But Peter had merely said, "You aren't afraid of anything, are you, Eliza?" and she had tossed her head and said, "Of course not. Why?"

Peter stopped and faced her. "Because if I do this thing, I'll be needing a wife who isn't afraid. I'll be needing a wife who's strong, who won't turn away from a hard job; because it will be hard, I don't want to lie to you, but we'd be starting a new life, a better life than we could ever have here, in a place where there's room to breathe, room to grow, room for any man with a fire in his belly and a good strong wife by his side."

Eliza caught her breath. She tried to make some sense of what he had just said, but one fact stood out clear and firm, like lightning ripping through a dark sky.

"Are you asking me to marry you?"

"Yes."

Eliza opened her mouth to speak, but no words came. She had thought, from the moment Peter had first asked her to walk out with him, that this day would come, but she had pictured it as something entirely different. He would not go down on bended knee—that, she suspected, only happened in novels—but it would be in her parents' front room, Peter dressed in his best, at some vague point in the far future, and Peter would stammer a little, as befitted a man asking a woman to marry him and unsure of her answer, even though Eliza knew that she would say yes, with one younger sister already married and the prospect of spinsterhood looming ever more strongly before her. She had never pictured it happening so soon, though, in a darkening lane, Peter's face glowing with a passion which—the thought came and went quickly, but was there nonetheless—had more to do with the wagon and the stranger than with her.

Her mind had now put his words into some kind of sense, and she realised with a shock the full implications of what he had said. He was asking her to marry him, yes, but he was also asking her to go with him to this vast new land, to leave behind everything and everyone she knew and trust herself to a place about which she knew nothing, to join him in a grand project about which they had both been ignorant a few hours before, and which, she could see, was now consuming him like a flame. An answering flame of resentment flared up within her for a moment; an anger against this place which had, in so short a time, inspired in him an ardour which she had imagined would be reserved for her.

Peter was looking at her anxiously, and Eliza realised that she needed to answer. There was no time for prevarication, for coyness, for protestations of how sudden this was, even if she had been inclined to indulge in such luxuries. She knew, as clearly as if Peter had shouted it to the heavens, that he was bent on doing this thing, and that he would only ask her once; if she refused him now, or hesitated, then all would be lost, for he would see that she was not a woman who could be trusted to be strong, unhesitating, fearless. She allowed herself one quick moment of calculation, a survey of her bleak prospects should she demur; then she met his gaze firmly, strongly, and said "I will marry you," and hoped that the flame that burned inside him would one day warm her too.

૪૦ ૦૪

Now, almost two years later, she stood under the pitiless eye of the prairie sun against which there was no defence, and which had turned her face, once so fair and fresh, first red and then brown. They had not married immediately; Peter had no home of his own to which to take her, and they had agreed, after due consideration and much discussion, that it would be best if they were married shortly before Peter left for Canada. He would go out alone to that new land. He did not expect Eliza to come until he had a home for her, and she had not argued, although when she said goodbye to him—her husband of three days—she had wondered, for a brief moment, if he had secretly hoped that she *would* argue with him, insist on going, on taking her place beside him, even though neither had any real idea of where that place would be or what it would look like. It had been too late, then, even had he or Eliza wanted it, and the last sight she had of him was his head looking at her from out the window of the train as it pulled away, and his arm waving, before his train vanished.

There began a curious, almost dream-like year in which Eliza felt as if she were two people living the same existence, each aware of the other but having little in common. She lived as she always had, performing her chores around the house and farm, walking to the village, sharing a room with her younger sister Jane, and there were times when she could almost feel that what had happened between her and Peter had been little more than a dream, a fancy spun out of her imagination. Then she would catch sight of the thin gold ring on her finger, and realise with a shock that she was now a married woman, her husband—the word sounded odd, almost nonsensical, like a child's made-up assortment of letters—far from her in a strange land. His occasional letters were a reminder of him, and she scanned them eagerly when they came, paying scant heed to the details of his new life, his new home—soon to be her home too—looking instead for anything more personal, more private, something of the man himself; but in this quest she was more often than not disappointed, and she would fold each new letter, once it had been read and remarked upon by her family, and place it with the others in the bottom of the large chest which she was slowly filling with clothes and linens and her few personal possessions, realising as she did so that when the chest was filled it would mark the end of all she had known of life until that point, and the beginning of another life which she was not even sure would be her own.

Occasionally, as she passed through her day, she would notice some small detail to which she had never really paid heed before; something which she had accepted as being a part of her life that would never change, and which she now realised would continue, unseen, without her. It seemed impossible; but she would look at the chestnut trees in bloom, their flowers creamy against the rich green leaves, or the bluebells carpeting the ground, or the redstarts and nightingales nesting in the hedgerows, and think for a moment "I shall not see this again," and the enormity of what she was about to do would well up inside her. Each detail she noticed marked the passage of time, every one reminding her inexorably that she had started down a road from which she could not turn back, and she would go back to the house and look at how full the chest now was, how little room there was in it, and realise how few were the days remaining to her in her old life.

≈

A year after Peter departed, Eliza made her own voyage, by train to Liverpool to board the *Numidian*, accompanied by her father, who was nervous of the city in a way that Eliza would never have suspected, and who stood twisting a large white handkerchief in his hands as he waved goodbye to her from the dockside. Then the long trip across the endless ocean, and the first blessed sight of land, of Halifax, swelling up out of the water until it filled her sight. Another train journey, longer than she had thought possible, to Montreal and then Toronto, and then through country which at first inspired Eliza with memories of home: there were towns and villages, farms and fields, if not quite of the shape and design to which she was accustomed then at least familiar, known, knowable. Then the train had swept north, around the great inland seas of which she had read, and slowly, inexorably, the traces of the world she had known at home, and half-glimpsed in this new land, vanished, and her only link with it was the iron rail under the wheels which bore her onward.

She gained her first glimpse of the prairie when they left Winnipeg, and she pressed her face to the glass of the carriage, first wiping away the dust which streaked the windows and coated everything else with a fine layer of grit. She had been unprepared for the vastness of it; another ocean, with an occasional town or farm doing nothing to make it seem any less implacable than the sea she had crossed. She began to have some dim sense of what she had taken on, and pulled back from the window with a small stifled gasp.

Her destination was, she knew, a place called Moose Jaw. The name had seemed impossibly foreign, even faintly exotic, in a way that Halifax, Montreal, Toronto had not when she read of it in the Wiltshire countryside in a letter from Peter; now it sounded almost sinister, hinting at something on which she dared not let her thoughts dwell. As the train drew in to the dusty station Eliza peered out the window into the harsh sun, looking for Peter, and for a moment did not see him. Her heart fluttered in something like panic. "Let him be here, please, let him be here," she heard herself say in a low voice that almost did not tremble; and then she saw him, standing beside a curious-looking cart drawn by a pair of massive, ungainly, dirty brown oxen, and she was off the train and into his arms, heedless of the people watching and Peter's faint air of embarrassment, burying her face in his shirt so

THE WIDE, WIDE SEA

that she could block out, if only for a moment, the vast blankness which surrounded them and that seemed to be searching for a foothold within her, the relentless wind which she could feel pushing at her, the dry, dusty air which filled her nostrils.

They would not stop in the town, which seemed bustling and purposeful. Peter was anxious to be away, explaining that he wanted to arrive home before dark. "But it's only noon!" said Eliza, puzzled; "how far away is our home? Can't we walk from there to town?"

Peter stared at her. "It's not far," he said slowly, after a pause. "Not here, at any rate."

"What do you mean, 'not here'?" Eliza said.

"Well——" There was another pause. "Things are different here, bigger," said Peter at last. "You have to realise that. Places aren't so close together. I told you, in my letters, that we weren't in the town. You knew that."

"Yes." He had said that their house was outside town; not far, he had added, but she realised now that he had never been more precise than that, and she had pictured the town, and their farm a short distance away, within an easy walk certainly, the town, or some of it, visible from where she was to live, full of the promise of life and noise and people. Memories of the land she had just passed through—of that wide ocean of grass and hills stretching away forever, unbroken, untouched—made the bright day seem chill. "How far?" she asked in a low voice.

"About twenty miles," replied Peter. She stood motionless, silent, taking in those three bare words. "I tried to get land closer to town," said Peter defensively, "but it was all gone, and what was left wasn't worth having. It's a fine spot, where we are; there's water, and a few trees, and I'll plant more, soon as I have a chance, around the house, make a wind-break, and some shade. It'll be the prettiest, snuggest spot you ever saw, Eliza, I promise."

He was almost cajoling, now, as if she were a child who had turned away, disappointed, from a gift that was not to her liking, and Eliza felt ashamed. He had worked so hard—she could see that in his hands, his face, the lines of his body, harder than they had been—and she knew that she had to say something to take away the hurt from his voice, his eyes. She said faintly, "Twenty miles; it's not so very far, is it?"

Peter smiled, relieved. "Course it's not. That's my girl." He hugged her clumsily, and Eliza hoped that he would say something else, add words of comfort, anything to chase away the thoughts which were prowling the corners of her mind. But he did not, and as he turned away and busied himself with her cases she realised dully that there was nothing he could say. She watched as her entire life was loaded into the back of the ungainly wagon, then took a deep breath and climbed up beside Peter, to start the final, and longest, stage of her journey.

The town was soon a distant blur behind them. Eliza kept turning to watch it, straining her eyes until it vanished altogether, and they were alone on the prairie. She tried to make some note of where they had come from and where they were going, but there were no signposts or markers—nothing except the road itself, a dusty, hard-packed, rutted ribbon, and the occasional homestead with small, huddled houses, a few outbuildings, and perhaps a straggling row of young trees, full of the promise of future shade and shelter but for the moment a reminder of how recently this old land had been settled. The high clouds overhead did little to dispel the glare of the sun, and all looked harsh, brassy beneath its rays, with not even the green and gold of the prairie grasses, the dark brown earth, or the occasional flowers—what looked to her like buttercups and pale crocuses—able to soften this first impression, and utterly unable to provide the familiarity which she suddenly craved.

Eventually they turned off the main road on to a dispirited track that wound southwards. The houses—although Eliza could hardly think of them as such—grew more sparse, and some struck her as odd, although they were far enough away that she could not say precisely why. As each one came into view she hoped Peter would announce that they were home, but the houses rose and then fell behind in turn as the oxen plodded on. Just as she was beginning to think that their journey was going to continue forever, Peter coaxed the team of oxen from their straight line towards a small house—what Eliza thought of as one of the "odd ones"—and she felt her spirits lift slightly. This, then, was their home, and she watched with some eagerness as they drew closer. When Peter stopped the cart she sat gazing at the building, her expression puzzled; then she turned to him, eyes wide, trying to take in what she was seeing.

"It's made of dirt!"

Peter, who had jumped down from the cart, looked up at her. "Sod," he corrected. "It's made of sod. They're called soddies. They're what folk build when they don't have enough money to buy lumber."

"But. . . . " She tried to find words. "This is our house?" she said faintly. "Made of dirt?"

"Our house?" Peter looked at her for a moment, puzzled, then laughed. "No! Our house is a little piece on. I just thought we'd stop and pick up a few things while we were here. This was the Olesons' place; Oleson said I could take what I needed."

A wave of tiredness swept over Eliza, and suddenly she felt like crying. Nothing seemed to make sense in this land; everything was changed, all the markers and boundaries she had known all her life swept away in a place where twenty miles was considered no distance and houses were made of dirt and they could help themselves to another's possessions. There were so many things she wanted to say, so many questions; but all she said was "Why?"

"Why?" Peter looked puzzled, and Eliza had to stop herself from shouting at him.

"Why can we take what we want?"

"Oh." Peter scratched his head. "Oleson cleared out, went back to Sweden after his wife died. Couldn't stand being alone, he said, though I don't think he was cut out for this kind of life. Didn't know what he was getting himself into. He was having a rough time of it before his wife died. If she'd lived then he might have made a go of it, with her and all—she were the strong one, I reckon—but after what happened . . . well, he just sort of gave up, and soon as spring came, and the roads were passable, he up and left. Said I could take what I wanted."

"What happened to her—to Mrs. Oleson?"

Peter paused and looked at her, as if weighing his answer. "It was in winter," he said finally. "You'd not think, to look at it now, what the winter can be like here. The snow comes, and it's like a curtain comes down, and you can't see a hand in front of your face, it's that fierce."

They walked towards the house, and Peter gestured towards a small wooden outbuilding some thirty yards away. "They had a cow, and some chickens, in the barn there; they had enough wood for that, but not for the house. Oleson used to make a sort of joke of it, that they lived in a soddie but the cow had a proper house." He paused. "Don't know what happened, exactly, but I reckon that Mrs. Oleson went out to the barn, and got lost in the storm. There was a fierce one, the day she died. I was glad enough to stay snug inside, myself."

Eliza stared in disbelief. "But . . . but it's no more than a few steps! How could someone get lost?"

Peter shrugged. "You'll see, come winter," he said, and though his tone was resolutely normal, as though he were discussing something of no more moment than the likelihood of another sunny day, Eliza felt a chill strike her. "The wind comes up, and it's as if the snow was a living thing, trying to beat you down. I told Oleson he should put a line up between the house and the barn, as a guide, and he said he would, but he never got round to it. Near as I can figure, his wife went out and got turned round by the wind and the snow. She wouldn't have realised until she'd walked far enough to know she'd missed the barn, and then she would have turned herself round and tried to follow her footprints back, but . . . well, they'd have been filled in already, and she'd have been good as blind in all that snow, just wandering, hoping to stumble across the house. Oleson found her next day, half-a-mile away, frozen to death."

Eliza stared, eyes wide, mouth open to frame words that she could not say. *What kind of land is this that you've brought me to?* she wanted to scream. *How can anyone live here, in dirt and snow, and freeze to death in sight of . . .*

Her thoughts broke off. In sight of what? In all the land

around there was nothing to be seen save the dirt house and the tiny barn, and a few straggling trees in the distance that would afford no shelter, no warmth, no aid. It would be a simple matter to freeze to death here, she thought, within steps of safety.

Some of what she was thinking must have been visible in her face, for Peter said soothingly, "Don't you fret, it won't happen. I'll string a line between our house and the barn, nearer to winter; long as you keep hold of that you'll be right as rain." He glanced up at the sky, to where the sun was gently dipping towards the horizon. "Best get what we want, and then we'll be off. I expect you could be doing with a cup of tea after your trip, make you feel better."

She looked at him for a moment, and then laughter rose up, unbidden, at the suggestion that a cup of tea would be sufficient to restore her. She saw Peter smile, and then as the laughter continued to spill out of her she saw his face change into something wary, almost frightened, and she wondered for a moment what he could be frightened of, before she realised that it was her; or rather her laughter, which had a cracked, brittle sound even to her own ears. That look sobered her in an instant. She forced herself to stop and draw a few ragged breaths while the echo of her laughter was caught by the wind and whirled away to dance across the prairie.

"I'm sorry, Peter." She did not know precisely what she was sorry for, but the words needed to be said, to erase that look from his face. "I'm just tired, is all." From some half-remembered place inside her she conjured up the ghost of a smile. "A cup of tea," she said carefully, not fully trusting herself, "would be lovely."

He watched her for a moment, thoughtfully, and nodded. "Right then. Best hurry along, in that case."

Eliza stood for a moment, drawing another deep breath. A sound behind her made her turn sharply, and her eyes swept the landscape. There was no one, nothing, except the wind, sighing over the bright grass, and surely it was only her imagination which had conjured her name out of the sound, as if someone had called her. She shivered once, then turned and followed Peter into the dimness of the house.

            ಹಿ   ೲ

Peter was proud of the fact that he could afford to build a house of wood during his first year, and Eliza had, at first, been reassured by it. The thought of living in a house made of dirt had appalled her; it was, she felt, something that she could simply not have borne. When she followed Peter into the Oleson house she had felt like an animal creeping into a burrow, and had stood uncertainly near the door, her eyes sweeping around the interior, dim despite the blazing sunshine outside. They had retrieved a few items—some cloth from which Eliza could make curtains; a few kitchen utensils; oddments of clothing left behind—the residue of a life begun in hope, and ended in . . . but Eliza did not want to think of that.

Her days settled into a routine that was not unfamiliar to her from her past life; what she could not accustom herself to was the intense loneliness of it. Peter was gone for most of the day, breaking more land with the oxen, tending the fields, maintaining the firebreak he had erected away from the house— "Just in case," he had tried to reassure her—and Eliza was busy around the house; there was so much to do, and no other pair of hands to do it. There were two cows in the barn—one had been the Olesons', Peter explained—and chickens, and a half-wild cat which stayed sleek on mice and rats but was rarely seen. Eliza had tried to coax it into the house, but the cat had glared at her with feral eyes and scorned her attempts at friendship. There was the house to tend, and the vegetable garden to hoe and plant and weed, water to be drawn and carried and wood to be chopped and carried and stacked, and always something to cook, or clean, or mend, or make. She did not mind the hard work—she was accustomed to that—but she could not rid herself of an ache, a hunger for the company of someone or something. Even a dog would have been some comfort, but a dog was not a necessity, not yet, and in this land anything that was not a necessity was relegated to some future day. Even the sight of another house on the horizon would have been enough, she told herself, to provide reassurance that she was not completely alone, unprotected; but no such reassurance was forthcoming.

She increasingly found herself stopping in the middle of what she was doing and listening, straining for the sound of something, anything, which would prove that she was not alone. It was not long before she thought she heard someone calling her name, as on the first day at the Olesons'; but it was the wind, she told herself, which never seemed to end, never rested. She could see it before she felt it, watch the grasses and the crops blowing before the gust swept over her, and if she was outside she would fight an urge to drop to the ground and try to dig her way in, like an animal seeking the safety of its den.

More and more she tried not to spend much time outside. The cry of the wind, and the sight of the wide sea of land stretching endlessly away, frightened her, and she kept her head down as much as possible, concentrating on the ground immediately beneath her feet, looking neither to left nor right. If she did not look up she could not see how alone she was.

Their closest neighbours lived two miles away, the house out of sight behind a fold of hill. Eliza walked over one day, not long after arriving, desperate for the sight of another person, another house, but she came away disappointed. Mrs. Reilly, a hearty, red-faced matron, was glad enough to see her, but was largely preoccupied with her five children, who ranged in age from a girl of about ten to a babe in arms of indeterminate sex who seemed to cry incessantly. The older children were scarcely less noisy, and the change from the silence of her own house made Eliza want to clap her hands to her ears. As it was, she emerged with a violent headache and a vague dull pain.

She started the weary walk back to her house, but before she was halfway there she thought of the Olesons' soddie. The house was still unoccupied, and Eliza had a sudden urge to see it again, justifying her curiosity with the excuse that there might well be more items which would be of use to her and Peter. She turned her footsteps in the direction of the abandoned house, which looked no less forlorn than the first time she had seen it when finally it came into view, alone on the prairie. Yet as she drew nearer Eliza realised that it seemed less of an intrusion on the land than their own home, of which Peter was so proud. The soddie was built from the land, the soil itself. It might even have grown up there, springing from the earth like the grass which surrounded it: part of the landscape, not an imposition upon it.

When she entered the soddie, Eliza was struck by how cool it was. Their own house she found stifling, with the sun beating relentlessly upon the thin roof and walls; but the soddie was deliciously refreshing, a welcome respite from the heat. She ran a hand over one of the walls, feeling the roughness. The dirt was dark and wholesome; life-giving, she thought, not like the thin, dry dust against which she waged a ceaseless war in her own home.

She glanced around the interior of the soddie, noting how compact it was, how well ordered. A few pieces of rough-made furniture remained, and a large trunk was pushed against one wall, where it had obviously served as a makeshift table. Eliza gazed at it, idly wondering why it had been left behind. Perhaps it contained his wife's things, for which Mr. Oleson presumably had no need after she died. What had they been like, this couple who now existed only as names? Peter had said that Mrs. Oleson had been the strong one of the pair, better suited to the life here than her husband. Would she and Mrs. Oleson have been friends? The answer darted through her mind, sharp and unwelcome, that they would not have been, and she brushed it away, wondering where Mr. Oleson was now. Home, she supposed, wherever that was. She felt a sudden ache at the thought. A picture arose before her, so vivid that she could almost touch and hear and smell it, of her home in England, and she closed her eyes to block out the vision and prevent the tears which she could feel rising.

She felt, rather than heard, a movement behind her, and whirled round, visions of home forgotten. She was facing the door, which she had left open. Framed in the glare of the sun was a figure: a woman, Eliza thought, although it was difficult to be sure. She squinted against the sunlight, trying to make out details, but the contrast between the dim interior of the soddie and the brightness outside made it impossible to register anything beyond a general impression of someone tall and pale, silent and watchful. She uttered a tremulous "Who is it? Who's there?" but there was no answer. Then, before Eliza could frame some faltering words of explanation or apology, there was nothing.

Eliza darted to the door and swept her gaze over the land in front of her. There was no one in sight, no sign that anyone was, or had been, there: no cart or wagon or horse, nothing to break the vastness except the small barn which stood thirty or so yards off to her left, impossible to reach in the short time it had taken her to leave the soddie.

Of course, if the woman had gone round the side of the house, she could even now be waiting, out of sight, for Eliza to follow. But that was ridiculous. What reason could anyone have for such an action? She had imagined the figure, that was all; the darkness within and the light without and her own loneliness had tricked her into thinking she had seen someone where there was no one. Her decision not to walk around the house was not inspired by fear, she told herself; she needed to start back to their house, as Peter would be back soon, and there were chores to do.

She did not look back at the soddie, not even when the sound of her name was borne to her on the wind. There could not be anyone there.

She asked Peter, later that evening, what the Olesons had been like; particularly Mrs. Oleson. Peter scratched his head ruminatively.

"Quiet," he said finally. "Hard workers. Leastways, she was. They both had fair hair, like all them Swedes seem to, and she were tall; as tall as him, with rough hands, like a farmhand's, on account of her working in the fields alongside her husband. Oh, not that he didn't do his fair share; but she were the strong one, I reckon. I saw a bit of them, what with being so close and all, and I got the feeling that coming here were her idea more'n it was his; he'd have been content to stay where they were, but she wanted something else." He stopped, and shook his head.

"That's why it struck so hard, when she died. If she hadn't, well, then, they'd have made a go of it; she'd have seen to that. But the heart just seemed to go out of him after. Terrible thing, it was. He came staggering up to the house, more dead than alive, soon as the storm were over and he could get out. Don't know how he made it; he were half-froze when he got here, and it were all I could do to get the story from him. Well, soon as I heard it I knew what must have happened, and so did he, but he kept saying she were out there, waiting for him, that he could hear her calling. I never heard anything except the wind, but . . . well, I didn't have the heart to say that, not with him standing there, with a look on his face like he was in hell itself. The way I reckon it, he'd been in hell for a fair time, and this put the cap on it. Soon as spring came he couldn't get away fast enough. Left most of his things behind; said I could have what I wanted, that maybe they'd bring us better luck than he'd had."

It was a long speech for Peter, who generally came back from his day's work so tired that he had scant energy left to waste on words, and Eliza had listened in horrified fascination. She could picture the scene: Peter, alone in the house, thankful that the storm had ended, and then the pounding at the door; Oleson's story, gasped out between sobbing breaths; the search for the missing woman, which could only end in one way; the broken man, wanting nothing but to leave this hard land which had cost him so dear.

But he got to leave, came the thought, unbidden, to Eliza's mind; *he was lucky, because he got to go home again*. Her hand flew to her mouth, as if she had spoken the words aloud, and Peter stared at her, puzzled. "What's wrong?" he asked.

"Nothing. I was . . . I was just thinking what a terrible thing to happen."

"Aye." Peter sighed. "It's a hard land, no denying that. I don't blame Oleson for leaving. She might have, though."

"What do you mean?" asked Eliza, more sharply than she intended.

Peter shrugged. "I mean that she weren't the kind to back down from a challenge. If it'd been the other way round—if anything had happened to her husband—I'd wager she'd have stayed on, by herself, made a go out of it, just to show she couldn't be beat. A strong woman—just like the one I've got, eh, lass?" He grinned at her. "A good, strong wife; that's what a man needs here. When I asked you to marry me and you said yes straight off, like, knowing what it meant, without having to think about it: well, I knew then and there I'd made the right choice."

"What would you have done if I'd not given you an answer when you asked?" said Eliza in a low voice.

"Why, I'd have said 'It's no good, my girl, I can't take a wife who doesn't know her own mind off to Canada with me!'" He laughed. "But you've always known your own mind, no fear of that." He yawned and stretched. "Best think about getting off to bed. You too, lass; you look a bit peaky. You're not sickening for something, are you, or . . . or anything else?"

"No," she replied, "I'm just a bit tired, is all. What else could there be?"

"Well"—Peter paused, and looked suddenly shy—"sometimes women . . . that is . . . when they're going to . . . well, when someone else is on the way . . . " His voice trailed off, and Eliza realised what he meant.

"No, Peter, I'm not going to have a baby; leastways, not yet."

"Aye. Just thought that . . . Plenty of time, eh?" He rose from his chair. "Are you coming?"

"In a few minutes, Peter; I have one or two things to do, then I'll be in."

"Right. Don't be too long."

"I won't, Peter."

She continued sitting after he had disappeared into their tiny bedroom, closing the door behind him. She knew that he would be asleep within moments of his head touching the pillow, and she sat waiting patiently until she heard the creak of the bed. Then she stood up and moved to the door, opening it wide and passing through so that she could stand in front of the house and feel the wind upon her hot face. She did not mind being outside at night; the darkness pressing down was every bit as merciless as the sun, but at night she could not see the vast landscape stretching away from her in all directions; could pretend that there would be houses, roads, signs of life visible were it not for the blackness which shrouded these things and hid them from her sight.

Peter did not feel this way. He exulted in the land, the space, in everything that made her shrink back and pull away. Mrs. Oleson would not have felt the way Eliza did. She had been strong, Peter said; the land had not frightened her. Hearing the way her husband spoke about the dead woman, Eliza knew that she could never speak of the way she herself felt, never let him know the thoughts which chased around inside her head as she went about her daily routine.

She looked back at the house, silvery in the moonlight. How flimsy it was! She tried to picture the house in winter, buffeted by wind and snow, and wondered how they could hope to keep safe in so meagre a shelter. She knew that it was possible to freeze to death in a house here; and what of Mrs. Oleson? She had frozen to death within sight of her own house, had got lost within a few feet of safety. She had never in her life imagined a place such as this, and no one had thought to warn her of it: not the smiling agent, who had been full of the promises of the new land and free with pictures that did nothing to show the reality of it, and not Peter, who had never once mentioned that they were so far from anyone, that days could pass when she would see no one but him, that a person could lose her way just a few steps from her own door, and wander the snowbound prairie, alone, unheeded, until she froze to death.

Eliza felt a surge of anger, sudden and biting: at the land, at the agent, at Peter. She hated them, hated them all. They had all lied to her, or if not lied then failed to speak the truth, to tell her how alien this place was, how lonely she would be, how she would feel the sky and the land beating down on her until she felt she had to scream and hide, find a place of safety. She wanted to scream now, scream to the uncaring heavens, to the stars shining coldly. She actually felt a scream rising, and clenched her hands so tightly that her nails, blunt as they were, dug semi-circles into the flesh of her palms.

A thread of movement out of the corner of her eye made her turn her head, eyes scanning the darkness. Had Peter come outside? No; the movement had been in the direction of the barn, and Peter could not have walked there without Eliza seeing him. There was no one, and nothing, there that she could see.

The Eliza of two years ago, of the new hat and blue ribbons, would have strode to the barn to see what was there. Now, however, she began to shiver, and backed towards the house, not wanting to turn her back on the barn until she was within reach of safety. She stumbled over the door sill and almost fell, and had just enough presence of mind to not slam the door. She was glad the curtains were drawn over the windows; the thought of something looking in was unbearable.

Peter was sound asleep, as she had known he would be. Quietly, furtively, Eliza undressed and slipped into her nightgown, then lay down on the bed and pulled the sheet over her, despite the warmth of the night. She wanted to move closer to Peter, cling to him, but she did not want him to wake, so she lay rigid on her side of the narrow bed, eyes closed, mouth set firm, her hands at her sides, formed into fists. At some point she slept, and was mercifully untroubled by dreams.

She said nothing of this to Peter next day. Her anger had passed, leaving her feeling weary to her very bones, unrefreshed by sleep. He was out all day, breaking land for next year's planting; every acre which he broke now would mean a larger crop the following season. When he came home, tired yet satisfied, speaking confidently of what they were accomplishing, she found she could not talk to him of how she felt, could not tell him that the vastness of the land terrified her, that she felt as if someone were watching her always, that she was desperate for human contact, the sound of voices, the sight of people and places. The only voice she heard—other than Peter's—was the one that called her name across the fields, the one which she had at first thought was the wind. But now she knew better; she knew who was calling.

Mrs. Oleson.

She knew it was Mrs. Oleson because she had seen her again that day, standing once more by the barn, silent, watchful. She was tall and fair-haired, and Eliza knew that her hands, could she see them, would be rough and chapped from working in the fields alongside her husband; she had to, Eliza knew, because it was the only way in which all the work would get done, the only way in which her dreams and hopes would be realised. She did not see her directly; it was only out of the corner of her eye, and when she turned to look there was no one there. But she was conscious of the woman, even when she could not see her, and she found herself trying to get a closer look, pretending to ignore the figure and then turning her head with sudden swiftness in an attempt to catch it. It was no use; Mrs. Oleson moved too swiftly for Eliza to see her clearly.

Over the next few days Mrs. Oleson was a constant presence every time Eliza went outside. She hurried about her chores as quickly as possible, seeking the solace of the inside of the house whenever she could, keeping the curtains drawn lest the face appear at the window. She wondered what she would do if the figure came into the house, then pushed the thought from her mind. That could not happen. The house was the only place left to her. If she was not safe in there . . . She let the thought trail off, as her thoughts did more and more often. Sometimes, when Peter was speaking to her, he had to repeat himself two, even three times before she took in what he was saying, and she often found that she had forgotten his words within minutes of his saying them. Sometimes she would look up and find Peter watching her, with a look in his eyes which worried her, although she could not say why.

One afternoon, when she had gone outside to tend to the garden after putting it off for as long as possible, she had been conscious of Mrs. Oleson standing by the barn, and had been trying without success to get a better look at her when Peter's voice broke the silence with a puzzled, "What's wrong with you, Eliza?"

She jerked herself upright, suppressing the cry which rose to her lips and willing her heart to stop its frantic beating. "Peter!" she said finally, when she could trust herself to speak. "You . . . you startled me."

"I'm sorry, lass. Thought you'd have heard me coming." He glanced in the direction of the barn. "What were you looking at?"

Eliza stopped herself following his gaze. Out of the corner of her eye she could still see the figure, tall and fair, beside the door which Peter was looking straight at.

"I . . . I thought I saw someone at the barn."

"Ah." Peter looked from the barn to Eliza and back again. "Your eyes must be playing tricks. Anyone had been there, I'd have seen them too."

"Yes." She straightened slowly, like an old woman, and turned to face the barn. There was no figure to be seen; only the blank face of the building, and the endless land stretching out behind it.

ဆ ⅋

Now she stood under the blue sky, looking at the endless plains, feeling the sun blazing down upon her and wondering vaguely what she was doing there, so far from the shelter of the house, and why she felt so cold. The thought came to her, slowly, as from a great distance, that it was because of Mrs. Oleson. That morning Eliza had seen her inside the house for the first time, standing motionless in the corner of the main room, and the sight had made her drop the bucket of milk which she had just carried in from the barn. She had not even tried to clean it up; her one thought had been that her sanctuary had been despoiled, and that she must leave, quickly, without looking back. It was only when she had found herself two hundred yards from the house that she had stopped, as if an invisible wall lay across her path. Ahead of her there was nothing but open plain; Peter was out there, somewhere, but she knew that she could not go to him, could not explain. The house was barred to her, now; she could not go back, could not face what was waiting patiently inside. She thought of the barn; that was possible. She might be safe there. . . .

She turned to look at the structure, and cried out when she saw the figure of Mrs. Oleson standing in front of the door to the barn, as if barring her way. It took a moment to register the fact that the woman had not disappeared when she looked full upon her, and, when the realisation hit her, she screamed once, a high, keening sound. The noise was picked up by the wind, which seemed to throw it back into her face, and she thought she could hear her own name amongst the rush of sound. She screamed again, trying to form the word "No!", but it did not come, and the dancing wind seemed to mock her, push at her, as if she were in a crowd of people all jostling her, trying to force her in the direction of the barn, and the woman in front of it.

She would not go there. Her feet turned, away from the house and barn, away from Peter, across the grass, and she began to run, blindly, heedlessly, knowing only that she needed to get away from this pitiless land, from the emptiness that consumed her, within and without. She had no clear idea of where she was going, but stumbled on, her breath coming in choked sobs, refusing to turn and look behind her at what might be following.

She had no idea how long she ran; she only knew that she must keep moving. She stumbled often, and fell more than once, but did not stop; and it was only when she saw the soddie looming up in front of her that she realised that this was where she had to go. She would find safety inside the house of earth; she could hide herself away in the cool shadows, let the land shelter her from itself.

She reached the door, which was hanging open. She could not remember whether or not she had closed it behind her, the last time she had been there. It did not matter. She plunged inside and stumbled over something on the floor, coming to rest against the far wall, where she huddled herself into a tight ball, trying to draw ragged gasps of breath. She felt the roughness of the dirt through her dress, and turned and dug her hands into it, clawing away clods of cool brown earth.

Over the sound of her laboured breathing and the pounding of her heart she heard a noise, faint as a whisper, from the door. She half-turned towards it, and thought she saw a movement outside, and knew that she had been followed. She was not safe. She would be found. Her eyes darted wildly about the interior of the soddie, searching for somewhere more sheltered. Her world had shrunk to these four dark walls, and still it was not small enough. Hide. She needed to hide. Under something, behind something, inside something, where she could not be seen, where she could not see the figure at the door, darker now, more solid. It would see her in a moment. She had no time; she must be quick, no time for thought, no time. . . .

ЕО СЯ

Peter found her that evening, when the harshness had gone out of the sun and the land was bathed in a soft light which tipped the grasses with gold. He might not have seen her inside the dimness of the soddie's interior had it not been for the dirty fringe of blue dress hanging out from under the closed lid of the trunk which, when opened, revealed Eliza's body, curled up like a broken doll discarded by a careless and uncaring child.

THE BRINK OF ETERNITY

THE KNIFE IS LONG AND LETHAL yet light, both in weight and appearance; a thing precise and definite, which he admires for those reasons. It has not been designed for the task at hand, but it will suffice.

The sound of a heart beating fills his ears, and he wonders if it is his heart or the other's. He will soon know.

The knife is raised, and then brought down in a swift movement. A moment of resistance, and then the flesh yields, and vivid spatters spread, staining the carpet of white, bright and beautiful.

He brings the knife down again, and again. He can still hear the beating, and knows it for his own heart, for the other's has stopped. He fumbles for a moment, dropping the knife, pulling off his gloves, then falls to his knees and plunges his bare hand into the bruised and bloody chest, pulling out the heart, warm and red and raw.

He eats.

ꙮ   ꙮ

WALLACE, William Henry (1799–?1839) was born in Richmond, Virginia. His family was well-to-do, and William was almost certainly expected to follow his father, grandfather, and two uncles into the legal profession. However, for reasons which remain unknown he abandoned his legal studies, and instead began work as a printer and occasional contributor of letters, articles, and reviews to various publications. In this respect there are interesting parallels between Wallace and Charles Francis HALL (q.v.), although where Hall's Arctic explorations were inspired by the fate of the Franklin Expedition, Wallace appears to have been motivated by the writings of John Cleve Symmes, Jr. (1779–1829), particularly Symmes's "hollow earth" theory—popular through the 1820s—which postulated gateways in the Polar regions which led to an underground world capable of sustaining life.

From *We Did Not All Come Back:
Polar Explorers, 1818–1909*
by Kenneth Turnbull
(HarperCollins Canada, 2005)

He could not remember a time when he did not long for something which he could not name, but which he knew he would not find in the course laid out for him. The best tutors and schools, a career in the law which would be eased by his family's name and wealth, marriage to one of the eligible young ladies whose mamas were so very assiduous in calling on his own mother, and whose eyes missed nothing, noting his manners, his well-made figure, strong and broad-shouldered, his prospects and future, of which they were as sure as he; surer, for his was an old story which they had read before.

But he chafed under his tutors, a steady stream of whom were dismissed by his father, certain that the next one would master the boy. School was no better; he was intelligent, even gifted, yet perpetually restless, dissatisfied, the despair of his teachers, who prophesied great things for him if he would only apply himself fully. He was polite to the mamas and their daughters, but no sparkling eyes enchanted him, no witty discourse ensnared him; his heart was not touched. He studied law because it was expected of him and he saw no other choice.

And then . . . and then came the miracle that snapped the shackles, removed the blinders, showed him the path he was to follow. It came in the unprepossessing form of a pamphlet, which he was later to discover had been distributed solely to institutes of higher learning throughout America, and which he almost certainly would never have seen had he not, however reluctantly, wearily, resignedly, followed the dictates of his family, if not his head and heart. Proof, if it were needed, that the Fate which guides each man was indeed watching over him.

The pamphlet had no title, and was addressed, with a forthright simplicity and earnestness Wallace could only admire, "To All The World". The author wrote:

> I declare the earth is hollow, and habitable within; containing a number of solid concentrick spheres, one within the other, and that it is open at the poles 12 or 16 degrees; I pledge my life in support of this truth, and am ready to explore the hollow, if the world will support and aid me in the undertaking.
>   JOHN CLEVES SYMMES
>   Of Ohio, Late Captain of Infantry.

He opened the pamphlet, his hands trembling. A passage caught his eye:

> I ask one hundred brave companions, well equipped, to start from Siberia in the fall season, with Reindeer and slays, on the ice of the frozen sea: I engage we find warm and rich land, stocked with thrifty vegetables and animals if not men, on reaching one degree northward of latitude 62; we will return in the succeeding spring.

The words seemed to inscribe themselves on his heart. "One hundred brave companions"; "start from Siberia"; "find warm and rich land"; "return in the succeeding spring".

In an instant he knew what it was that he had to do. After long years of wandering and searching, his restless feet were halted and pointed in the only true direction.

80 03

It is his first food in—how long? He has lost count of the days and weeks; all is the same here in this wasteland of white. He remembers Symmes's "warm and rich land" and a laugh escapes his throat. It is a rough, harsh, scratched sound, not because its maker is unamused, but because it has been so long since he has uttered a sound that it is as if he has forgotten how.

The remains of the seal lie scattered at his feet; food enough to last for several days if carefully husbanded. There will be more seals now, further south, the way he has come, the way he should go. Salvation lies to the south; reason tells him this. But that would be salvation of the body only. If he does not continue he will never know. *He fears this more than he fears the dissolution of his physical self.*

He grasps the knife firmly in his hand—he can at least be firm about this—and begins to cut up the seal, while all around the ice cracks and cries.

ಬ ಅ

One of the earliest pieces of writing identified as being by Wallace is a review of James McBride's *Symmes' Theory of Concentric Spheres* (1826), in which Wallace praises the ingenuity and breadth of Symmes's theory, and encourages the American government to fund a North Polar expedition "with all due speed, to investigate those claims which have been advanced so persuasively, by Mr. Symmes and Mr. Reynolds, regarding the Polar Regions, which endeavor can only result in the advancement of knowledge and refute the cant, prejudice, ignorance, and unbelief of those whose long-cherished, and wholly unfounded, theories would seek to deny what they themselves can barely comprehend."

From *We Did Not All Come Back*

His path was set. He threw over his legal studies, to the anger of his father and the dismay of his mother, and waited anxiously for further word of Symmes's glorious venture. How could anyone fail to be moved by such passion, such selfless determination, such a quest for knowledge that would surely be to the betterment of Mankind?

Yet no expedition was forthcoming. Symmes's words had, it

seemed, fallen on the ears of people too deaf to hear, too selfish to abandon their petty lives and transient pleasures. Wallace had fully expected to be a part of the glorious expedition; now, faced with its failure, he cast round for something that would enable him to dedicate his life—or a large part of it—to those Polar realms which now haunted him, in preparation for the day when Symmes's vision would prevail, and he could fulfil the destiny which awaited him.

He became a printer, for it seemed that his only connection with that region which so fascinated him was through words; so words would become his trade. He found work with a printer willing—for a consideration—to employ him as an apprentice, and learned the trade quickly and readily. When he was not working he was reading, anything and everything he could to prepare himself. He read Scoresby's two volume *Account of the Arctic Regions* and found, for the first time, pictures of that region of snow and ice, and of the strange creatures living there, seals and whales and the fearsome Polar Bear and, strangest of all, the Esquimaux who, in their furs, resembled not so much men as another type of animal. It was true that Scoresby scorned the idea of a "hollow earth"; yet he was only a whaling captain, and could not be expected to appreciate, embrace the ideas of someone like Symmes, a man of vision, of thought. Wallace expected more from Parry, that great explorer, and was heartened to find that the captain believed firmly in the idea of an Open Polar Sea, although he, like Scoresby, declined to accept a hollow earth.

Wallace knew that it existed, knew with his whole heart and soul that such a thing must be; those who denied it, even those who had been to the North, were either wilfully blind, or jealous that they had not yet managed to discover it, and thereby accrue to themselves the glory which belonged to Symmes. When Symmes came to Richmond on a speaking tour Wallace obtained a ticket to the lecture and sat, enthralled, while Symmes and his friend Joshua Reynolds preached their doctrine, hanging on to every word, eyes greedily devouring the wooden globe which was used by way of illustration, and displayed the hollows in the earth at the Polar extremities which led to a fantastic world of pale beings and weak sunlight.

In 1823 he heard that Symmes's friend, the businessman James McBride, had submitted a proposal to Congress, asking for funding to explore the North Polar region expressly to investigate Symmes's theory. Here at last was his opportunity; and he waited in a fever of excitement for the passing of the proposal, the call to arms, the expedition, the discovery, the triumphant return, the vindication.

The proposal was voted down.

ᛒ   ☙

He has been living thus for so long that his body now works like a thing independent of his mind, an automaton. The seal meat is still red, but no longer warm; the strips are hardening, freezing. He must . . . what must he do? Build a snow house for the night; yes. And then he must load the seal meat on to his sledge, in preparation for the next day's travel. In which direction that will be he can not say. He does not know what lies ahead, what awaits, and it frightens him as much as it elates him; he does know what lies behind, what awaits there, *and that frightens him even more, with no trace of elation whatever.*

ᛒ   ☙

Following Symmes's death in 1829 his theory largely fell out of favour, as a wave of Polar exploration failed to find any evidence of a "hollow earth". Symmes's adherents gradually deserted him, or turned their attentions elsewhere; Joshua Reynolds successfully lobbied Congress for funding for a South Seas expedition which would also, as an aside, search for any traces of a "Symmes hole", as it came to be known, in the Antarctic. Although no sign of such a hole was found, the voyage did have far-reaching literary consequences, inspiring both Edgar Allan Poe's *The Narrative of Arthur Gordon Pym* and Herman Melville's *Moby-Dick*.

Poe published an article in praise of Reynolds, and the South Sea expedition, in the *Southern Literary Messenger* in January 1837; a reply to this article, penned by Wallace, appeared in the March 1837 issue. Wallace commends Poe on his "far-sighted and clear-headed praise of what will surely be a great endeavor, and one which promises to answer many of the questions which, at present, remain beyond our understanding", but laments the abandonment of American exploration in the North. "A golden opportunity is slipping through our fingers; for while the British Navy must needs sail across an ocean and attack from the east, through a maze of channels and islands which has defied all attempts and presents one of the most formidable barriers on Earth, the United States need only reach out along our western coast and sail through Bering's Strait to determine, for once and all, the geography of the Northern Polar regions."

Elsewhere in the article Wallace writes of the Arctic as "this Fearsome place, designed by Nature to hold and keep her secrets" and of "the noble Esquimaux, who have made their peace with a land so seemingly unable to support human existence, and who have much to teach us". These references make it clear that Wallace had, by 1837, already spent time in the Eastern Arctic, a fact borne out by the logbook of the whaling ship *Christina*, covering the period 1833–5. On board when the ship left New London in May 1833 was one "Wm. H. Wallace, gent., late of Richmond" listed as "passenger". In late August the log notes starkly that "Mr. Wallace disembarked at Southampton Island." Where he lived, and what he did, between August 1833 and March 1837 remains a mystery; Wallace left behind few letters, no journals or diaries that have been discovered, and did not publish any accounts of his travels. It has been assumed that he, like later explorers such as Hall and John RAE (q.v.), spent time living among the Inuit people and learning their way of life; if so, it is unfortunate that Wallace left no account of this time, as his adoption of the traditional Inuit way of life, in the 1830s, would mark him as one of the first white men to do so.

From *We Did Not All Come Back*

Even when Symmes died, and his theory looked set to die with him, Wallace kept faith. There would, he now knew, be no government-backed venture in search of the hollow earth; it would be up to one man of vision, daring, resolve to make his own way north. That man, he swore, would be William Henry Wallace, whose name would ever after ring down the annals of history.

Yet it was not fame, or the thought of fame, which spurred him on; rather, it was the rightness of the cause, the opportunity to prove the naysayers wrong, and a chance to break truly free from the shackles of his life and upbringing and venture, alone, to a place which was shrouded in mystery, to see for himself the wonders which were, as yet, no more than etchings in books, tales told by travellers. He had lived frugally, not touching the allowance still provided by his father, who hoped that the Prodigal Son would one day return to the family home; and with this he set out, early in 1833, for New England, where he persuaded a reluctant—until he saw the banknotes in the stranger's pocketbook—whaling captain to let him take passage on board his ship. Only when the *Christina* had set sail for the north did William Henry Wallace, for the first time in many years, know a kind of peace.

But it was a restless peace, short-lived. He spent the days pacing the deck with anxious feet, eyes ever northward, scanning the horizon for any signs of that frozen land for which he longed. When the first icebergs came in sight he was overcome with their terrible beauty, so imperfectly captured in the drawings he had pored over until he knew their every detail as well as if he himself had been the artist. Soon the ice was all around, and while captain and crew kept a fearful eye on it always, Wallace drank in its solemn majesty, and rejoiced that each day brought him closer to his goal.

When the *Christina* left him at Southampton Island he was oblivious to the crew's concern for a man whom they obviously thought mad. Yet they did not try to dissuade him; they had business to attend to, and only a short time before the ice closed in and either forced them home or sealed them in place for long, dreary months. The captain did try, on one occasion, to stop Wallace; but after a few moments he ceased his efforts, for the look in the other's eyes showed that no words the captain could muster would mean anything. At least the man was well provisioned; whatever qualms the captain might have about his mental state, his physical well-being was assured for a time. And once off the ship he was no longer the captain's concern.

Wallace had studied well the texts with which he had provided himself. In addition to clothing and food and tools, he had purchased numerous small trinkets—mirrors, knives, sewing needles, nails—and they paid handsome dividends amongst the Esquimaux, who were at first inclined to laugh at the *kabloona* come to live among them, but soon learned that he was in earnest about learning their ways. Before long Wallace had shed the outward garb of the white man and adopted the clothing of the Esquimaux, their furs and skins so much better suited to the land than his own cotton and wool garments. Their food he found more difficult, at first, to tolerate; it took many attempts before his stomach could accept the raw blubber and meat without convulsing, but little by little he came to relish it. His first clumsy attempts at building a snow house, or igloo, were met with good-natured laughter, but before long he was adept at wielding the snow knife, a seemingly delicate instrument carved from a single piece of bone which ended in a triangular blade of surprising sharpness. He learned to judge the snow needed for blocks, neither too heavy nor too light, and fashion the bricks so they were tapered where necessary. He learned to make windows of clear ice, and of the importance not only of a ventilation hole at the top of the structure, but of ensuring that it was kept free of the ice that formed from the condensation caused by breath and body warmth, lest the shelter become a tomb for those inside.

The casual way in which the Esquimaux men and women shared their bodies with each other shocked him, at first; after a time he came to see the practicality of sleeping, unclothed under furs, in a group, but he remained aloof from the women who plainly showed that they would welcome him as a partner. In all other ways he admired the natives of that cold land: what other travellers remarked on as their cruelty he saw as a necessity. Illness or frailty in one could mean death for all; there was no room in that place for pity, or sentiment, and he abandoned without regret the last traces of those feelings within his own soul.

He became skilled at traversing the fields of ice and snow, and would often set out alone. The Esquimaux, who only ventured across the ice when necessity compelled them in search of food, were puzzled by his expeditions, which seemed to serve no purpose. In reality he was searching, always searching, for any indication that he was drawing closer to the proof he sought, the proof that would vindicate Symmes, and his own life. He did not mark, in that realm of endless snow, how long he searched; but eventually he realised that he would not find the answers he was seeking in this place of maze-like channels. Symmes had been correct when he said that the answer lay from the west, not the east; and if he had been correct in this, why should he not be correct in much else?

When the *Christina* put in at Southampton Island in 1836 he had been cut off from his own kind for three years. The captain— the same man who had left him there—was astounded when he recognised, among the natives who crowded to the ship to trade for goods, the figure whom he had long thought dead. He was even more astounded when Wallace indicated—in the halting tones of one speaking a foreign tongue—that he sought passage back to New London. He spoke vaguely of business, but further than that he would not be drawn, except to say, of his time in the north, that he did not know whether he had found heaven on earth or an earthly heaven.

          ℘   ℘

His igloo is finished. Small as it is, he has had difficulty lifting the last few blocks in to place. He is vaguely surprised that the seal meat, coming as it did to revive him after his body's stores had been depleted, has not given him more energy. Instead, it seems almost as if his body, having achieved surfeit in one respect, is now demanding payment in another regard. After days, weeks, months of driving his body ever onward, all he can think of now is sleep; of the beauty of lying down under his fur robes and drifting into slumber even as the ice bearing him drifts closer to those unknown regions about which he has dreamed for so long.

          ℘   ℘

Wallace's reference, in his article, to the west coast of America and "Bering's Strait" suggests that he felt an attempt on the Arctic should be made from that side of the continent, and this would have been in keeping with Symmes's own beliefs. No such formal expedition along the west coast was to be made until 1848, when the first of the expeditions in search of the Franklin party set out, but it is clear that Wallace undertook an informal— and ultimately fatal—journey of his own more than a decade earlier. An open letter from Wallace, published in the Richmond *Enquirer* in April 1837, states his intention of travelling via Honolulu to Hong Kong and thence to Siberia, "which location is ideally placed as a base for the enterprising Polar traveller, and has inexplicably been ignored as such by successive governments, which have declined to take the sound advice of men such as Mr. Symmes, whose work I humbly continue, and whose theories I shall strive to prove to the satisfaction of all save those who are immune to reason, and who refuse to acknowledge any thing with which they do not have personal acquaintance."

Wallace's letter continues, "I shall be travelling without companions, and with a minimum of provisions and the accoutrements of our modern existence, for I have no doubt that I shall be able to obtain sustenance and shelter from the land, as the hardy Esquimaux do, until such time as I reach my journey's end, where I shall doubtless be shown the hospitality of those people who are as yet a mystery to us, but from whom we shall undoubtedly learn much which is presently hidden."

It is not known when Wallace left Virginia, but the diary of the Revd. Francis Kilmartin—now in the possession of the Mission Houses Museum in Honolulu—confirms that he had arrived in the Sandwich Islands, as they were then known, by March 1838, when he is mentioned in Kilmartin's diary. "Mr. Wallace is a curious mixture of the refined gentleman and the mystic, at one moment entertaining us all with his vivid and stirring tales of life among the Esquimaux, at another displaying an almost painful interest in any news from the ships' Captains arriving in port from eastern realms. His theories about the Polar region seem scarcely credible, and yet he appears to believe in them with every fiber of his being." In an entry from April 1838 Kilmartin writes "We have said our farewells and God speeds to Mr. Wallace, who departed this day on board the *Helena* bound for Hong Kong. While I am, I confess, loath to see him go—for I do not foresee a happy outcome to his voyage—it is also a relief that he has found passage for the next stage of his journey, which he has been anticipating for so long, and which consumes his mind to the exclusion of all else."

From *We Did Not All Come Back*

໒ð ᴄ୫

He had not wanted to return to Virginia, but there was that which needed to be done, preparations he needed to make, before setting out once more. He was uncomfortable with his parents, although not as uncomfortable as they with him. His father declared, publicly, that he would wash his hands of the boy, as if Wallace were still the feckless lad who had abandoned his studies so long ago; his mother thought, privately, that she would give much to have that feckless lad back once more if only for a moment, for she found herself frightened of the man who had returned from a place she could barely imagine.

He left Richmond—which he had long since ceased to think of as home—in early summer of 1837, and made his way to the Sandwich Islands, thence to Hong Kong, and thence—but later he could hardly remember the route by which he had attained the frozen shore of that far country about which he had dreamed for so long. He seemed to pass through his journey as one travels through a dream world, the people and places he saw like little more than ghosts, pale and inconsequent shadows. It was not until he stood on that northern coast, saw once more the ice stretching out before him, that he seemed to awaken. All that he had passed through was forgotten; all that existed now was the journey ahead, through the ice which stretched as far as his eyes could see.

໒ð ᴄ୫

The ice moves, obeying laws which have existed since the beginning of time. Currents swirl in the dark depths below, carrying the ice floe upon which he has erected his igloo, carrying it—where? He does not know. It is carrying him onward; that is all he knows.

໒ð ᴄ୫

Kilmartin's fears were well founded, for it is at this point that William Henry Wallace disappears from history. What befell him after he left Honolulu is one of the minor mysteries of Arctic exploration, for no further word is heard of him; we do not even know if he successfully reached Hong Kong, and from there north his passage would have been difficult. His most likely course would have been to travel the sea trading route north to the Kamtschatka Peninsula and then across the Gulf of Anadyr to Siberia's easternmost tip and the shore of the Chukchi Sea, from whence he would have been able to start out across the treacherous pack ice toward the North Pole.

Whether or not he made it this far is, of course, unknown, and likely to remain so at this remove, although one tantalising clue exists. When the crew of the *Plover* were forced to spend the winter of 1848-9 in Chukotka, on the northeast tip of the Gulf of Anadyr, they heard many tales of the rugged coastline to the west, and met many of the inhabitants of the villages, who came to Chukotka to trade. One of the party—Lieutenant William Hulme Hooper—later wrote *Ten Months Among the Tents of the Tuski* about the *Plover*'s experience, and in one chapter touches on the character of these hardy coastal people. "They are superstitious almost to a fault," he wrote, "and signs and events that would be dismissed by most are seized on by them as omens and portents of the most awful type. . . . One native told of a man who appeared like a ghost from the south, who had no dogs and pulled his own sledge, and whose wild eyes, strange clothes, and terrible demeanor so frightened the villagers that they—who are among the most hospitable people on Earth, even if they have but little to offer—would not allow him a space in their huts for the night. When day came they were much relieved to find that he had departed, across the ice in the direction of Wrangel Land to the north, where the natives do not venture, upon seeing which they

were convinced that he was come from—and gone
to—another world."

Historians have debated the meaning behind
Hooper's "a man who appeared like a ghost from
the south". The author would, of course, have been
hearing the native's words through an interpreter,
who might himself have been imprecise in his
translation. Hooper's phraseology, if it is a faithful
transcription of what he was told, could mean that
the stranger appeared in ghost-like fashion; that
is, unexpectedly. However, another interpretation
is that the man appeared pale, like a ghost, to the
dark-skinned Chukchi people; this, when taken
with the direction from which the man appeared
(which is the course Wallace would almost certainly
have taken) and his decision to head northeast
toward Wrangel, means that Hooper's description
of "the man like a ghost" might be our last glimpse
of William Henry Wallace, who would have gone to
certain death in the treacherous ice field; although
whether before, or after, finding that Symmes's
theory was just that—a theory only—will never be
known.

From *We Did Not All Come Back*

The land ice—the shelf of ice permanently attached to the
shore—was easy enough to traverse. He towed a light sledge
of his own devising behind him; he had no need of dogs, and
now laughed at Symmes's idea that reindeer would have been a
practical means of transport. Here there was one thing, and one
thing only, on which he could depend, and that was himself.

An open lead of water separated the land ice from the pack
ice, and it was with difficulty that he traversed it. From that
moment his journey became a landscape of towering ice rafters
and almost impenetrable pressure ridges, formed by the colliding
sheets of ice. On some days he spent more time hacking a trail

through the pressure ridges, or drying himself and his clothes after falling through young ice or misjudging his way across a lead, than he did travelling, and would advance less than a mile; on other days, when his progress seemed steady, he would find that the currents carrying the ice had taken him further forward than he anticipated.

He headed ever northward. He passed Wrangel Land on his left, and could have confirmed that it was an island, not a land bridge across the Pole connecting with Greenland; but by now such distinctions were beyond him. All was one here, the ice and snow and he himself, a tiny dot in the landscape of white. Did he believe, still, in Symmes? Would he have recalled the name, had there been anyone to mention it? But there was no one, and with every step forward he left the world, and his part in it, further behind.

Each night he built his house of snow. The Esquimaux had built their igloos large enough to accommodate several people; his own houses were small, large enough to accommodate only one, and consequently he had had to train himself to wake every hour or so, to clear the ventilation hole of ice so that he could breathe. It was not difficult to wake at regular intervals; the ice cracked and groaned and spoke almost as a living person, and more than once he sat in the Arctic night, listening to the voices, trying to discern what they were saying. One day, perhaps; one day.

His provisions, despite careful husbanding, gave out eventually, and for several days he subsisted on melted snow, and by chewing on the leather traces of the harness which connected him to his sledge, his only remaining link with his past. In reality, he was almost beyond bodily needs; he only remembered that it was time to eat when the increasing darkness reminded him that another day was drawing to a close. The seal was the first living thing that he had seen in—how long? He did not remember; yet instinct took over, and he killed and ate it, and when he had sated his hunger he had a moment of clarity, almost, when his course seemed laid out, stark and level. Either he hoarded the seal meat, turned, and set back for the coast, or he continued, onward through the ice, toward: what? An Open Polar Sea? Symmes's hollow earth?

It did not matter.

Nothing mattered.

His destiny was here, in the north, in the ice. It was all he had wanted, since—he could not remember when. Time meant nothing. The life he had left behind was less than dust. This was the place that he was meant to be.

He would go on.

჻ ჻

He crawls into the igloo and fastens the covering over the opening, making a tight seal. His fur-covered bed beckons, and he pulls the robes over himself. Around and below him the ice cracks and cries, a litany lilting as a lullaby which slowly, gradually, lulls him to sleep.

The ventilation hole at the top of the igloo becomes crusted with ice, condensed from his own breath.

He does not wake to clear it.

And the ice carries him, ever onward.

TOURIST TRAP

THE LEAFLET WAS THRUST into Charlotte's hand before she could refuse it. She had not seen the boy distributing flyers; he had been hidden by a pillar and, swept up by the flow of people on the pavement, she had been carried inexorably forward, with nowhere to go when the boy appeared before her, turned, and held out his hand in one fluid motion. Before she had had a chance to notice his face the leaflet was in her hand and, his mission accomplished, he had disappeared into the crowd, suddenly and completely.

She did not want to dispose of the leaflet while there was a possibility he might still be watching, and she could see no rubbish bin where it could conveniently be deposited. She had travelled some twenty yards before she spotted one; but before dropping it into the bin she smoothed the piece of paper out and looked at it.

The flyer consisted of a single, narrow strip of bright yellow paper with "Trotter's Tours Bring You The Best Of Britain" emblazoned across the top. Charlotte looked back in the direction she had come. She could no longer see the boy; possibly he had now moved to the other side of the pillar, or had taken himself off to another location in search of a more receptive audience. He certainly seemed to have been unlucky with the people behind her: she could see no one clutching the telltale yellow sheets. Perhaps they had been bolder than she, and had already discarded them.

Charlotte turned her attention back to the leaflet.

BARBARA RODEN

Specialists In Local Sightseeing
We Go That Extra Mile For You
DON'T MISS OUR FABULOUS
OFF-SEASON RATES!

Charlotte felt a bang on the side of her leg, and looked up to see a woman furiously manouevring a pram backwards. Two children, both under six, clung to either side of her, and the pram—from which the sound of a crying baby could be heard—appeared to be full of shopping. The two older children were in the middle of an argument which, from the well-worn taunts, was obviously a performance that had been given many times before. The mother caught Charlotte's eye and glared at her, as if everything was her fault; then, with a sharp word to both children that made Charlotte wince, she continued down the pavement. The sound of the children arguing lingered on the air for a few moments and then mercifully faded and died. Charlotte looked down at the leaflet once more.

> Forget about it all for a day and relax in the professional hands of Trotter's Tours. Our luxurious, fully-equipped, air-conditioned coach will whisk you away on a day of adventure. In the morning, you'll visit the picturesque ruins of Snaresbury Abbey, as seen in the film *One Day Last Summer*. Then it's on to the beautiful village of Brindford, "Heronsbrook" in the long-running television series *Blue Skies*, where there will be time for lunch before travelling on to the magnificent estate of Wynsford, used as the setting for the acclaimed miniseries *Soldier of Fortune*. Tour price includes admission fees; lunch, tea, and gratuities extra.

There was more in the fine print, including the price of the tour and the departure points and times. Charlotte read the blurb again, shivering a little in the early October breeze. Well, there would be no need for air-conditioning, at any rate. She looked up at the sky, where the sun was playing hide-and-seek with clouds which were clearly winning. She had made no clear plans for the day: she knew no one in the town, which had merely been another stop on her fortnight-long holiday. It was late in the year to be taking holidays, but there had been such good reasons for everyone else in the office to go during the prime summer months, and Charlotte had found her two weeks getting pushed further and further back. At least, she had told herself, it would give the tourists—the *other* tourists—a chance to thin out.

The tourists may well have vanished—hence the disappearance of the boy with the leaflets—but the residents of the ancient city in which she found herself certainly made up for them. They took over the pavements with a proprietary air: mothers with pushchairs walked two and sometimes three abreast, seemingly oblivious to everyone behind them, while gangs of children (surely they should be at school?) stood in front of any shop that promised food or loud music or both. Even as she stood pondering the leaflet, three schoolboys in navy blue blazers came charging down the pavement towards her, narrowly missing her at the last moment. Two of them exchanged a joke—almost certainly at her expense—and laughed as they ran past, while the third stopped for a moment and looked impassively back at Charlotte before turning and following the others.

Charlotte decided. She had spent two days in the city already, and had another night booked at a bed-and-breakfast near the train station. She didn't want to have to cancel, and disappoint the sad-eyed proprietor; but neither did she want to spend another day in the city, being jostled and pushed, especially as it looked as if it might well start to rain before long. A relaxing trip on a coach, with lunch in Brindford and perhaps a cream tea at Wynsford, would get her away from the crowds; and if it rained, at least she'd be warm and dry. She assumed the coach had heating as well as air-conditioning.

The coach departed from the train station at 10.30. Charlotte glanced at her watch. Just before 10.00; and she had with her everything she would need. Her heavy-duty, plastic-lined carrier bag, printed over with cats and flowers, contained a rolled-up plastic mac and a collapsible umbrella, as well as a guidebook, a bottle of water, and a packet of biscuits. She had also, at the last minute, added a scarf; after all, you never knew what the weather would do at this time of year, and it was better to be safe than sorry.

She turned her back on the city centre and set out for the station, following the stream of black taxis making their way to it. As she walked she noted, somewhat sadly but without surprise, that her way led past branches of the same chain stores which dominated every other town of any size in Britain. She could have been anywhere; if someone had blindfolded her and plumped her down in the city centre, it might have taken her some time to decide precisely where she was. The thought depressed her. All of her holidays were spent in the British Isles; her only trip abroad had been on a school visit to France when she was seventeen, and she had been dismayed and somewhat frightened to find that her schoolgirl French had done little to prepare her for the realities of getting by in a foreign country. Perhaps, she thought, she should spread her horizons a little on her next trip: Eire, or the Channel Islands (which she knew were British, but which somehow seemed "abroad" to her).

This somewhat daring train of thought was halted by her arrival at the station. She pulled the leaflet out of her bag and looked at it again. "Coaches depart outside the train station", it read, which, considering the long sweep of pavement outside the building, was not as helpful as it might have been. She was on the point of finding the Tourist Information booth and asking for help when a group of people noisily saying goodbye to a bored-looking teenage boy moved away from the curb, revealing a wooden signboard set on the pavement. "Trotter's Tours: Departure Point" it announced, while a clock below was headed by the legend "Next tour departs at ———". Someone had pointed both hands to twelve.

Charlotte looked around to see if anyone else appeared to be waiting for the coach, but could not spot any telltale slips of yellow paper. She checked her watch; just ten past ten. There was still plenty of time for others to arrive; and there could well be a few people inside the station, seeking the dubious comfort of a cup of railway coffee. She would give it ten minutes; if no one had arrived by then, she would go back to town and try to find some other way to occupy her day.

A clock perched high above the station ostentatiously ticked away the minutes, and as Charlotte's self-imposed deadline approached it seemed that no one else had found the tour an attractive proposition. However, just as the minute hand struck twenty past the hour, and Charlotte reluctantly decided she would have to seek out some other amusement for the day, a number of people suddenly converged on the signboard, as if a pub somewhere in the area had just turned out and the patrons had decided that this was the next best option. Little knots of two or three people stood in clusters on the pavement, all peering at the board and checking various brochures and leaflets.

A moment later a coach pulled up to the kerb, the words "Trotter's Tours" and "We go that extra mile for you" emblazoned on the front and side. It was an undistinguished vehicle in all other respects; when Charlotte boarded she wrinkled her nose at the smell—admittedly faint, but persistent—of stale tobacco, kept at bay, but not vanquished, by the aggressive use of air freshener. A professionally enthusiastic guide, who had a name badge reading "Ron" pinned crookedly to his jacket, kept up a running commentary as he greeted each arrival and collected their fare.

"Hello there, luv," he said cheerily to Charlotte as she boarded, "ay-up, mind the step, that's a girl . . . take any seat you fancy, there're views from all sides . . . now don't you worry about missing anything, I'm here to make sure you don't . . . you can put yourself in my hands, ha-ha, been doing these tours since Adam was a lad . . . that's it, in you go . . . Hello there, mate . . . mind the step, that's the way . . . ah, one of our American friends, I see . . . "

His patter faded as Charlotte made her way down the coach and settled on a seat near the back with an unobstructed window view. A quick check of the queue showed that there would be a number of empty seats, so she did not feel guilty about placing her bag on the seat beside her rather than at her feet or in the overhead bin. She had noticed one or two other "singles" in line, and had no wish to have one of them latch on to her for the duration of the tour. She had an uncanny knack for attracting the wrong sort of person; whenever she travelled by train or bus she invariably found herself sitting beside someone garrulous or drunk or both.

She was gazing at the coloured brochure Ron had given her upon boarding the coach, when she became aware that someone had stopped in the aisle beside her. She looked up to see a man standing there, gazing at the remaining seats as if weighing them up. He caught Charlotte's eye, smiled, and made as if to sit beside her; then, catching sight of her bag ostentatiously perched on the seat, he asked, "Are you saving this for someone?"

"No, not really," Charlotte was forced to admit.

"Oh, good. Then you don't mind . . . ?"

His unspoken question hung there for perhaps a second too long before Charlotte heard herself say, "No, of course not." She reached over for her bag, her glance, as she did so, taking in the empty seats, of which there were quite a few.

"My name's Frank," her seat-mate said. "Frank Miller. I'm from Chicago; well, not *really* Chicago, you know, but pretty close, and at least people over here have heard of Chicago; most of them, anyway. You from here?"

Charlotte was unsure whether by "here" he meant England or something more specific. "I'm from Guildford," she replied. Then, realising that that probably meant little to him, she added, "That's south of London. My name's Charlotte."

"Well, Charlotte, I'm really glad to meet you. I have to say, I didn't know what to expect from you English people." He affected a dreadful British accent. "Stiff upper lips, what, old chap?" He resumed his normal tone. "I mean, you've kind of got this reputation, you know, of being a bit—well, stand-offish, I guess, but everyone has been just great since I got here. Some of my friends warned me before I came: 'Don't expect them to be too friendly; they like to keep to themselves; it takes ages for them to get to like you', that sort of thing, but people have been incredible. I love the way all the guys call me 'mate', like they've known me for years! Just goes to show, doesn't it?"

It took Charlotte a moment to realise she was being included in the conversation. "Goes to show what?"

"Well, that you can't believe everything you hear! I mean, if I'd listened to my friends, I never would've come, and then I'd have missed all this." He gave an expansive wave, which Charlotte interpreted as taking in England and its inhabitants as a whole; she could hardly imagine that he would wax so enthusiastic about the coach and the train station.

Further comments were curtailed by the *whoosh* of the coach door shutting and a muttered conversation between Ron and the driver. The vehicle pulled out into traffic, and Ron, swaying slightly with the coach's movement, began what was obviously a well-rehearsed spiel.

"Good morning, ladies and gents, and welcome to Trotter's Tours, where we go that extra mile for you. Actually, these days that should be 'We go that extra 1.6 kilometres for you', but somehow the powers-that-be didn't think that was quite so catchy." Polite titters greeted this little sally. "Well, I'm really glad to have you all with me today, because of all the many tours that Trotter's does, this one has to be my absolute favourite, and I think you'll see why by the end of the afternoon."

The coach made a sudden swerve into another lane, which caused Ron to stumble and provoked a horn blast from a fellow motorist. Ron regained his balance. "Before we go much further, everyone, I should introduce you to Terry, our driver." Terry raised a hand slightly in acknowledgement of this introduction. "Terry's one of our most experienced drivers; he should be, the number of refresher courses he's been on! I'm not saying he's a bad driver, mind, but he *is* on a first-name basis with most of the policemen in the county, and the lads in the service department say he's single-handedly responsible for keeping most of them in a job."

More polite titters. Frank laughed aloud, and turned to Charlotte. "You Brits kill me with your humour," he said. "Benny

Hill, Monty Python; and that *Are You Being Served?*—it just kills me every time. You know that show?"

"A little."

"It's *great*! We get it every night on one of our local channels. It's a real classic, believe me!"

At the front, Ron was continuing his well-worn patter, and Frank turned his attention back to the guide. Charlotte breathed a small sigh; partly of relief, partly of dismay. It was going to be a long day.

ॐ ஐ

Their first stop was Snaresbury Abbey, already familiar to Charlotte (and, it appeared, to everyone else on the coach) from its appearance in the Academy Award-winning film *One Day Last Summer*. The lushly romantic epic had come along at a time when such qualities had almost been forgotten by the British film industry, and the movie-going public, in Britain and abroad, had lapped up its gorgeous settings and costumes, sumptuous score, and doomed central romance. Snaresbury Abbey had been one of the film's key settings, and soon after the party had filed off the coach, excited little groups of people were pointing out familiar scenes and vistas, and taking pictures of each other waving and smiling.

Charlotte had hoped that Frank would leave her once they were off the coach, and perhaps attach himself to another group; but a glance at her fellow travellers showed this to be an unlikely prospect. Most of their companions were elderly—or at least older—women travelling in twos and threes, although there were a few couples, one with a bored-looking boy of twelve or thirteen in tow. A group of foreign-looking people offered a brief promise of hope, but when she got close enough to hear them speaking Charlotte realised that they were German, and thus unlikely to prove an attraction to Frank. She was right.

"I just *loved* that film," confided Frank, as they milled about the abbey ruins. "You Brits sure know how to make great movies! And you're lucky: when you need to film at a castle or palace or cathedral or whatever, you just have to go out and find the nearest one! In America we'd have to build it all from scratch, and then it wouldn't look anything like the real thing; more likely end up looking like something that belonged in Vegas or Reno or somewhere. You ever been to Vegas?"

The thought of going somewhere like Las Vegas made Charlotte wince. "No."

"I tell you, you're not missing much. I mean, it's okay for a little while, but then you just get bored with the whole thing, unless you like to gamble, and I can't see the point in throwing my money away like that. Everyone knows it's all rigged anyway. A lot of my friends, though—*they* think that Vegas is just great. Well, they can have it! Give me something like this any time."

Charlotte looked around her. The abbey, while undeniably beautiful in its angular way, looked vaguely unsettling, like the carcass of some once-noble beast which had been left to rot itself quietly away in this corner of English countryside. She shivered slightly. Everyone else was now well scattered through the ruins, and she could hear low exclamations and cries of delight as yet another familiar vista was spotted. The young boy had wandered a considerable distance from his parents; indeed, Charlotte was startled to see that he had managed to climb to some height, and was now surveying the scene from a position half-hidden by crumbled stonework. He must have felt her looking at him, for he turned towards her, and she caught a glimpse of dark, unsmiling eyes before he darted from sight.

Frank pointed something out to her, and she dutifully looked, realising that she had not taken in a word he had said. Fortunately, he did not seem to require her input in any way; her mere presence was enough, and Charlotte realised that if he insisted on attaching himself to her for the rest of the trip, she could at least tune his voice out to a large extent.

With this somewhat cheering thought firmly wedged into her mind, Charlotte surveyed her surroundings once more. Most of the party, having exhausted the immediate pleasure of seeing the abbey, were making their way to the gift shop, a red brick structure which seemed to have been designed and built with the one aim of clashing as jarringly as possible with the abbey ruins. The young boy had caught up with his parents; he must have moved quickly after Charlotte had spied him. Perhaps he had thought she would cause trouble for him by reporting his actions to someone. Climbing on the ruins was not, she suspected, looked upon favourably by those in charge.

Charlotte and Frank inevitably found themselves in the gift shop, which was doing a thriving business in the sale of merchandise related to *One Day Last Summer*. Charlotte had a quick look round, bought a token postcard or two, and then escaped from the shop while Frank was trying to decide whether to get an expensive coffee-table book about Snaresbury and its vicinity, or an equally expensive "making of" book about the film. As she left the building, she passed the boy, who was clearly bored rigid with the proceedings and was waiting for his parents to finish in the shop. As Charlotte walked by he gazed at her with a sullenness which she guessed was habitual, and not directed at her personally.

Ron was waiting at the door of the coach, smoking a cigarette and exchanging bored chit-chat with the driver. When he saw the first of the passengers heading his way he took a last drag at his cigarette before stubbing it out and resuming his professional manner with long-practised ease.

"Well, well, well, glad to see you all back again so punctually. I wish I could add another hour or so to each day, but that's beyond even me, I'm afraid, and we have schedules to keep to; at least, *I* have a schedule to keep *you* to, so that we can get the most out of everywhere we see, and the longer we have to wait the shorter the time we have somewhere else, which *would* be a shame, as I know that you're all looking forward to getting to Brindford, which is our next stop. So if you'll all just take your seats, ladies and gents, then I can do a quick head count and we'll be on our way."

Frank was the last person back on the coach, which earned him a ribbing from Ron: "Usually it's one of the ladies we have to wait for; you'll have to do better at the next stop, mate, and not let the side down." Frank, sinking down into his seat as the coach lurched into movement, grinned good-naturedly and pointed proudly to the plastic carrier bag he was holding.

"Bought them both," he said, fishing the books out to show Charlotte. "Well, I'm not going to get this way again, am I? Seemed a shame to leave one behind. It's not like I can get them at home this easily."

"No, I suppose not." *Perhaps*, thought Charlotte, *he'll look at his books for a little while, and I'll get some peace.* But it was not to be.

"Well, I don't want to spoil them." He tucked them carefully back into the bag. "Besides, I'll have plenty of time to read them. I hope my pictures turn out. I'll have to watch the movie again when I get home; it'll mean a lot more now that I've seen the place. I've got it on DVD; you should see how great it looks! And there are all sorts of extra things on it, too; behind the scenes stuff, really great. Did you know . . . "

And he was off. Charlotte, who had seen the film once and enjoyed it well enough, found herself listening to an extended lecture on the finer points of the filming of *One Day Last Summer*, interspersed with encomiums on Frank's DVD player, which was, she gathered, absolutely top of the line. She had only the faintest idea of what a DVD actually was, but she did not want to expose her ignorance on the matter. Besides, it was easier to let Frank talk, and merely chime in with the odd comment when a pause alerted her to the fact that something in the way of a response was required.

When they arrived in Brindford, Ron was most explicit on the matter of timing. "I need everyone back here by two o'clock sharp," he said, in a tone which made Charlotte think he would follow this up with "Synchronise watches!" "Keep an eye on the time, ladies and gents," he continued. "There's a lot to see at Wynsford, and we don't want to keep everyone waiting here. Now, I can recommend a couple of good places for lunch, if anyone's interested . . . "

They spread out from the coach, and Charlotte found that Frank had once more attached himself firmly to her. For a brief moment she wondered if he had any amorous inclinations in her direction; but the thought was gone almost as soon as it had arrived. She had long since abandoned any notion that men found her a romantically attractive prospect. She was a good listener, and that attracted men of a certain type, who wanted little more than to have someone to talk to, someone who would not interrupt or argue or want to tell a story of their own in turn. Charlotte never interrupted or argued, and any stories which she might have had she kept to herself.

Stepping into the High Street of Brindford was rather like visiting once more a place she had not seen for many years, but which had not changed an iota in the intervening time. It was, of course, familiar to the millions of viewers of the long-running show *Blue Skies*, which had occupied a much coveted spot on BBC-1's early Sunday evening line-up for many years. It was, or had been, a show which revolved around the lives and loves, fortunes and misfortunes—some comic, some dramatic— of three generations of one family living in a small village; but over the years the three generations had become four, and the characters had seeped into the nation's consciousness. Had she been asked, Charlotte would not have called herself a particularly avid watcher of the show; but she knew enough about it to feel vaguely excited to be in the actual village where the outdoor scenes were shot, and to spot locations which were familiar in an oddly distant way.

Frank, of course, was a dyed-in-the-wool enthusiast.

"Oh yes, we get it at home; it's been on for ages. I think we're maybe a season or two behind, so I haven't been watching it while I've been here, in case I spoil anything. It's a great show; really makes you think that this is how people in England live. I mean, I know that they don't, most of them, but it's how people *should* live, if you see what I mean. Hey, that's Jim Anstruther's house! Can you take a picture of me in front of the door?"

The people of Brindford must, Charlotte reflected, be used to hordes of tourists wandering their streets, taking pictures, and generally acting as if they'd returned to their dearly-beloved homes after several years away. Being used to a thing wasn't the same as enjoying it, though, and she wondered if the people living in the neatly kept houses and working in the trim shops ever cursed the fame which had come to their sleepy village. She waited patiently while Frank found the perfect place to stand to have his picture taken. The house, which in the show belonged to curmudgeonly old Jim Anstruther, gave little sign of anyone being home, and Charlotte was therefore startled when the net curtain of one of the windows twitched and a face appeared briefly behind it. It looked like a young boy or girl—boy, she thought— and she had an impression of malevolence and something else, something less easily defined.

The face disappeared almost immediately, leaving Charlotte blinking dazedly, as if trying to focus. She heard Frank calling her; he sounded puzzled, as if a dependable piece of electrical equipment had suddenly malfunctioned.

"Hey, Charlotte, you okay? Have you got the picture yet? I want to get a few more shots before we have some lunch."

"Yes, just a minute," she mumbled, swinging the camera up into position. It took her a moment to focus properly, and when she had taken the picture Frank paused only long enough to retrieve his camera before heading off down the street to the next location. Charlotte glanced once more at the house, but there was no further movement from behind the curtain. Whoever it was must have gone. Still, she had no inclination to linger; and for the first time that day she felt almost glad of Frank's company.

They had lunch with Ron and several other members of the party in a pub, the exterior of which played the part of The Cross Keys in *Blue Skies*. The interior, Charlotte noted with some surprise, looked nothing like its television counterpart, but the walls were hung with dozens of photographs from the show, black-and-white giving way to colour as the years went by. The talk was mostly about the show, and Frank took an eager part in it, while Charlotte picked at her ploughman's lunch. The thought of the face in the window was making her shiver. Much of Brindford seemed to enjoy basking in the reflected glow from the TV series; but at least one person appeared hostile. How many people, she wondered, had posed in front of that door, trampled through the garden, and peered in the windows? It must take a toll. Whoever it had been, though—and she was inclined to think that it *had* been a young boy, certainly no older than twelve or so—must surely be used to it by now. More likely it was merely a case of pre-teen resentment of the world at large. Still, she would be glad when they were safely on their way to Wynsford.

Charlotte and Frank were back at the coach before the appointed time, earning them an approving nod from Ron, who was casting appraising glances at the sky.

"Won't be surprised if we get a spot of rain before the afternoon's out," he announced. "Shame, that; the grounds are magnificent, some of the finest in England. Still, the house is well worth seeing; you could spend a whole day just looking around *that*, if you had a mind to. And maybe the rain'll hold off; you never can tell."

No indeed; you never could tell, thought Charlotte, as she glanced at Frank, who was mercifully quiet for a few moments, looking through some of his Brindford purchases. She sighed. She wasn't having a *bad* time—not *exactly*—but she wished that Frank didn't feel the need to comment on absolutely everything they saw. Perhaps things would be better at Wynsford.

And things *were* better, at least for a time. Frank had filled the trip there with his eager, excited chatter, and Charlotte had managed to allow most of it to flow over and around her, responding only when pauses informed her that some input was expected. The sight of the great house, looming before them in its Capability Brown-designed park, had been enough to silence even Frank, however, and by the time he regained his tongue they were inside the house and in the hands of a professional guide, who left only miserly pockets of silence for the group to fill as she shepherded them from one stately room to the next. As soon as they had all assembled at the next point she would be in full flow again, rattling off names and dates, identifying portraits, pointing out significant pieces of furniture or china or silverware, and answering questions from the group. Charlotte noted that the guide seemed impatient with any questions having to do with the TV miniseries which had brought the house, some four hundred years after it was built, a new fame. It was almost as if she was resentful of the intrusion which had been made into the well-ordered house, the inevitable upset of routine, the sudden superficial fame which had doubtless attracted many people who would otherwise never have darkened the door of Wynsford.

They proceeded to another room, Frank filling the silence with a whispered, "No wonder they needed so many servants! I'd hate to have to dust *this* place. And how can one house need so many sitting-rooms, anyway?"

It was, thought Charlotte, an unexpectedly apt question. She was becoming rather tired of the guide's incessant drone, which had started as a welcome change to Frank's but had quickly grown just as tiresome. She turned her attention away, towards the windows, and through them to the coolness and silence of the grounds beyond. It was not raining, although the sky was a dull, heavy grey which promised rain before the afternoon was over. Suddenly Charlotte was impatient to be outside; to leave the stifling house and relentless guide behind and wander through the gardens, restore to herself some of the tranquility which she had sought, and thus far not found, on the trip.

She chafed restlessly as the tour proceeded to its close. The guide, who was clearly more at home indoors than out, gave what Charlotte thought was a somewhat grudging run-down of a few of the delights available to them outdoors and then left them to find their way out; a way which led, Charlotte was not surprised to see, through a well-stocked, and expensive, gift shop. She made her way determinedly to the door, leaving the rest of the party clustered around the displays of boxed soaps and tea towels.

Once outside she paused and took several deep breaths, like one who has just escaped from terrible danger. A glance at the sky showed that the rain was still in abeyance; with luck it would hold for another hour or so, and see them safely back on the coach. She pulled out the information leaflet she had been given about the house, and examined the list of possibilities.

There was a great lake with bridge, a waterfall, several temples and follies of various periods and/or historical interest, a grotto, an Italian garden, a conservatory, something depressingly called "The Wynsford Experience", and, of course, the famous water terraces, without a view of which no visit to Wynsford was complete (or so the leaflet claimed). Charlotte hesitated, trying to decide; and in that moment was lost, for the door behind her opened and Frank and a number of others from their party emerged into what was left of the day. Frank hailed her.

"I was hoping you hadn't gone too far! We've decided to come back to the shop before we leave; one of the guys inside says it's going to rain soon, and pretty hard, so if we want to see anything outside we should do it now. We're all going to walk up to the water terraces; come on!"

There was no room for disagreement or, indeed, for talk of any kind, as the group moved off in the direction of the water terraces. Charlotte noted that the couple with the boy were part of the group, and caught the lad's eye as he turned to follow his parents. The look of sullen resentment had gone; now there was just apathy. He shuffled off after the group, head down, hands in his pockets, kicking aimlessly at loose stones on the walkway.

Charlotte reluctantly started after them, drawn on by the mechanics of the group. Better, after all, to be with someone—*anyone*—than to be alone. Wasn't that right? Yes.

No. A voice from somewhere surprised her. It was not from inside her head; indeed, it was almost as if she had someone perched on her shoulder, speaking into her ear, like those cartoons of people with an angel on one side of them and a devil on the other, both trying to put forward their cases. *No*, said the voice again, *that's* not *right. You don't have to go with them. Do what* you *want to do! Go off on your own! See something else!*

She slowed her steps, allowing the group to gain distance. Frank was near the front; mercifully, he was buried in conversation with someone else, and was oblivious to Charlotte's absence. In a moment they would be out of sight around a bend in the path. She stopped and watched as they gradually disappeared, swallowed up by the trees. The only one who noticed her was the boy, who turned at the last moment and caught her eye briefly. Then he, too, was gone.

Charlotte stood, savouring her freedom, feeling like a prisoner who has unexpectedly been granted parole and who stands, blinking, on the outside of the prison door. With a small shake of her head she focussed her attention once more on the leaflet. The water terraces were definitely out; what else did she want to see? The lake and its bridge were justly famous, but Charlotte felt that she was already overly familiar with that image, it having featured in the opening credits of *Soldier of Fortune* every week for thirteen weeks. The grotto sounded interesting. She would make for that, and if something else came up along the way, then she could always stop and see that instead; as long as the rain held off.

Wrought-iron signposts with long, elegant fingers pointed the way to the various attractions which Wynsford had to offer, and Charlotte set off in the direction of the grotto. She saw few other people, and most of them were heading in the opposite direction, back towards the house, in anticipation of the rain. She patted her bag with a small smile. She had her mac and umbrella; even if the rain started before she got back to the coach, she'd be able to escape the worst of it. Preparation; that was the key.

The path twisted and turned, but every now and then a signpost appeared to point the way to the grotto. Looking behind her, she saw that the house had disappeared from sight. Once or twice she thought that someone was on the path, a little way behind her, but to her relief no one appeared to break the stillness with their presence. She walked briskly, swinging her arms, breathing deeply, letting the silence wash over her, cleanse her, refresh her.

She came to a junction where a small path led off to the right. There was no signpost to guide her, but she supposed that the grotto must be further along the main, better-travelled, path. Odd that there was no sign.

Now that she had stopped, Charlotte realised how immense and total the silence was. There was nothing to indicate the presence of any living thing, other than herself: not even a bird.

Did they hide in their nests when it threatened rain? Charlotte wondered. She wasn't sure. But the stillness was what she had been hoping for, longing for; wasn't it?

Yes; but not this *still* another voice whispered. She shook her head, as if trying to dislodge something. This was silly. She had come out here to get away from people; she had *got* away from people; so why was she suddenly nervous? The grotto; she had said she would find the grotto. Well, she *would* find it, and then she would head straight back to the house. After all, it wasn't sensible to get caught in a rainstorm, no matter how well prepared she was. She didn't want a long ride back to town in damp clothes.

A movement out of the corner of her eye caught her attention, and she turned and looked down the path along which she had come. There was nothing there. "A squirrel," she thought; "it must have been a squirrel, darting across the path." She had seen no other squirrels during her walk.

Charlotte looked about once more, hoping to find some indication that she should continue down the main path. She was grimly determined to find the grotto now that she had come so far. *If I had known it was such a distance from the house I wouldn't have come*, she thought. *Perhaps the water terraces would have been a safer bet after all.*

"Safer"; odd word to choose. Before she could pursue this thought further, however, she spotted a small sign, close to the ground and partly obscured by foliage and leaves. It had obviously been there for some time; probably this sign, and others like it, had been forerunners of the obviously much newer, shinier, more tourist-friendly wrought-iron signposts she had been following. One finger, marked "Grotto", pointed clearly down the main path; but she was intrigued to note that another finger, pointing down the smaller path, read "Maze".

A maze! There was nothing about a maze marked on the leaflet she had been given; she was positive of that. Just to be sure, she dug it out of her pocket and checked. No; not a word. That was odd. Perhaps it was being built, or whatever you called it when you were putting together a maze. Cultivated, she supposed.

But no; this sign had clearly been there for some time. Perhaps the maze had been grubbed up, like a hedgerow, or had been infested with something or caught some botanical disease.

Well, the best way to find out would be to go and look. She checked her watch and calculated how long it would take her to walk back to the house and coach. She estimated that she had about twenty minutes to spare to find the maze—or what was left of it—have a quick look, and then start back. It would certainly give her something to talk about on the way back; not even Frank would be able to top *this*.

Charlotte started off down the smaller path, all thoughts of the grotto forgotten. She was fascinated with the idea of seeing a maze; the only one she had ever been in was the one at Hampton Court, and it had been so full of tourists that any element of mystery or delicious confusion had been lost in a babble of voices, shrieks, and laughter. This promised to be quite different, if it was still in existence.

The smaller path was clearly not frequented; foliage was encroaching from both sides, and tufts of grass were springing up here and there, in contrast to the tidy paths along which she had previously walked. It was impossible to say how long it had been since anyone had been that way. She hoped it wouldn't take too long to get to the maze; she wanted to have a chance to look around it before she had to start back.

As if in answer to her unspoken wish, the path took a sharp turn to the left and disclosed, to her delighted vision, what was clearly an extensive and ornate yew hedge, set in a clearing amid overhanging trees. She imagined that when it had been laid out, the trees had been much smaller, and the whole construction had been much more open. Now, however, the trees, clearly unchecked, were spreading dark branches over the maze, as if trying to claim it, and the effect was somewhat oppressive. It needed someone to come in and do some extensive trimming. Perhaps that was why the maze was closed; work had started—or was about to start, she corrected herself; there was certainly no sign of anything currently going on—and the owners wanted to keep people away for the duration.

An elaborate wrought-iron gate was set in the centre of the wall of hedge facing her. Charlotte approached it, expecting it to be firmly shut and padlocked, and was pleased to find that the gate was unlocked, and actually hanging open a few feet, as if in invitation. Should she go in? Her ambition had been merely to satisfy her curiosity as to the maze's existence, and she didn't have very much time. But a glance at her watch showed her that she had a few minutes to spare; long enough to go a short way in, satisfy herself as to the maze's condition, and then return to the house.

She pushed at the gate so that it was almost completely open and went in a few feet. The hedges rose up two or three feet above her head; there was certainly no possibility of cheating by peering over the tops to ascertain the best route! She must be sure that she didn't go in too far, or she might find herself unable to find her way back to the entrance.

She remembered having read somewhere that if you always chose the left fork in a maze, you would find yourself in the centre in no time. Or was it the right-hand path you were supposed to take? She was sure it was left. Anyway, it didn't matter, as she wasn't trying to find the centre. She'd just go in a short distance, so she could say she'd been in the maze, and then come straight back out again. She didn't have time to do much more than that, anyway.

But as she made her way into the maze, she was beckoned onwards—or so it seemed—by a seductive siren call, inviting her to go just a little further, see what was around the next corner, and then the next, and then the one after. And it all seemed so *easy*. She had obviously remembered correctly, for whenever Charlotte came to a choice of ways she took the left-hand path, which always seemed to be correct, for she met with no dead ends and never seemed to double back on her own tracks. It was easy to tell that she had been the only one in the maze for some time: the long grass was untrodden save where she had walked.

Almost before she knew it, Charlotte had reached the centre. She did not know what to expect: a sundial, perhaps, or pond, or a small garden. There were none of these things: merely two stone benches, facing each other across a square some twenty or so feet across. There might once, perhaps, have been a garden of some sort between them, but it had obviously been pulled up or left to die at some point, and never been replanted.

A small, soft sound reached her ears as something landed in the long grass at her feet. Then another sound, and another, and Charlotte looked up to see that the promised rain had now arrived. She sighed, pulled open her bag, and shrugged her way into her plastic mac, then fished her umbrella from out of the bag's depths. She struggled to get it to open properly —collapsible umbrellas *never* opened without a struggle—then stood for a moment, surveying her surroundings. She wished that she had someone there with whom to share her experience. Even Frank would have been a relief, for she had to admit that the silence was now oppressive. She smiled faintly at the thought that she could consider Frank's presence at all welcome. It seemed almost odd, somehow, that he wasn't hovering nearby, like a shadow.

"It's too bad you're not here, Frank," Charlotte said aloud, more to break the silence than anything else. "You'd have liked this. You picked the wrong time to leave me on my own."

From somewhere close by she heard the unmistakable sound of laughter.

It was only the slightest of sounds, low and soft, but *gloating*, somehow. She stood stock still, eyes darting about the small clearing. Nothing.

Of course there's nothing said a voice. *You've made sure of that, haven't you? No one even knows you're here.*

And somehow that thought made things much worse.

A few moments ago she had been surprised to find that she wouldn't have minded Frank's company. Now she would have given just about anything to see him come walking around the corner, chattering non-stop about how great the maze was. But no one came around the corner. *Because no one's here except you* came a voice. *And if you've got any sense, you'll get yourself out of here, too, before you get soaked.*

Charlotte shivered and realised that the rain was coming down harder now; much harder, in fact. She raised her umbrella and, huddling under it, turned towards the opening out of the centre of the maze. As she did so, she thought she saw someone slip thinly through the gap in the hedge, out into the maze. She could not be positive, but she thought she heard, over the steady patter of the raindrops, another laugh.

Charlotte stood motionless in the centre of the maze, her heart pounding, her eyes fixed on the gap in the hedge. Someone was out there; she was sure of it. Someone *had* been following her! But who? Frank? No; she didn't think that he was capable of something quite so subtle. Had Frank decided to follow her, he could never have kept silent for so long. Who then?.

The boy! Yes, that had to be it. She remembered him turning to look at her as the group moved away. He had been at the back; perhaps he had slipped away, unbeknownst to his parents, and had decided to brighten his day by following the unsuspecting Charlotte. Well, a schoolboy was someone she felt she could deal with. She raised her voice to ensure she was heard above the sound of the rain.

"I don't know your name, but I recognised you, so you might as well give up this silly game." Silence. "Come on, you can't have gone very far, you must be able to hear me. Just call a halt now, and we'll head back to the house together." Still nothing. "Look, this isn't remotely funny. If you're waiting there to jump out and yell boo, then don't bother. Just show yourself like a sensible lad, and we can both get out of here. You can share my umbrella, if you want."

Only the sound of the rain greeted her. If he was out there, then the boy was ignoring her well-meaning efforts to smooth things over. Perhaps he had already gone, the surprise of having been recognised speeding him back to his parents so that he could deny anything should Charlotte accuse him when she returned to the coach.

The coach! Charlotte fumbled for her watch, and was shocked to find that the time, which had seemed to be passing so gently, had now flown by. They were supposed to be back at the coach at 4.30; it was now almost twenty-five past. She was going to be terribly late.

She turned once more to the entrance. It seemed to be harder to make out now, and she realised that the rain and the coming dusk were conspiring with the surrounding trees to bring the darkness on. Much as she disliked the idea of stepping out into the maze again, she couldn't stand there all day. She took a deep breath.

"Okay; if you're still there, I just want you to know I'm coming out now, so no stupid tricks, please. I won't say anything to your parents if you'll just behave sensibly. Deal?"

No answer. Either he was intent on playing some silly prank, or—she fervently hoped—he was far away, legging it back to his parents. She took another deep breath and, squaring her shoulders, started back into the maze.

Almost immediately she found herself in difficulty. Her umbrella, although fairly compact even when opened, was still too wide for the overgrown maze, and was continually snagging itself on overhanging branches. Worse still, her sense of direction, so sure before, seemed to have completely deserted her. Charlotte had reasoned that if she kept to the right at each junction, she would make her way out as easily as she had got in; but this was not the case, and the steady rain was beating down the grass, obscuring the marks she had made on the way in. She found herself walking up blind alleys, then retracing her steps, only to grow confused as to which way she had just come. The rain was falling ceaselessly and relentlessly, and her umbrella was more hindrance than help. It snagged again on a particularly ruthless branch, and as she struggled to free it Charlotte saw someone standing at the end of the alley she was in. As soon as her eyes were turned directly on the spot, the figure slipped sideways and was gone; but she was positive she had recognised the boy. Only surely he hadn't been that thin . . .

"All right, so you want to play stupid games then, do you?" she shouted into the gathering gloom. "Fine! I'll have a thing or two to say to your parents, young man; just you wait!"

ᙏ ᘉ

Ron drummed his fingers impatiently on the door of the coach and tried to ignore the low murmurs of his bored and restless passengers. He checked his watch again. Past five o'clock. He turned once more to Frank, who was sitting behind the driver, and who had been uncharacteristically silent for the last few minutes.

"You *sure* you don't know where she's got herself off to?"

"I've told you!" Frank's voice contained a mixture of annoyance, perplexity, resentment, and worry. All four emotions had been struggling for mastery each time Ron had questioned him; worry was now emerging as a clear winner. "We ran into her outside the gift shop and told her we were going to the water terraces before it started to rain. As far as I knew, she was with us; it was only when we got there that I saw she hadn't come, and then I just figured she'd decided to go off somewhere else on her own. I thought she'd be back here waiting for us; she didn't seem the kind of gal who'd be late for things."

Ron turned to the young boy, who was sitting with his mother. The apathy had vanished from his face; he seemed, if anything, rather pleased to have a part to play in the drama which appeared to be unfolding around him.

"And you, son; you said that you saw her as you were heading up to the water terraces. What was she doing?"

"She weren't doing nothing," he said.

"*Anything*, William; she weren't doing anything," his mother corrected automatically.

"Weren't doing *anything*, then," said William. "She were just standing there, watching us, like; then I went round a corner and couldn't see her."

"And she didn't follow the group after that?"

"Nope. I were in back all the time, and no one were behind me."

"And we didn't see her after that," chimed in Frank. "I thought it kind of funny that she wasn't there; I was sort of expecting her, I guess. I kept looking for her all the way back here."

"Right," said Ron heavily. He pointed to Frank. "You'd better come with me."

"Why me? Where're we going?" asked Frank, rather nervously. A stranger in a foreign country, he didn't like the direction events were taking.

"We're going to have to find someone in charge here, and tell them we've got a missing passenger. And you're the one who can give the best description of her." Ron squinted out into the rain. "Come on, mate; ready when you are."

ℬ ℭ

Charlotte stumbled down another dark alleyway. Her umbrella had long since been discarded as useless, and her plastic mac hung open. Rain soaked her hair, rolled down her neck in clammy tracks, streaked her face, blurred her vision. The ground underfoot was slick and treacherous; several times she had stumbled and fallen, and from the pain in her left ankle she thought it likely that she had done some fairly serious injury to herself. Twice now she had found herself back in the centre of the maze; the second time she had stood and cried, uselessly and helplessly, until the sound of laughter had cut through her tears like a knife.

She looked up quickly, as something at the end of the alley caught the edge of her vision, although she knew it was no use; whoever it was was always too quick for her. She didn't think it was the boy from the coach party; he had been big for his age, bulky. This person was smaller, thinner. She thought back to the figure she had seen in the ruins at Snaresbury, and the face she had seen in the window in Brindford; even the boy distributing leaflets. Yes; that was who it looked like.

But how could that be? asked a small, tired voice. *He couldn't be in all four places, could he? Well?*

But the part of her that would once have looked seriously at this undeniably sensible question had gone away somewhere, and could not be reached.

"Go away!" she screamed into the rain. "Go *away*, do you hear me? Just leave me alone! Why are you doing this to me?"

As if it had at last tired of its game, the figure sidled back into view, slowly, almost shyly. As she finally got a full look at its face, Charlotte realised, belatedly, that she did not really want an answer to her question. It was undoubtedly the boy she had seen in Brindford; the boy whose face had radiated malevolence, and something else she had not been able to place. Now, however, she saw clearly what it was.

Hunger.

ॐ ॐ

Ron and Frank hurried along the path to the grotto, flanking a large, burly man in gum boots and a wax jacket. The rain had stopped a few minutes earlier, but they remained huddled inside their jackets, hands in pockets, heads down. They came to a junction, where a smaller path led away to the right.

"That's the way to the grotto, down there." The burly man pointed ahead of them along the main path. Harry Wainwright had been in charge of the grounds at Wynsford for nine years, and this was hardly the first time that someone had gone missing; but usually the someone was a youngster who got separated from his parents, or teens larking about, not realising how big the grounds really were. Respectable, sensible, intelligent women did not, as a rule, disappear in Wynsford's grounds, and Wainwright was more concerned than he cared to let on to the other two. He turned to Frank.

"What makes you think she might have come down here? It's a long way from the house, and you didn't have a lot of time, did you?"

Frank shrugged. "I don't know," he said. "I just—well, it seems like the sort of place she might have been interested in seeing, somehow. I can't explain it any better. Besides, she isn't anywhere closer to the house."

"No." Wainwright knew that for a fact. Several of his staff were searching the grounds, and he was in constant radio communication with them. If Charlotte had been found, he'd have been told.

"We'll go on to the grotto—it's not much further—and

178

search there. Then, if we don't find her, we'll head back to the house. No point in staying out here; it'll soon be too dark to see anything anyway."

"What'll happen when we get back to the house?" Frank thought he knew the answer already, and didn't really want to hear it pass the other man's lips, but something forced him to ask the question.

"It'll become a police matter then." Wainwright saw the look on the other men's faces and shrugged. "We can only do so much. Of course, I don't know how seriously the police will treat it; people, at least adults, have to be missing for a certain period of time before they're *legally* missing, if you see what I mean; but under the circumstances . . . " His voice trailed away.

"What about checking down there?" Frank pointed in the direction of the other, smaller path. "What's along there, anyway?"

"Nothing," said Wainwright. "Used to be the maze. Still is, technically, at least until it comes out next month. The only way she'd find it is if she went down there, and she'd have no reason to do that. All the old signposts were pulled up last year, and replaced with the wrought-iron ones. And the maze isn't marked on any of them."

Frank looked around. Wainwright was correct—there were no signs to be seen. "Still," he argued, "she might have followed the path, just to see what was there. Shouldn't we check?"

Wainwright shrugged. "Suit yourself. It's not very far; we'll check, then go to the grotto—after that it's back to the house. Come on."

It was not, as he said, very far to the maze. The dark clearing was oppressive, and did not incline them to linger; once they had checked the gate they turned and retraced their steps to the main path. It was, after all, abundantly clear that no one had been inside the maze for some time: a thick chain and stout, rusty padlock held the gate firmly, unflinchingly, uncompromisingly shut.

NORTHWEST PASSAGE

How then am I so different
    from the first men through this way?
Like them I left a settled life, I threw it all away
To seek a Northwest Passage at the call of many men
To find there but the road back home again.

           —Stan Rogers, "Northwest Passage"

THEY VARY IN DETAIL, the stories, but the broad outline is the same. Someone—hiker, hunter, tourist—goes missing, or is reported overdue, and there is an appeal to the public for information; the police become involved, and search and rescue teams, and there are interviews with friends and relatives, and statements by increasingly grim-faced officials, as the days tick by and hope begins to crack and waver and fade, like colour leaching out of a picture left too long in a window. Then there is the official calling off of the search, and gradually the story fades from sight, leaving family and friends with questions, an endless round of what ifs and how coulds and where dids pursuing each other like restless children.

Occasionally there is a coda, weeks or months or years later, when another hiker or hunter or tourist—more skilled, or perhaps more fortunate—stumbles across evidence and carries the news back, prompting a small piece in the "In Brief" section of the *Vancouver Sun* which is skimmed over by urban readers safe in a place of straight lines and clearly delineated routes. They gaze at the expanse of Stanley Park on their daily commute, and wonder how a person could vanish so easily in a landscape so seemingly benign.

Peggy Malone does not wonder this, nor does she ask herself any questions. She suspects she already knows the answers, and it is safer to keep the questions which prompt them locked away. Sometimes, though, they arise unbidden: when outside her window the breeze rustles the leaves of the maple, the one she asked the Strata Council to cut down, or the wind chimes three doors down are set ringing. Then the questions come back, eagerly, like a dog left on its own too long, and she turns on the television—not the radio, she rarely listens to that now—and turns on the lights and tries, for a time, to forget.

ℬ ℰ

The road was, as back roads in the Interior go, a good one: Len had always ensured that it was graded regularly. Peggy, bumping her way up it in the Jeep, added "get road seen to" to her mental checklist of things to do. She could not let it go another summer; next spring's meltwater would eat away even further at the dirt and rocks, and her sixty-three-year-old bones could do without the added wear and tear.

She followed the twists and turns of the road, threading her way through stands of cottonwood and birch and Ponderosa pine. Here and there the bright yellow of an arrowleaf balsam flashed into sight beneath the trees, enjoying a brief moment of glory before withering and dying, leaving the silver-green leaves as the only evidence of its passing. Overhead the sky was clear blue, but the breeze, when she pulled the Jeep in front of the cabin, was cool, a reminder that spring, not summer, held sway.

Peggy opened the rear of the Jeep and began unloading bags of supplies, which seemed, as always, to have proliferated during the drive. There was nothing to be done about it, however; the nearest town was an hour away, and she had long since learned that it was better to err on the side of too much than too little. Even though she was only buying for one now, the old habits died hard, and she usually managed to avoid making the journey more than once every two weeks or so.

She loaded the last of the milk into the fridge, which, like the other appliances and some of the lights, ran off propane; the light switch on the wall near the door had been installed by Len in a fit of whimsy when the cabin was being built, and served no useful purpose, as electricity did not extend up the valley from the highway some miles distant. The radio was battery operated, but seldom used: reception was poor during the day and sporadic at night, with stations alternately competing with each other and then fading away into a buzz of static. Kerosene lanterns and a generator could be used in an emergency, and an airtight fireplace kept the cabin more than warm enough in spring and fall. In winter she stayed with a nephew and his family on Vancouver Island; Len's brother's son, Paul, a good, steady lad who had given up urging his aunt to make the move to the Island permanent when he saw that it did no good. She would move when she was ready, Peggy always replied; she would know when the time came, and as long as she was able to drive and look after herself she was happy with the way things were.

Supplies unloaded, she set the kettle to boiling. A cup of tea would be just the thing, before she went out and did some gardening. It was not gardening in the sense that any of her acquaintances on the Island would understand it, with their immaculate, English-style flowerbeds and neatly edged, emerald green lawns which would not have looked out of place on a golf course; she called it that out of habit. She had learned, early on, that this land was tolerant of imposition only up to a point, and for some years her gardening had been confined to planting a few annuals—marigolds did well—in pots and hanging baskets.

Of course, she now had the grass to cut, and there were the paths to work on. It was Len who had suggested them, the summer before he died, while watching her struggle to keep the sagebrush and wild grass at bay. The cabin was built on a natural bench which overlooked the thickly treed valley, and was in turn overlooked by hills, rising relentlessly above until they lost themselves in the mountains behind. On three sides of the cabin the grassland stretched away to the trees, and Peggy had fought with it, trying, with her lawn and her flowers, to impose some sense of order on the landscape. She had resisted the idea of the paths at first, feeling that it would be giving in; but about what, and to whom, she could not have said. Still, she had started them for Len, who had taken comfort, that last summer, in watching her going about her normal tasks, and then she had continued them, partly because she felt she owed it to Len, and partly to fill the hours.

The paths now wound through a large part of the grassy area around the cabin. They were edged with rocks, and there were forks and intersections, and it was possible to walk them for some time without doubling back on oneself; not unlike, thought Peggy, one of those labyrinths in which people were meant to think contemplative thoughts as they followed the path. She was not much given to contemplation herself, but keeping the existing paths free of weeds occupied her hands, and she supposed vaguely that it was good for her mind as well.

Now she stood looking at the paths, wondering whether she should do some weeding or check the mower and make sure it was in working order. It might have seized up over the winter; if so, then a good dose of WD-40 should take care of matters. She knew precisely where the tin was—Peggy knew precisely where everything in the cabin was—and was just turning towards the shed where the mower was stored when she heard the unmistakable sound of a vehicle coming up the road.

It was such an unusual sound that she stopped in her tracks and turned to face the gate, which hung open on its support, the only break in the fence of slender pine logs which encircled the property and served to keep out the cattle which occasionally wandered past. The road did not lead anywhere except to the cabin, and visitors were few and far between, for the simple reason that there was almost no one in the area to pay a visit. Peggy stood, waiting expectantly, and after a few moments a ramshackle Volkswagen van swung round the curve and started up the slight incline which levelled off fifty yards inside the gate, not far from the front of the cabin where her Jeep was parked.

It pulled to a halt just inside the gate, and Peggy watched it. There were two people in the front seat, and for a minute no one made a move to get out; she got the impression that there was an argument going on. Then the passenger door opened, and a boy emerged, waving a tentative hand at her. She nodded her head, and the boy said something to the driver. Again Peggy got the impression that there was a disagreement of some sort; then the driver's door opened slowly, and another boy emerged.

She would have been a fool not to feel a slight sense of apprehension, and Peggy was not a fool. But she prided herself on being able to assess a situation quickly and accurately, and she did not feel any sense of threat. So she stood and waited as they approached her, taking in their appearance: one tall and fair-haired, the other shorter and dark; both in their late teens or early twenties, with longish hair and rumpled clothing and a general impression of needing a good square meal or two, but nothing that made her wish that the .202 she kept inside the cabin was close to hand.

The pair stopped a few feet from her, and the fair-haired boy spoke first.

"Hi. We, uh, we were just passing by, and we thought . . . " He trailed off, as if appreciating that "just passing by" was not something easily done in the area. There was a pause. Then he continued, "We heard your Jeep, and were kinda surprised; we didn't think anyone lived up here. So we thought that . . . well, that we'd come by and see who was here, and . . . "

The trickle of words stopped again, and the boy shrugged helplessly, as if making an appeal. It was clear the other boy was not about to come to his aid, so Peggy picked up the thread.

"Margaret Malone," she said, moving forward, her hand extended. "Call me Peggy."

The fair-haired boy smiled hesitantly and stuck out his own hand. "Hiya, Peggy. I'm John Carlisle, but everyone calls me Jack."

"Nice to meet you, Jack." Peggy turned to Jack's companion and looked at him evenly. "And you are . . . ?"

There was a pause, as if the boy was weighing the effect of not answering. Jack nudged him, and he said in a low voice, "Robert. Robert Parker."

Something about the way he said it discouraged any thoughts of Bob or Robbie. The conversation ground to a halt again, and once more Peggy took the initiative.

"So, you two boys students?" she asked pleasantly. Jack shook his head and said, "No, why d'you ask?" at the same moment that Robert said sullenly, "We're not boys."

Peggy took a moment to reply. "To answer you first," she said finally, nodding towards Jack, "we sometimes get students up here, from UBC or SFU, studying insects or infestation patterns, so it seemed likely. And to reply to your comment, Robert," she said, looking him directly in the eye, "when you get to my age you start to look at anyone under a certain age as being a boy; I didn't intend it as an insult. If I want to insult someone I don't leave them in any doubt."

Jack gave a sudden smile, which twitched across his face and was gone in an instant. Robert glared at him.

"If you don't mind my asking, what brings you to this neck of the woods? Seems kind of an out of the way spot for two . . . people . . . of your age, especially this time of year."

Nothing.

Really, thought Peggy, *was my generation as inarticulate as this when we were young? You'd think they'd never spoken to anyone else before.*

Again it was Jack who broke the silence.

"We're just, well, travelling around, you know? Taking some time out, doing something different, that kind of thing." Seeing the look in Peggy's eyes, he added, "We just wanted to go somewhere we wouldn't be bumping into people, somewhere we could do what we wanted. We've been up here for a few weeks now, staying in an old place we found over there." He pointed an arm in an easterly direction. "It was falling to pieces," he added, as if he was apologising. "No one's lived there for ages, we figured it'd be okay."

Peggy held up a hand. "No problem as far as I'm concerned, if it's the place I think you mean. Used to be a prospector's cabin, but no one's used it for years. You're welcome to it. Last time I hiked over that way was some time ago, and it was a real

handyman's special then. You must have done a lot of work to
get it fixed up so that you could live in it."

Jack shrugged. "Yeah, but we're used to that. Lots of stuff
lying around we could use."

"What do you do about food?"

"We stocked up in town; and there's an old woodstove in the
cabin. We don't need a lot; we're used to roughing it."

Peggy eyed them both. "Seems to me you could do with
something more than just roughing it in the food line for a
couple of days."

"We do okay." It was Robert who spoke, as if challenging
Peggy. "We do just fine. We don't want any help."

"I wasn't offering any, just making a comment. Last time I
checked it was still a free country."

"Yeah, course it is," Jack said quickly. He glanced at Robert and
shook his head; a small gesture, but Peggy noticed it. "Anyway,
we heard your Jeep; we were kinda surprised to see someone
living up here. We figured it was only a summer place."

"No, I'm up here spring through fall," said Peggy. "Afraid
you're stuck with me as your nearest neighbour. Don't worry, I
don't play the electric guitar or throw loud parties."

It was a small joke, but Jack smiled again, as if he appreciated
Peggy's attempt to lighten the mood. Robert nodded his head in
the direction of the van, and Jack's smile vanished.

"Well, we've got to get going," he said obediently. "Nice
meeting you, Peggy."

"Nice meeting you two," she said. "If you need anything . . . "

"Thanks, that's really kind of you," said Jack. He seemed
about to add something, but Robert cut in.

"Can't think we'll need any help," he said curtly. "C'mon,
Jack. Lots to do."

"Yeah, right, lots to do. Thanks again though, Peggy. See you
around."

"Probably. It's a big country, but a small world."

"Hey, that's good." Jack smiled. "Big country, small
world."

Robert, who had already climbed into the driver's seat,

honked the horn, and Jack turned almost guiltily towards the van. The passenger door had hardly closed before Robert was turning the van around. Jack waved as they passed, and Peggy waved back, but Robert kept his eyes on the road and his hands on the wheel. Within moments they were through the gate, and the curve of the road had swallowed them up.

₧   ⁣

Over the next few days Peggy replayed this encounter in her head, trying to put her finger on what bothered her. Yes, Robert had been rude—well, brusque, at least—but then a lot of young people were, these days; some old people, too. Their story about wanting to see something different; that wasn't unusual, exactly, but Peggy could think of quite a few places which were different but which didn't involve fixing up a dilapidated shack in the middle of nowhere. Yet Jack had said they'd done that sort of thing before, so it was obviously nothing new for them.

Were they runaways? That might explain why they came to check out who was in the cabin. But if they were running away from someone, they would hardly have driven right up to her front door. Drugs crossed her mind; it was almost impossible to pick up the paper or turn on the news without hearing about another marijuana grow-op being raided by police. Most of them were in the city or up the Fraser Valley, but she had heard about such places in the country, too; and didn't they grow marijuana openly in some rural spots, far away from the prying eyes of the police and neighbours? That might explain why Jack had looked so nervous . . . but, when she recalled the conversation, and the way Jack had looked at his friend, she realised that he was not nervous on his own account, he was nervous for, or about, Robert, who had seemed not in the least bit nervous for, or about, anything. He had merely been extremely uncomfortable, as if being in the proximity of someone other than Jack, even for five minutes, made him want to escape. What had Jack said? They wanted to go somewhere they wouldn't be bumping into people.

Robert must have had a shock when he saw me here, thought Peggy. *Bet I was the last thing he expected—or wanted—to run into.*

She did not see the pair again for almost three weeks. Once she saw their van at the side of the road as she drove out towards the highway and town, but there was no sign of Jack or Robert, and on another occasion she thought she saw the pair of them far up on the hillside above her, but the sun was in her eyes and she couldn't be sure. She thought once or twice about hiking over to their cabin, which was two miles or so away. There had been a decent trail over there at one time, which she and Len had often walked; but the days were getting hotter, and her legs weren't what they once were, and when she reflected on her likely reception she decided she was better off staying put. If they wanted anything, or needed any help, they knew where to find her.

It was late morning, and Peggy had been clearing a new path. A wind had been gusting out of the northwest; when she stopped work and looked up the hill she could see it before she heard or felt it, sweeping through the trees, bearing down on her, carrying the scent of pine and upland meadows before rushing past and down the hill, setting the wind chimes by the front door tinkling, branches bending and swinging before it as if an unseen giant had passed. Sometimes a smaller eddy seemed to linger behind, puffing up dust on the paths, swirling round and about like something trapped and lost and trying to escape. But Peggy did not think of it like this; at least not then. Those thoughts did not come until later.

She straightened up, one hand flat against her lower back, stretching, and it was then that she saw the boy standing at the edge of the property, by the mouth of the trail leading to the prospector's cabin. She had no idea how long he had been standing there, but she realised that he must have been waiting for her to notice him before he came closer, for as soon as he knew he had been spotted he headed in her direction.

"Hello there," she said. "Jack, isn't it? Haven't seen you for a while; I was beginning to wonder if you'd moved on."

"No, we're still here." He gave a little laugh. "Kind of obvious, I guess."

"A bit. Your friend with you?"

"No."

"I'm not surprised. He didn't seem the dropping-in type."

"No." Jack seemed to feel that something more was needed. "He was a bit pissed off when he found someone was living here. He thought we had the place to ourselves, you see, no one around for miles."

"He likes his solitude, then."

"You could say that."

"Still, it's not as if I'm on your doorstep," said Peggy reasonably, "or, to be strictly accurate, that you're on mine. If your friend doesn't want to run into anyone, he's picked as good a spot as any."

"Yeah, that's what I've been telling him, but I think we'll be heading out before the end of the summer."

"Because of me?"

"Well, no; I mean, sort of, but that's not the whole reason. Robert"—he paused, looking for words—"Robert likes to keep on moving. Restless, I guess you could say. He's always been like that; always wants to see what's over the next hill, around the next corner, always figures there's somewhere better out there."

"Better than what?"

Jack shrugged. "I don't know. He gets somewhere, and he seems happy enough for a while, and then, just when I think 'Right, this is it, this is the place he's been looking for' off he goes again."

"Do you always go with him?"

"Yeah, usually. We've known each other a long time, since elementary school. His family moved from back east and we wound up in the same grade three class."

"Where was that?"

"Down in Vancouver. Point Grey."

Peggy nodded. Point Grey usually, but not always, meant

money, respectability, expectations. She could see Robert, from what little she knew of him, being from, but not of, that world. Jack, though, looked like Point Grey, and she wondered how he had found himself caught up in Robert's orbit.

"He's always been my best friend," the boy said, as if reading her thoughts. "We hung out together. I mean, I had other friends, but Robert just had me. It didn't bother him, though. If he wanted to do something and I couldn't, he'd just go off on his own, no problem. It's like he always knew I'd be there when he needed me."

"Has he always liked the outdoor life?"

Jack nodded. "Yeah, he's always been happiest when he's outside." He shook his head. "I remember this one time I got him to go along with a group of us who were going camping for the weekend. We were all eleven, twelve; our parents didn't mind, they figured there were enough of us that we'd be safe." He paused, remembering. "We rode our bikes from Point Grey out to Sea Island; you know, behind the airport." Peggy nodded. "There used to be a big subdivision out there, years ago, but then they were going to build another runway and the houses got . . . what's the word . . . expropriated, and torn down, and then nothing happened, and it all got pretty wild, the gardens and trees and everything.

"Well, we all had the usual shit . . . I mean stuff; dinky pup tents and old sleeping bags and things, and chocolate bars and pop, but not Robert. He had a tarp, and a plastic sheet, and a blanket, matches, a compass, trail mix, bottled water; he even had an axe. You'd've thought he was on a military exercise, or one of those survival weekends, instead of in the suburbs. We goofed around, and ate, and told stories, and then we crawled into our tents, all except Robert. He'd built a fire, and a lean-to out of branches and the tarp, and he said he'd stay where he was, even when it started to rain. Rain in Vancouver: who'd think it?

"Anyway, when morning came round we were a pretty miserable bunch of kids; the tents had leaked, and our sleeping bags were soaked, and we'd eaten almost everything we'd brought. And there was Robert, dry as a bone, making a fire out of wood he'd put under cover the night before, with food and water to spare. Made us all look like a bunch of idiots."

"Sounds like a good person to have around you in a place like this."

"Yeah, you could say that." He scuffed the toe of one foot against the dirt, watching puffs of dust swirl up into the air.

"So where is he this morning?"

Jack stopped scuffing and looked up at Peggy. "He went off a couple of hours ago; said he needed to get away for a while, be on his own. He gets like that sometimes. I hung around for a bit by myself and then . . . " His look was almost pleading. "It just got so quiet, you know? You don't realise how quiet it is till you're by yourself. Robert doesn't mind; sometimes I think he'd rather be by himself all the time, that he wouldn't even notice if I never came back."

Peggy tried to think of something to say. Jack went back to scuffing the dirt, and a breeze picked up the cloud of dust, swirling it in the direction of the paths. Jack followed the cloud with his eyes, and seemed to notice the paths through the grass for the first time.

"Hey, that's pretty cool." He took a couple of steps forward, and she could see his head moving as he followed the curves of the paths with his eyes. "Bet it would look neat from overhead, like in one of those old Hollywood musicals."

Peggy had not recognised the tension in the situation until it was gone; its sudden disappearance left her feeling slightly off-balance, like an actor momentarily surprised by the unexpected ad-lib of someone else on stage. Jack was still gazing out over the paths.

"Must've taken a long time to do this," he said. "What's it for?"

"Nothing, really." Peggy moved forward so that she was standing beside him. "It was my husband's idea; he said he got tired of watching me trying to control the brush, that I should work with it, not against it."

If you can't beat 'em, join 'em, she heard Len's voice say. *And looking at all that*—he had waved his hand towards the expanse of scrub and the hills beyond—*I don't think you're ever going to beat 'em, Peg.*

"If you can't beat them, join them," said Jack, and Peggy started slightly and looked sideways at him. "That's how I feel about Robert sometimes. Can I take a closer look?"

"Go ahead." Peggy looked at her watch. "I'm going to go and make some lunch; nothing fancy, just sandwiches and some fruit, but if you want to stay then you're more than welcome."

"Could I?" he asked eagerly. "I'd really like that. Our cooking's pretty . . . basic."

Peggy, noting Jack's pinched face and pale complexion, could believe it. "I'll go and rustle something up; come in when you're ready."

She stood at the kitchen counter, letting her hands move through the familiar motions of spreading butter and mayonnaise, slicing tomatoes and cucumber, while in her head she went over the conversation with Jack. There were undercurrents she could not fathom, depths she could not chart. She had thought of them as two boys from the city playing at wilderness life, and Jack's words had not dismissed this as a possibility; but there was something else going on, she was sure of it. Were they lovers? Had they had a fight? That could be it, but she did not think so. She could not connect the dark, intense figure she had seen three weeks ago with something as essentially banal as a lovers' tiff.

Through the window she could see Jack moving slowly along one of the paths, his head down as if deep in concentration. He stopped, as if aware of her gaze upon him, but instead of turning towards the cabin he looked up at the hillside above, intently, his head cocked a little to one side as if he had heard something. Peggy followed his gaze, but could see nothing on the bare slope, or in the air above; certainly nothing that would inspire such rapt attention.

She stacked the sandwiches on a plate, then sliced some

cheese and put it, with some crackers and grapes, on another plate. She wondered what to offer as a drink. Beer would have been the obvious choice, but she had none. Milk or orange juice; or perhaps he'd like a cup of coffee or tea afterwards. . . .

Still pondering beverage choices, she put the plates on the table, then went to the door. Jack had not altered his position; he seemed transfixed by something up the hill. Peggy looked again, sure that he was watching an animal, but there was nothing to be seen.

She called his name, and he turned to her with a startled look on his face, as if he could not quite remember who she was or how he had got there. Then he shook his head slightly and trotted towards her, like a dog who has heard the rattle of the can opener and knows his supper is ready.

"Sorry it's nothing more elegant," said Peggy, pointing to the table, "but help yourself. Don't be shy."

She soon realised that her words were unnecessary. Jack fell on the meal as if he had not eaten in days, and for some minutes the only sound was him asking if he could have another sandwich. Peggy got up twice to refill his milk glass before finally placing the jug on the table so he could help himself, and watched as the cheese and cracker supply dwindled. Finally Jack drained his glass and sighed contentedly.

"Thanks, Peggy, that was great, really. Didn't know how hungry I was until I saw the food. Guess I wouldn't win any awards for politeness."

Peggy laughed. "That's okay. It's been a long time since I saw someone eat something I'd made with that much pleasure. I'm sorry it wasn't anything more substantial."

Jack looked at his watch. "Geez, is that the time? I better be going; Robert'll be back soon, he'll wonder where I am, and I'll bet you've got things to do."

"Don't worry, my time's my own. Nice watch."

Jack smiled proudly, and held up his wrist so Peggy could see it better. Silver glinted at her. "Swiss Army. My parents gave it to me when I graduated. Keeps perfect time." He sat back in his chair and looked around the cabin. "You live here by yourself? You said something about your husband. Is he . . . ?" He stopped, as if unsure how to continue the sentence to its natural conclusion, so Peggy did it for him.

". . . dead, yes. Four years ago. Cancer. It was pretty sudden; there was very little the doctors could do."

"I'm sorry."

"That's okay. You didn't know him. He went quite quickly, which is what he wanted. Len was never a great one for lingering."

"So you live up here for most of the year on your own? That's pretty gutsy."

Peggy could not recall having been called gutsy before. "You think so?"

"Yeah, sure. I mean, this place is pretty isolated, and you're . . . well, you're not exactly young." His face went pink. "I don't mean that . . . it just must be tough, that's all, on your own. Don't you ever get lonely?"

"No, there's always something to do. I spend the winter with family on the Island; I get more than enough company then to see me through the rest of the year."

Jack nodded. His eyes continued moving around the cabin, and he spotted the light switch. "Hey, I didn't think you had power up here."

"We don't. That's a bit of a joke, for visitors."

"Bet you don't get too many of those."

"You'd be right. My nephew and his family have been up a couple of times, but not for a while. He doesn't like it much up here; says it makes him uncomfortable. This sort of place isn't for everyone."

Jack nodded. "You've got that right." He looked through the screen door towards the hillside and gestured with his head. "You ever feel that something's up there watching you?"

Peggy considered. "No, not really. An animal sometimes, maybe; but we don't get too many animals up there. Odd, really, you'd think it would be a natural place to spot them." A memory came back to her; Paul, her nephew, on one of his rare visits, standing on the porch looking up at the hills. "My nephew said once it reminded him of a horror movie his sons rented: *The Eyes on the Hill* or something."

"*The Hills Have Eyes*," Jack corrected automatically. "Yeah, I've seen it." He was silent for a moment. "Do you believe that?"

"What—that the hills have eyes? No."

"But don't you feel it?" he persisted. "Like there's something there, watching, waiting, something really old and . . . I don't know, part of this place, guarding it, protecting it, looking for something?"

Peggy couldn't keep the astonishment out of her face and voice. "No, I can honestly say I've never felt that at all." She considered him. "Is that what you think?"

"I don't know." He paused. "There's just something weird about this spot. I mean, we've been in some out of the way places, Robert and me, but nowhere like this. I'll be kind of glad when he decides to move on. I hope it'll be soon."

"I thought you wanted him to settle down somewhere."

"Yeah, I do, but not here."

"Why don't you leave? Robert seems able to fend for himself, and he seems to like this sort of life better than you do. Why do you stay with him?"

"I've always stayed with him."

"But you said that he likes to go off on his own, that you don't think he'd notice if you didn't come back."

Jack looked uncomfortable, like a witness caught out by a clever lawyer. "Oh, I just said that 'cause I was pissed off. He'd notice."

"Is he your boyfriend? Is that why you stay?"

Jack looked shocked. "God, no! It's nothing like that. It goes back a long way. . . . Remember I told you about that camping trip out to Sea Island? Well, when I went round to Robert's house to get him his mom was there, fussing, you know, the way moms do, and he was getting kind of impatient, and finally he just said 'Bye, mom' really suddenly and went to get his bike, and his mom turned to me and said 'Look after him.' Which was kind of a weird thing to say, 'cause I was only eleven, and

Robert wasn't the kind of kid who you'd think needed looking after—well, we found that out next day. But I knew what she meant. She didn't mean he needed looking after 'cause he'd do something stupid, she meant that he needed someone to . . . bring him back, almost, make sure he didn't go off and just keep on going."

"Is that why you stay with him? So he doesn't just keep on going?"

"I guess." His smile was tinged with sadness. "I'm not doing such a great job, am I?"

"You're a long way from Point Grey, if that's what you mean."

"Yeah, and I can't see us making it back anytime soon. Robert wants to keep heading north, up to the Yukon, and then head east."

"What on earth for?"

Jack shrugged. "He does a lot of reading; he's got a box of books in the van, all about explorers and people who go off into the wilderness with just some matches and a rifle and a sack of flour and live off the land. I think that's what he wants to do; go up north and see what's there, see what he can do, what he can find. He loves reading about the Franklin expedition; you know, the one that disappeared when they were searching for the Northwest Passage, and no one knew for years what happened to them. I think he likes the idea of just vanishing, and no one knows where you are, and then you come out when you're ready, and tell people what you've found."

"The Franklin expedition didn't come out."

"Robert figures he can do better than them."

"Well then, you should break it to him that the Northwest Passage was found a long time ago, and tell him he should maybe stick closer to home."

"He doesn't want to find the Northwest Passage; anyway, he says it doesn't really exist, there is no Northwest Passage, not like everyone thought back in Franklin's time."

"And you'll go with him?"

"I suppose so."

"You do have a choice, you know."

"Yeah, like you said, it's a free country. But I kind of feel like I have to go with him, to . . . "

"Look after him?"

"I guess." He shrugged. "It's like there's something out there, waiting for him, and I have to make sure he comes back okay, otherwise he'd just keep on going, and he'd be like those Franklin guys, he'd never come out."

The conversation was interrupted by the unmistakable sound of a vehicle coming up the road towards the cabin. Jack stood up so quickly his chair fell over.

"Shit, it's Robert."

"Probably," Peggy agreed drily. "Don't worry, there's nothing criminal about having lunch with someone."

"No, but . . . Robert can be . . . funny, weird, sometimes. Don't tell him what I said about looking after him, he'd be really pissed off."

"Your secret is safe with me."

They went out on to the porch and watched the van drive up. Robert climbed out and glared at Jack.

"Thought you'd be here," he said, ignoring Peggy. "C'mon, let's go."

"Hello to you too," said Peggy. "You're a friendly sort, aren't you? In my day we'd have considered it bad manners to order a person out from under someone else's roof. Guess times have changed. Or are you just naturally rude?" Robert stared at her, but she gave him no chance to speak. "Jack's here as my guest; he's had a good lunch, which I must say he needed, and you look like you could do with something decent inside you, whatever you might think. So you can either stay here and let me fix you some sandwiches, which I'm more than prepared to do if you're prepared to be civil, or you can climb back into your van and drive away, with or without Jack, but I think that's his decision to make, not yours. He found his way here by himself, and I'd guess he can find his way back if he decides to stay a bit longer."

Robert started to say something; something not very pleasant, if the look that flashed across his face was anything to go by. Then he took a deep breath.

"Yeah, you're right. He can stay if he wants. No problem." He turned towards the van.

"Wait a minute," said Jack, moving off the porch. "Don't go. Peggy said you could stay, she'll fix you some sandwiches. Don't be a jerk. You must be as hungry as me."

"We've got food back at our place," said Robert; but he slowed down. Jack turned and threw a pleading look back at Peggy. *What can I do?* was written on his face.

"Robert. *Robert.*" He stopped, but kept his back turned to Peggy. "If you don't want to stay now, that's fine; maybe this isn't a good time, maybe you've got things to do, I don't know. But why don't you both come back over for supper? I've got some steaks in the fridge that need using up, and I can do salad and baked potatoes. Sound good?"

"What do you say, Robert?' said Jack eagerly. "I'll come back with you now, then we both come back later and have supper."

Robert looked at Jack, then at Peggy. She put her hands in front of her, palms out, like a traffic policeman. "No ulterior motive, no strings, just a chance to give you both a good meal and talk to someone other than myself. You'd be doing me a big favour, both of you."

"Yeah," said Robert finally, slowly, "yeah, okay, supper would be great."

"Fine! About six, then."

Robert climbed in the driver's seat, and Jack mouthed *Thanks!* and gave a wave; the sun glinted off the face of his watch, making her blink. He got in the other side, and once more she watched as the van rattled out the gate and round the curve.

"I hope I've done the right thing," she said aloud. "Why can't things be simple?"

The afternoon drew on. Peggy did a bit more work on the paths, clearing some errant weeds. She straightened up at last, and glanced down across the valley below. It was her favourite view, particularly in the late afternoon sun, and she stood admiring it for a few moments, watching the play of light and shade across the trees. The wind, which had been playing fitfully about her all day, had at last died down, and everything was still and calm and clear.

Suddenly she turned and looked up behind her. She could have sworn that she heard someone call her name, but there was no one there; at least no one she could see. Still, the feeling persisted that someone was there; she felt eyes on her, watching.

The hills have eyes.

For the first time she realised how exposed she and the cabin were, and how small. Crazy, really, to think that something as essentially puny and inconsequential as a human could try to impose anything of himself on this land. How long had all this been here? How long would it endure after she was gone? *Work with it, not against it* Len had said. *If you can't beat 'em, join 'em.* But how could you work with something, join with something, that you couldn't understand?

She shook her head. This was the sort of craziness that came from too much living alone. Maybe Paul was right; maybe it was time to start thinking about moving to the Island permanently.

Or maybe you just need a good hot meal said a voice inside her head. *Those boys will be here soon; better get going.* She took one last look at the hill, then turned towards the cabin. The wind chimes were ringing faintly as she passed, the only sound in the stillness.

Inside, she turned on the radio; for some reason which she did not want to analyse she found the silence oppressive. The signal was not strong, but the announcer's voice, promising "your favourite good-time oldies", was better than nothing. She started the oven warming and wrapped half a dozen potatoes in foil, to the accompaniment of Simon and Garfunkel's "The Sound of Silence", then started on the salad fixings: lettuce, cucumber, radishes, tomatoes, mushrooms. As she scraped the last of the mushrooms off the board and into the bowl she glanced out the window, and saw a figure standing on one of the paths, looking back at the hillside. *Jack*, she thought to herself, recognizing the fair hair, and looked at her watch. It was ten past five. *They're early. Must be hungry.*

Simon and Garfunkel gave way to Buddy Holly and "Peggy Sue". The oven pinged, indicating it was up to temperature, and she bundled the potatoes into it. When she returned to the window, the figure was gone.

"C'mon in," she called out, "door's open, make yourselves at home." She put the last of the sliced tomatoes on top of the salad, then realised no one had come in. "Hello?" she called out. "Anyone there?" Buddy Holly warbling about pretty Peggy Sue was the only reply.

Peggy went to the door and looked out. There was no one in sight. The van was not there, and it registered that she had not heard it come up the road. *It's such a nice night, maybe they walked.* She looked to her right, to where the trail they would have taken came out of the woods, but no one was there.

A squawk of static from the radio made her jump. For a moment there was only a low buzzing noise; then Buddy Holly came back on, fighting through the static, for she heard "Peggy" repeated. Another burst of noise, then the signal came through more clearly; only now it was the Beatles, who were halfway through "Help!".

"Interference," she muttered to herself. They often got overlapping channels at night; another station was crossing with the first one. She went outside and looked round the corner of the cabin, but there was no one in sight. When she went back in, "Help!" was ending, and she heard the voice of the announcer. "We've got more good-time oldies coming up after the break," he said, and she realised the radio had been broadcasting the same station all along. They must have got their records, or CDs, or whatever they used now mixed-up, she decided.

She placed the salad on the table and got the steaks out of the fridge. She was beginning to trim the fat away from around the edges when the radio gave another burst of static, then faded away altogether. She flicked the on/off switch, and tried the tuner, but was unable to raise a signal. *Dead batteries*, she thought. *I only replaced them last week; honestly, they don't make things like . . .*

She broke off mid-thought at the sound of a voice calling her name. *Definitely not Buddy Holly this time*, she thought, and walked to the door, ready to call a greeting. What she saw made her freeze in the doorway.

Robert was running towards her across the grass; running wildly, carelessly, frantically even, as if something was chasing him, calling out her name with all the breath he could muster. In a moment she shook off her fear and began crossing the yard towards him, meeting him near the back of her Jeep. He collapsed on the ground at her feet, and she knelt down beside him as he gasped for breath.

"Robert! Robert, what's wrong? What's happened?"

"Jack," he gasped; "Jack . . . he's gone . . . got to help me . . . just gone . . . "

"Gone! What do you mean? Gone where?"

He was still panting, and she saw that his face was white. He struggled to his knees and swung round so that he could look behind him, in the direction of the blank and staring hillside.

"Don't know . . . we were coming over here . . . walking . . . and then he was gone . . . didn't see him . . . "

"Right." Peggy spoke crisply, calmly. "Just take another deep breath . . . and another . . . that's it, that's better. Now then"—when his breathing had slowed somewhat—"you and Jack were walking over here—why didn't you come in the van?"

"It wouldn't start; battery's dead or something."

"Okay, so you decided to walk, and Jack went on ahead, and you lost sight of him. Well, as mysteries go it's not a hard one; he's already here."

Robert stared at her. "What do you mean, he's already here?" he almost whispered.

"I saw him, over there." Peggy pointed towards the paths. "I looked out the window and there he was."

"Where is he now?"

Peggy frowned. "Well, I don't know; I went outside, but

couldn't see him. I thought you'd both come early and were looking around."

"What time was this?"

"Ten past five; I looked at my watch."

"That's impossible," said Robert flatly, in a voice tinged with despair. "At ten past five he'd only just gone missing, and I was looking for him a mile from here. There's no way he could have got here that fast."

Peggy felt as if something was spiralling out of control, and she made a grab at the first thing she could think of. "How do you know exactly when he went missing?"

"I'd just looked at my watch, to see how we were doing for time; then he was gone."

"Maybe there's something wrong with your watch."

Robert shook his head. "It keeps perfect time." He looked down at his left wrist, and Peggy saw him go pale again.

"What the fuck . . . " he whispered, and Peggy bent her head to look.

The face of the digital watch was blank.

Robert began to shiver. "What's going on?" he said, in a voice that was a long way from that of the sullen youth she had seen earlier. "Where's Jack?"

"I don't know; but he can't have gone far. Did you two have a fight about something? Could that be why he went on ahead?"

"But he didn't go on ahead," said Robert, in a voice that sounded perilously close to tears. "That's just it. We were walking along, and he asked what time it was, and I looked at my watch—it was only for a couple of seconds, you know how long it takes to look at a watch—and then he was just . . . gone."

"Could he have . . . I don't know . . . gone off the trail? Gone behind a tree?"

Robert looked at her blankly. "Why would he do that?"

"I don't know!" Peggy took a deep breath. The boy was distraught enough, without her losing control as well. "Playing a joke? Looking at something? Call of nature?"

He shook his head. "No."

"Think! Are you sure you didn't just miss him?"

"I'm positive. There wasn't time for him to go anywhere, not even if he ran like Donovan Bailey. I'd have seen him."

"Okay." Peggy thought for a moment. "You say you were both a mile from here, at ten past five, which is the same time I looked outside and saw Jack here, at my cabin. I'd say that your watch battery was going then, and it wasn't giving you an accurate time, which is how Jack seemed to be in two places at once."

Robert shook his head again. "No." He looked straight at Peggy. His breath was still ragged; he must have run the mile to her cabin. "Jack's gone." Then, more quietly, "What am I going to do?"

Peggy got him inside the cabin and into an armchair, then went back out on the porch. The clock on the radio had died with the batteries, but her old wind-up wristwatch told her it was almost six. *Time for Jack and Robert to be arriving. . . .*

She called out "Jack!" and the sound of her voice in the stillness startled her. She waited a moment, then called again, but the only reply was the tinkle of the wind chimes. She walked round the cabin, not really knowing why; Jack hadn't seemed the kind to play senseless tricks, and she didn't expect to see him, but still she looked, because it seemed the right—the only—thing to do.

She stood at the front of the cabin, looking down over the valley. All those trees; if someone wandered off into them they could disappear forever. She shivered, then shook her head. Jack hadn't disappeared; there had to be an explanation. He and Robert had had a fight; Jack had stormed off, and Robert was too embarrassed to tell her about it. Jack was probably back at their place by now . . . but that didn't explain how he had been outside the cabin at ten past five. Unless he had come to the cabin as originally planned, then decided he couldn't face Robert, and gone back to their camp by road . . . no, it was all getting too complex. She took a deep breath and walked round the side of the cabin . . . and stopped short at the sight of a figure over on the paths.

Only it wasn't a figure, she realised a split second later; there was no one, nothing, there. She had imagined it, that was all; perhaps that's what she had done earlier, looked up and remembered the image of Jack standing there from before lunch. He hadn't been there at all; Robert was quite right. In which case . . .

"We need to go looking for Jack."

Robert looked up at her as if he did not understand. Peggy resisted the urge to shake him.

"Did you hear me? I said we need to go look for Jack."

"Shouldn't we . . . shouldn't we call the police?"

"Yes; but first we need to go looking for him." She told him about her mistake with the figure. "He was never here at all. So you must have missed him on the path. And he must be injured, or lost, or he'd be here now. So yes, we'll call the police when we get back. Even if we called them now, though, it would be almost dark before they could get here; they wouldn't be able to start a search until daybreak. We're here now; we have the best chance of finding him."

She turned the oven off—*last thing I need now is to come back and find the place burned down*—then gathered together some supplies: two flashlights, a first aid kit, a couple of bottles of water, a sheath knife. She put them in a knapsack, which she handed to Robert. Then she went into her bedroom and got the .202 out from the back of the cupboard. The sight of it seemed to make Robert realise how serious the situation was.

"What do you need that for?"

"There's all sorts of animals out there, and a lot of them start to get active around this time of day. It's their country, not ours, but that doesn't mean I want to become a meal."

"Do you know how to use it?"

Peggy stared at him levelly. "It wouldn't be much use having it around if I couldn't use it. I'm not an Olympic marksman, but if it's within fifty yards of me I can hit it. Let's go."

They headed out towards the trail, skirting the paths. A little gust of wind was eddying dust along one of them. Peggy was conscious of the hillside above them to their left, and could not shake off the sense that something was watching. What was it Jack had said? *Something there, watching, waiting, something really old . . . part of this place, guarding it, protecting it, looking for something.* No; she had to stop it, stop it now. Thoughts like that were no good. She needed to concentrate.

"Come on, Robert," she called over her shoulder, "let's go. We have a lot of ground to cover, and it'll be dark in another couple of hours. You better go first; it's been a while since I was last through here. Keep yelling Jack's name, and keep your eyes open."

They started along the trail. It was fainter than Peggy remembered, but still distinguishable as such; more than clear enough to act as a guide, even for the most inexperienced eye. They took turns calling, and stared intently about them, looking from side to side, searching for any signs of Jack; but there was nothing, not a trace of his passage, not a hint that he was calling or signalling to them. They stopped every so often to listen, and to give them both a chance to rest; but they only lingered in one place, when Robert indicated that they were at the spot where he had last seen Jack.

"Here," he said, pointing. "I was standing here, and Jack was about fifteen feet in front of me, and then . . . he wasn't."

Peggy looked around, trying to will some sign, some clue into being, but there was nothing that marked the spot out as any different to anywhere else they had passed. Birch and poplar and pine crowded round them, but not so thickly, she thought, that someone could disappear into them and be lost to sight in a matter of seconds. A breeze rustled the branches, and something skittered through the undergrowth; a squirrel, she thought, from the sound. They called, but there was no reply, and searched either side of the trail, but there was no sign of Jack. Without a word they continued on their way.

Robert was still in front, Peggy behind; the trail was not wide enough to allow more than single file passage. *Indian file.* The phrase from her childhood popped unbidden into Peggy's mind, along with the accompanying thought, *I suppose you can't call it that anymore, but Aboriginal file doesn't sound right. Or would it be Native file?* Natives . . . now what did that . . .

"Natives don't like that place." Who had said that? Someone, years before, who she and Len had run into in town, someone who knew the area and was surprised when they told him where they lived. "Natives don't like that place," he had said. "Never have. Don't know why; you can't pin 'em down. Used to be a prospector lived back in there, not far from where you are, I guess, and there was a feeling he was tempting . . . well, fate, I suppose, or the gods, or something. . . . What happened to him? He just up and left one day; disappeared. Some people figured he'd hit it lucky at last and had cleared out with his gold, others said it was cabin fever; whatever happened, it didn't do anything for the place's reputation."

Why had she thought of that now, of all times? She shivered uncontrollably, and was glad that Robert was up ahead and couldn't see her. She hurried to close the distance between them; and although her breath was becoming more ragged, and the ache in her legs more pronounced, she did not stop again until they were at the cabin.

It was much as she remembered it; a low, crudely built structure of weathered pine logs, with a single door and one window in front, and a tin chimney pipe leaning out from the roof at an angle. There was no smoke from the chimney, no movement within or without; only the sound of the wind, and a far-off crow cawing hoarsely, and their own breath. The dying sun reflected off the one window, creating a momentary illusion of life, but neither one spoke. There was no need. Jack was not here.

They checked the cabin, just to be sure, and the van, sitting uselessly in front, and they called until they were hoarse, but they were merely going through the motions, and Peggy knew it. Robert tried the van again, but the battery was irrevocably dead. Still silent, they turned and headed back the way they had come.

They did not call out now, or search for signs; their one thought, albeit an unspoken one, was to get back to Peggy's before dark. The sun had dipped well below the hills now, and the shadows were lengthening fast, and Peggy found herself keeping her eyes on the trail ahead. Once she thought she heard movement in the trees to their right, and stopped, clutching Robert's arm; but it was only the wind. They continued on their silent way, and did not stop again.

They reached the cabin as the last of the light flickered and died in the western sky. Peggy ached in every joint and muscle in her body, but she lit the propane lamps and put water on to boil for coffee while Robert collapsed into a chair and put his head in his hands. Finally, when she could think of nothing else to do to keep herself busy, Peggy sat down opposite him.

"Robert." He looked up at her with tired eyes. "Robert, it's time to phone the police. I'll do it, if you'd like."

"Yeah, that'd be good. Thanks."

She would not have thought that this was the same Robert she had seen earlier in the day. He seemed lost, diminished, and she realised with a start that Jack had been wrong, completely wrong, when he had told her that Robert wouldn't have minded if Jack had gone off and never come back. Something inside Robert compelled him, but Jack, she thought, had always been there, a link with the life he had left behind, and a way back to it. As long as Jack had been with him, Robert would have kept moving; now, without him, Peggy had the feeling that there'd be no Northwest Passage. She wished that Jack could know that, somehow. Perhaps he already did.

She moved to the phone, an old-fashioned one with a dial. She picked up the receiver and listened for a moment, then jiggled the cradle two, three, four times, while the look on her face changed from puzzled to worried to frightened. She replaced the receiver.

"No dial tone."

Robert stared at her. "What do you mean, no dial tone?"

"Just what I said. The line must be down somewhere. We can't call out."

"Great. Just fucking great." Anger mixed with fear flashed across his face, and for a moment he looked like the Robert of old. "What do we do now?"

"We have a cup of coffee and something to eat; then we get in my Jeep and drive to town and tell the police what's happened. After that it's in their hands."

"Shouldn't we go now?"

"Frankly, until I get some coffee into me I won't be in a fit state to drive anywhere, and I'd be surprised if you're any different. And the police won't be able to start a search until morning; another half an hour or so isn't going to make much difference now."

Robert looked at her bleakly. "I guess not," he said finally.

She busied herself with the ritual of making coffee. As she measured and poured, something caught her eye at the window, and she looked up automatically.

A face was staring in at her.

She gave a brief, choked cry and dropped the teaspoon, which clattered on to the counter. It took her a moment to realise that what she saw was her own reflection, framed in the darkness of the window and what lay beyond. That was all it could be. There was no one out there.

But she had seen something at the window, out of the corner of her eye, before she looked up. No; it had been a reflection of something in the room. The cabin was brightly lit, and the windows were acting like mirrors.

From the front of the cabin the wind chimes rang.

Peggy was suddenly conscious of feeling exposed. The little cabin, lights streaming out the windows into the darkness, did not belong here; it was an intruder, and therefore a target. She turned to Robert.

"Close the curtains."

"What?"

She pointed to the picture windows overlooking the valley. "Leave the windows open, but close the curtains."

He did as she asked, while Peggy reached for the blind cord by the kitchen window. The Venetian blinds rattled into place. *That's better*, she thought, and took the coffee in to the living-room.

They sat and sipped, both unconsciously seeking refuge in

this ordinary, everyday act. There was silence between them, for there was nothing to be said, or nothing they wanted to say. The wind chimes were louder now, the only sound in the vast expanse around them. The only sound. . . .

A thought which had been at the back of Peggy's mind for some time came into focus then, and she looked up, listening intently. She placed her cup on the table in front of her so hard that coffee sloshed over the side. Robert looked up, startled.

"What . . . " he began, but Peggy held up her hand.

"Listen!" she whispered urgently. Robert looked at her, puzzled. "What do you hear? Tell me. . . . "

Robert tried to concentrate. "Nothing," he said finally. "Just that chiming noise, that's all. Why, did you hear something? Do you think it's . . . "

"*Listen*. We can hear the chimes, yes, but there's no wind in the trees; we should be able to hear it in the branches, shouldn't we? And the windows are open, but the curtains aren't moving, they're absolutely still. *So why can we hear the wind chimes, if there isn't a wind?*"

Robert stared at her for a moment, uncomprehending. Then he went pale.

"What are you saying?" he asked; but she saw in his eyes that he already knew the answer, or some of it. Enough, anyway.

"I'm saying we have to leave," said Peggy, startled by the firmness in her voice. "Now. Don't bother about the lights. Let's *go*."

She picked up her purse and keys from the shelf where they lay, and moved to the door. She did not want to go out there, did not want to leave the cabin, and it was only with a tremendous effort of will that she put her hand on the knob and pulled open the wooden door, letting a bright trail of light stream out over the rocky ground. She thought she saw something move at the far end of it, something tall and thin, but she did not, *would not* look, concentrating instead on walking to the driver's door of the Jeep with her eyes on the ground, walking, not running, she would not run. . . .

"Hey!" Robert's voice rang out behind her, and she turned

to see him still on the porch, looking not towards the Jeep, but towards the paths. She followed his gaze, and in the faint light cast by a three-quarter moon could just see a figure standing silent, fifty yards or so from them.

"Jack!" cried Robert, relief flooding his voice. He stepped off the porch and moved towards the figure. "Hey, man, you had us worried! Where've you been? What happened?"

Peggy felt a trickle of ice down her back. "Robert—Robert, come here," she called out, fear making her voice tremble. "Come here now; we have to go."

He stopped and looked back at her. "Can't you see?" he said, puzzled. "It's Jack!" He turned back to the figure. "C'mon, come inside, get something to eat, tell us what happened. You hurt?"

"Robert!" Peggy's voice cracked like a gunshot. "That isn't Jack. Can't you see? *It isn't Jack.*"

"What do you mean? Of course it is! C'mon over here, man, let Peggy take a look at you, you're frightening her. . . . "

All the time Robert had been moving closer to the figure, which remained motionless and silent. Suddenly, when he was only twenty feet away, he stopped, and she heard him give a strangled cry.

"What the . . . what are you? What's going on?" Then, higher, broken, like a child, "Peggy, what's happening?" He seemed frozen, and Peggy thought for a moment that she would have to go to him, pull him forcibly to the Jeep, and realised that she could not go any closer to that figure. A warning shot, if she had thought to bring the rifle, might have broken the spell, but it was back in the cabin . . . She wrenched open the driver's door and leaned on the horn with all her might.

The sound made her jump, even though she was expecting it, and the effect on Robert was galvanic. He turned and began moving towards the Jeep in a stumbling, shambling run; as he got closer she could hear him sobbing between breaths, ragged, gasping sobs, and she was glad that she had not been close enough to see the figure clearly.

She had dropped the keys twice from fingers that suddenly

felt like dry twigs. Now, on the third try, she slammed the key into the ignition and turned it. Nothing. She turned it again. No response. She tried to turn on the headlights, but there was no answering flare of brightness. The battery was dead, and she realised, deep down in a corner of her mind, that she should have expected this.

Robert turned to her, eyes glittering with panic. "C'mon, get it started, let's go! What are you waiting for?"

"The battery's dead." Her chest was heaving as she tried to bite down the panic welling up inside her. Robert began to moan, a thin, keening sound, as Peggy forced her mind back. *Think, think*, she told herself. *There's a way to do this, you know there is, you just have to calm down, remember. . . .*

Len's voice sounded in her ear, so clearly that for a moment she thought he was beside her. "It's not difficult," she heard him say, "as long as it's a standard; automatics are trickier." And she remembered; she had asked him, once, what they'd do if the battery went dead, up here with no other car for miles. "We make sure the battery doesn't go dead," he'd said with a laugh, but when she pressed him—she was serious, it could happen, what would they *do?*—he had replied cheerfully, "Not a problem; just put the clutch in, put it in second, let gravity start to work, let out the clutch, and there you go, easy-peasy. Make sure the ignition's on, and just keep driving for a bit; as long as the engine doesn't stop you'll charge the battery back up."

She had no intention of stopping once she got the engine started.

She took a deep breath. The Jeep was parked on the flat, with the downward slope beginning twenty feet away. She would need help.

"Robert." He was still moaning, looking out the passenger window, and Peggy risked a look too. The figure seemed closer. "Robert! Listen to me!" Nothing. She reached out and shook him, and he turned to her, his eyes wide and scared. She hoped he could hear her.

"You need to get out and push the car," she said, slowly and clearly. He started to say something, and she cut him short. "Just do it, Robert. Do it now."

"I can't get out, I can't, I don't . . . "

"You have to. You can do this, Robert, but you have to hurry. Just to the top of the slope. Twenty feet; then you can get back in."

For a moment she thought that he was going to refuse; then, without a word, he opened his door and half-fell, half-scrambled out. Peggy turned the ignition on, pushed in the clutch, put the Jeep in second, and they began to roll, slowly at first, then faster, Robert pushing with all his strength.

It seemed to take hours to cover the short distance; then Peggy felt the car start to pick up momentum, and Robert jumped in, slamming the passenger door. She said under her breath, "Work, please, work," and let out the clutch.

For one brief, terrible second she thought that it wasn't going to work, that she had done something wrong, missed something out. Then the engine shuddered into life, and she switched on the headlights, and they were through the gate and round the curve, and the cabin had disappeared behind them, along with everything else that was waiting in the darkness.

They did not speak during the drive to town. Peggy concentrated on the road with a fierceness that made her head ache, glad she had something to think about other than what they had left, while Robert sat huddled down in his seat. She did not ask him what he had seen, and he did not volunteer any information. The only thing she said, as they drew near the police station, was "Keep to the facts. That's all they want to hear. Nothing else. Do you understand?" And Robert, pale, shaking, had nodded.

They told their story, for the first of several times, and answered questions, together and separately. Peggy did not know exactly what they asked Robert; she gathered, from some of the questions directed at her, that he was under suspicion, although in the end nothing came of this.

Officialdom swung into action, clearly following the procedures and guidelines laid out for just such a situation. Appeals for help were made; search parties were sent out; a spotter plane was employed. There were more questions, although no more answers. Peggy sometimes wondered where they would fit all the pieces she had not told them: eddies of dust and the ringing of chimes on a windless day, someone (not Buddy Holly) calling her name, the figure they had seen outside the cabin, the battery failures, the phone going dead. She imagined the response if she told the police that they should examine local Native legends and the vanishing of a prospector years earlier, or that she had felt that the hillside was watching her, or that Jack had not disappeared at all, he was still there, watching too, that he had only been looking after Robert.

All the searches came to nothing; no further traces of Jack were found. A casual question to one of the volunteers elicited the information that the phone in the cabin was working perfectly. Peggy herself did not go back; no one expected a sixty-three-year-old woman to participate in the search, and everyone told her they understood why she preferred to stay in a hotel in town. They did not understand, of course, not at all, but Peggy did not try to explain.

Paul came up as soon as he could. He, too, was very understanding, although he was surprised at his aunt's decision to put the property on the market immediately. She was welcome to stay with him and the family for as long as she needed to, that went without saying; but wasn't she being a bit hasty? Yes, it had been a terrible, tragic event, but perhaps she should wait a bit, hold off making a decision . . . she didn't want to do something she would regret. . . .

But Peggy was insistent. If Paul would go with her while she collected some clothing and personal items, she would be grateful; she would arrange with a moving company for everything else to be packed up and put into storage until she had found somewhere to live. She had clearly made up her mind, and although he did not agree with her, Paul did not argue the point any further.

They went up early in the morning, the first day after the search had been called off. Peggy worked quickly, packing up the things she wanted to take with her, while Paul cleared out the food from the fridge and cupboards. When everything had been loaded into his SUV he went round the cabin, making sure that everything was shut off and locked up, while Peggy waited outside.

Now, in the daylight, with the sun high overhead and birds wheeling against the blue of the sky, everything looked peaceful. A gentle wind ruffled the branches of the trees, and a piece of paper fluttered along—left by one of the searchers, no doubt. It blew across the grass, and landed in the middle of one of the pathways. Out of habit, she walked over to where it lay, picked it up, and put it in her pocket.

She looked up at the hills above her, then back at the cabin, realising that this was the same spot where she had seen—or thought she had seen—Jack on the afternoon he had disappeared. She shivered slightly, even though the day was hot, and started towards the SUV, anxious to be gone.

It was as she moved away that she saw it, a glint of something metallic at the edge of the path near her foot. She bent down and picked it up. A Swiss Army watch, silver, with a worn black leather band. Although she knew what she would find, she looked at the face. The hands showed ten past five.

When Paul came out and locked the front door, his aunt was already in the SUV. She did not look back as he drove away.

THE HIDING PLACE

ALLIE FOUND THE HIDING PLACE when she had almost given up looking. And it was so safe, so dark and quiet, that no one would ever find her, and she wondered why she had not thought of it before.

She needed somewhere to hide herself away; away from the Words and, even worse, the sullen Silences which hung over the bright little house with its three bedrooms and finished basement and neatly kept lawn. At least, it had been neatly kept once; now the grass overlapping the plastic edging, and the dandelions sprouting up like miniature islands in a sea of green, were another source of the Words and the Silences.

The yellow patches were filling in, which Allie thought was something her parents—especially her father—should be happy about. "Witch peas", her father had called them once, when Allie was only three and he had thought she was inside the house, and Allie, intrigued, had gone looking for the magic vegetables in the back yard. But she found no magic, only the bare yellow patches to which she had grown accustomed, and when she asked her father about the witch peas he gave a snort of disgust and said "Not witch peas, bitch pee, from that dog of your mother's." That had been the signal for her mother to leap to Sadie's defence: she was only a dog, it wasn't her fault, she didn't know any better. Her father had muttered something, and her mother had demanded, her voice growing shrill, that he repeat what he'd said, and he had replied "If I'd meant for you to hear it I would have said it louder", and then her mother had said "If you didn't want me to hear it then you shouldn't have said it in the first place, and anyway I heard what you said", and her father had said coldly "Then why did you ask me to repeat it?", and then they had sent Allie to her room, and the Words had started again, the Words that had been a constant backdrop, like a radio that no one ever turned off, for as long as Allie could remember. She wondered if there had ever been a time with just words. She would have to ask Maddie.

She was in her room now, lying on her bed and looking up at the stipples on the ceiling, seeing if she could find a new pattern in them; perhaps Sadie. She wished that Sadie was still alive; she might have helped, a little. She wanted to ask if they could get a new dog—maybe a puppy like Pamela's family had just got—but she had already asked that once, three months earlier, and her mother had rounded on her, furious, demanding to know how she could ask that so soon after Sadie . . . after Maddie . . . and then her mother's face had crumpled up like a tissue, and she had started to cry.

Allie wondered if her mother would cry like that over her.

There was nowhere in her room in which to hide; nowhere that she considered a good enough spot. There was no space under the bed, or beside the dresser, and her cupboard was full. Besides, it was too obvious a place, and too bright, crammed as it was with clothes and toys and games, and her own stuffies and the ones that Maddie, six years older, wasn't using anymore.

She had taken them from Maddie's room, one by one, after Maddie's accident, and no one had noticed. She had considered Maddie's room as a hiding place, but only briefly: she knew the trouble she would be in if she got caught. She had been found in there once before, by her mother, who had first become angry—"How *dare* you come in here!"—and had then started crying—"Your poor sister, she loves this room"—and Allie knew better than to be found there again. She did not want to contribute to the Words or the Silences any more than she already did.

The neighbourhood offered no help. The suburban rows of neatly laid out streets and carefully planned green spaces left nowhere to hide, could even have been built with this fact in mind. "We will have no secret places here," a stern and forbidding voice might have said, like the voice of the Wizard in *The Wizard of Oz* before Toto pulled back the curtain.

This made Allie think of Sadie again. She wondered if dogs went to heaven when they died, and if that was where Sadie was now. She wondered if Sadie was lonely, without her and Maddie.

Allie rolled over onto her tummy, still considering the problem of the hiding place. She could not ask her parents, or her teacher Ms. Cameron, who was always trying to be *understanding*—Allie hated that word—and who would not *understand* at all. Other children, she suspected, would be no help. They would keep their own hiding places as secret from her as they would from everyone else, even if they deigned to speak with her, which they did less and less these days.

That left Maddie. She never really had a chance to talk to Maddie, even if Maddie had been able to talk to her, which she hadn't, not since The Accident, and anyway she was never alone with Maddie anymore. Allie wondered if Maddie had had her own hiding place when she was Allie's age, and if so where it was. She had never shared it, even though they had once shared everything. They even seemed to know each other's thoughts; Allie would sometimes be thinking something and Maddie would come out and say it and they would both laugh while their parents looked on, bemused. There had also been secret, silent games, the silence so different from the one which enveloped the house and seemed to weigh everything down, like the accumulated dust of hundreds of thousands of dead Words.

The shared thoughts and secret games had stopped now, since The Accident. Allie had thought that, since their thoughts and games needed no words, they might have continued; but Maddie lay on her unnaturally neat hospital bed, silent in all ways, despite Allie's efforts to draw her out on the occasions—strained and formal, broken by her mother's crying and her father's anger—when she was able to visit. Maybe if her parents hadn't been there Maddie would have been more forthcoming.

Still, perhaps one day soon Maddie would be able to provide an answer, somehow. She looked at the clock on her dresser, considered the time, then rolled off the bed and went downstairs, where the Silence was thickest, where she knew her parents would be.

Her father was standing on one side of the kitchen counter, her mother facing him from across the room, the car keys on the work surface between them. The air was full of Words unsaid but perfectly understood, a well-rehearsed conversation that both knew by heart. Allie looked at the keys, then from one parent to the other.

"Can I come with you today?"

"No." The word came without hesitation from her father, while her mother said automatically "What's wrong with that sentence?"

"Can I *please* come with you today?"

"No!" Her father looked angry and, Allie thought, a little embarrassed, while her mother's eyes gleamed with—anger? pleasure? some unholy mixture of both? No matter. With all the cunning of a six-year-old who immediately senses weakness, Allie turned to her mother. "Please, Mom, can I come with you today? I promise I'll be good, and I won't touch anything, and I'll be very quiet."

Her father started to say something, but her mother overrode him. "Why not?" She smiled then, but her teeth remained hidden behind her tight lips, and the smile did not reach her eyes. "We can all do something together; be a proper little family."

"But Caitlin is coming over to . . . "

"I'll call and tell her we don't need a babysitter today." The smile that wasn't a smile flashed again. "And it will save us a little money. As you're always telling me, every penny counts now."

Her mother drove, as she always did these days, ever since The Accident, making a point of checking all the mirrors and over both shoulders before backing up or changing lanes, while her father fidgeted in the passenger seat and stared out the window. Allie didn't like this car as much as their old one, but she had learned not to say that more than the once. At one point her father said "You can go a bit faster, you know," and her mother replied carefully "I'm the one driving, thank you. And we don't want any *more* accidents, do we?" and her father subsided into silence.

ᛒᚩ   ᚲᛉ

When they got home her mother said she was too tired to cook supper. There was some leftover lasagna in the fridge and they could have that; she was going to bed.

Allie escaped as soon after the meal as she could, eager to pore over the day's events. There had been a moment in the hospital when she had been left alone with Maddie—her parents had gone outside to speak with a doctor—and while her sister had still not been able to talk, she had managed to give Allie the answer she was looking for. And it had been so very simple; the answer had been lying there in front of her all along.

She bathed herself after supper, tiptoed into her parents' room and kissed her mother, then said goodnight to her father in the living-room. He had a glass of something beside him which he tried to hide when she came in; but when he saw it was Allie he placed the tumbler back on the table beside his chair. She leaned in for a hug and he held her to him for a moment, in a big bear hug, the type of hug he hadn't seemed to be able to give for some time. His breath smelled the way it used to, too. It had stopped smelling that way for a time; Allie suspected that her mother would have more Words if she knew it smelled like that again. Or perhaps she knew, and that was what caused the Silences.

"I'm sorry, honey," her father whispered. When Allie drew her head back she saw that he was crying. "I'm so sorry for everything. Do you understand that?"

"Yes." She looked at him for a moment. "Will it get better?"

"I hope so."

"But do you think it will?"

"I don't know, Allie. I just don't know."

ᛒᚩ   ᚲᛉ

Allie lay in her bed, staring at the ceiling. The stipples were obscured by darkness now; she couldn't make out any patterns.

She thought about the hiding place. She didn't know when would be the best time to test it out. Now that she had found it, she was reluctant to take advantage of it. It could be dangerous, and there was no one she could ask. Maybe she should wait until the next time she could see Maddie again, see if her sister could tell her a little more.

Voices from downstairs. Her mother had obviously woken up and was in the living-room with her father. She could hear their voices through the heating ducts; only isolated Words, but none that she had not heard many times before over the last four months, and she could reconstruct the conversation easily enough. "Drinking again", "accident", "sorry", and "you'll never change" figured largely, punctuated by tears, shrill cries, and the sound of something breaking. The slam of the front door made the house shake.

Allie took a deep breath. She would not wait until she could see Maddie again. She would go now.

⁊ ʘ

The doctors at the hospital were full of reassuring words, but underneath there was a sense that something had happened for which they did not have a name. Allie was not responding—yet—but they were sure it was only a mater of time. A specialist was on the way, and a child psychologist. Until they arrived there was nothing more that could be done. At least she did not seem to be in any pain.

⁊ ʘ

A nurse with a kind face and tired brown eyes stepped out of a hospital room and closed the door softly behind her. She glanced down the hallway to where the parents were standing, and smoothed a strand of hair behind her right ear. She considered having a word with them, but decided against it. They were obviously distraught enough, and it was not as if she had anything positive to report about Maddie. There had been a moment, earlier in the evening, when the machines keeping her alive had alerted the nurse to a possible change, but by the time she had arrived in the room everything was the same as it had been for the past four months. She had written it up, and would talk to them later, when they were less upset.

Such a terrible shame, she thought. *Both daughters in here now.*

℞ ℟

Allie had found the perfect hiding place. And it was so safe, so dark and quiet, that no one would ever find her.

She wondered why she had not thought of it before.

She was glad she could talk to Maddie again. They had so much to catch up on, so many lovely secrets to share.

AFTER

" 'ONCE UPON A TIME there lived a gentleman who, having lost his first wife, of whom he had been exceedingly fond, married again, thinking that by this means he should be as happy as before.' Do sit still and stop fussing, Saville. See? You have quite disarranged my dress."

"Do all fairy tales begin 'Once upon a time'?"

"Yes, they mostly do. 'He had, by his first wife, a daughter of unparalleled goodness and sweetness, whom the second wife promised to love as her own. However, no sooner were the wedding ceremonies over than the stepmother began to show herself in her true colours. She could not bear the good qualities of her husband's daughter, the less because . . . ' "

"Mama is not your mama, is she? She is your stepmama, like the fairy tale."

"Yes. ' . . . because she made her own daughters appear the more odious. She employed her in the meanest work of the establishment, and caused her to sleep in a sorry garret at the top of the house, on a poor straw mattress which . . . ' "

"Do all fairy tales end with 'happily ever after'?"

"If you do not stop interrupting me, we shall never finish the story."

"But do they?"

"Yes, they do."

This is not a fairy tale.

ᛞ ᛉ

"Once upon a time" is, for the girl, past midnight; the clocks, out of unison, have told her so, and the last chimes have been absorbed into the fabric of the house and the silence of the cold, wet night. She turns slightly in the narrow bed in her room on the top floor of the house, her rough white nightdress chafing slightly against her skin, and imagines that she can feel, through mattress and bedclothes and gown, the razor which she placed there several days earlier. She wonders for how many more nights it will remain there. It has not thus far been missed, but it will be.

She reaches down to rub her right leg, still sore after she stumbled on the walk to Beckington made earlier in the day at her stepmother's behest, to pay a bill which was due. Glad of the excuse to leave the house, she had nonetheless asked why one of the servants could not go to pay it, to which her stepmother had replied that the servants were all busy. "Now that you are home from school, you must not expect to be waited on hand and foot, a great healthy girl like you." She had placed her hands on her rounded belly, full and ripe, and the girl had looked away. "I would go, but the doctor has ordered me to rest, with my confinement so close upon me. In another month's time there will be much more to be done about the house, and I shall need all your assistance. The devil makes work for idle hands, and you must see to it that you occupy both your mind and body, lest you suffer the same fate as your mother. The taint of madness was in her, and you must ensure that it finds no foothold in you."

The girl's hands clench, and for a moment a touch of colour burns in her pale face. It is another to add to the collection of remarks—cold, cutting, dismissive—which she has been storing up for months, years beyond counting, for at sixteen her life seems to be a place where months and years have no meaning. Instead it is divided into two parts: Before and After. In Before there were her mother and father, two sisters and two brothers and herself, all sleeping on the same floor, the servants above and below. In After there are three sisters still, but only one brother; the other, having turned his back on the family upon learning of his father's remarriage, had died alone in a foreign land. The four remaining siblings, clinging together like survivors of shipwreck, now sleep on the second floor, with the servants; the middle floor, with its thicker carpets, richer furnishings, larger rooms, is reserved for her father and stepmother and the children of their union, two nondescript girls and Saville, almost four and looking like a cherub, with his bright round face and yellow curls, the pet of the household. Her father is proud of his golden son, and looks at the remaining son of his first marriage with disapproval, heaping words of opprobrium on his head, forcing the boy to wheel Saville about in a pram like a nursemaid or a prating girl.

The spark of anger flares up in her again, brighter this time, and a red glow burns before her eyes, so bright that she feels it must illuminate the dark room. She closes her eyes against it and forces her hands to unclench, her breathing to slow, the red glow to fade to a dim spark. She has had ample practice in such matters. When she opens her eyes once more, she notes without surprise that the gentleman is standing inside the plain wooden door of her room, regarding her. She raises herself on one elbow.

"You have come, then," she says in a low voice. "I thought you had forgotten."

"I could not forget you, Constance Kent," he replies, his own voice friendly, almost laughing, as if it is not past midnight, and they are not alone in her room, the house sleeping around them. "You are an extraordinary girl."

ဆ   ၓ

Constance had met him a fortnight earlier, on the road to Beckington. Only one day home from school, and already she was seeking reasons to escape from the house, from the watchful eye of her stepmother, the prattling talk and silly games of her younger half-brother and -sisters. The road had been reduced to a muddy morass by the rain which looked set to continue all summer, and the hem of her dress had been caked with dirt, but she did not care. At least the weather had discouraged other travellers, and she was spared having to make conversation with any wayfarers. She thought longingly for a moment of the school in Beckington at which she had boarded for the last six months, so close to her home and family and yet as distant from that life as Sleeping Beauty in her briar-choked palace. Some of the other girls, she knew, thought it odd that she boarded when she lived so close, but her manner forbade enquiry, and she did not vouchsafe any information.

She rounded a bend, and was surprised and not a little displeased to see the figure of a man standing near a gate set into the hedge which bordered the road. He was not, as strangers often were, admiring the countryside around, lush and green, but was gazing in her direction as if in expectation of her arrival. Indeed, upon seeing her he called out "Miss Kent! The very girl I was hoping to see."

Constance halted, conscious of the mud and damp of her skirts, the dishevelment of her dress. She felt momentarily discomfited, unnerved; an unusual feeling for her, and it lent her voice an even more challenging tone than usual when she replied, "And how, might I ask, do you know my name?"

"Ah, I know many of the folk hereabouts, and very well, too."

"Have we met, sir? I do not call your face or name to mind."

"No, we have not met, Miss Kent; but I certainly know of you. Your father and mother, too. A very fine couple, well suited to each other, if I may say so."

Constance eyed him, her gaze direct. "My mother, sir, is dead. The—lady—to whom you refer is my stepmother."

The man made a slight bow. "My apologies, Miss Kent. I was not as precise in my language as I should have been. Your stepmother, to be sure. Formerly your governess, was she not? A very enterprising young woman."

"You seem to know a good deal about my family, sir. And you have the advantage of me: you know my name, but I do not know yours."

Again the slight bow. Was it her imagination, or was there an air of faint mockery behind it? "My apologies again, Miss Kent. Your sudden appearance has made me entirely forget any good manners which I possess. You may call me Mr. Hobbes."

Constance inclined her head slightly. "Mr. Hobbes. And now, if you will excuse me, I have business in the village."

"An errand, Miss Kent? Surely, on a day such as this, these

things might be better left to a servant. And so soon after the start of your holiday, an event which I am sure you were anticipating with great excitement. Indeed, I happened to overhear one of your school friends discussing the matter with you only last week, saying how pleasant it would be to go home for the holidays."

"That was a private conversation, sir. How did you happen to overhear it? I do not recall seeing you."

Mr. Hobbes smiled. "As I said, I know a great many people. I overhear a good deal."

"Then you cannot have failed to overhear my reply to Emma, which was that it might be pleasant at her home, but that mine was different."

"Ah yes. I had forgotten that." Mr. Hobbes indicated the gate. "May I suggest this way instead? A shortcut, if you will. I, too, have business in that direction, and will accompany you, if you do not object. The countryside, for all its pleasant face, may harbour treachery and danger, and I would not care to see anything untoward happen to you."

Constance hesitated for a moment. She did not know him, but he appeared to know her and her family, and seemed to be a gentleman: his dress and manners and mode of speech indicated as much. She glanced down the muddy ribbon of road, and then at the path, glinting green and wet on the other side of the gate. Her stepmother had told her to stay to the road and avoid getting her dress too dirty. Constance turned her level gaze back to Mr. Hobbes.

"Thank you," she said. "I will take the path, if you will be so kind as to open the gate for me."

They walked in silence for a time, Mr. Hobbes in front where the path was narrow, alerting her to pitfalls in her way. When the path widened enough to allow them to walk abreast, he slowed his pace until she drew level.

"Yes, I have known of your family for some time," he said easily, returning to his earlier comments. "Quite a remarkable one, if I may say so. There are surely many households where the governess aspires to the position of mistress of the house, but few where she is able to achieve that station. Your father was fortunate indeed to find such an able and willing helpmeet within the bosom of his own family, as it were. Yet it must have been difficult for you, to see your governess replace your own mother, and become a parent to you. A transition smoothed, no doubt, by the fond feelings between you. Surely you recall those days when your mother was still alive, and yet you would sit for hours on end with your governess, listening as she described your mother as a 'Certain Person' or 'That Woman'; those occasions when you were rude to your mother's face and then repeated the words to your approving governess. What a pretty pair you must have made!"

Constance, after a first flush of anger, grew pale. She stopped on the pathway, and Mr. Hobbes turned to face her.

"It is true that at one time I took against my poor mother; behaviour for which I am now truly sorry. And as for *her*"—Constance fairly spat the word—"any fond feelings which I might once have felt for her have long since evaporated. She showed herself to be a false friend, winning my father with a smiling face and soothing words, while behind his back she sought out every opportunity to treat my sisters and brothers and me with cruelty and meanness."

"Strong words, Miss Kent! I am certain that she had only your best interests at heart."

"Our best interests? Insisting, when our brother Edward sent us two tropical birds, that they be kept away from us in a cold back room, where they died? Locking me in the attic, or in the beer cellar, because I could not master the printing of the letter H? Banishing me to my room for two days, with only dry bread and milk and water to eat and drink, because I failed to spell a word correctly? Indeed, she kept all of us like prisoners. William and I were forbidden from playing with the neighbouring children, even though we begged to be allowed to do so."

"I am sure that she did not want you corrupted by outside influences."

"These were children of our own class, not urchins from the slums of London, or common labourers' children! What harm could have come from associating with them?"

Mr. Hobbes shrugged, and brushed a blade of grass from the cuff of his trousers. "I am sure that she had good reasons. You did defy her once, though, did you not?"

"Yes, William and I crept through the hedge when we heard the children playing one day. And do you know what she did when she found out? She tore up the little gardens that we had planted and cultivated ourselves! Was that not a harsh punishment for what was surely a minor transgression?"

"Perhaps. I have never been a parent myself, so cannot say what is and is not a fitting penalty. However, you certainly had any number of siblings to play with; could you not have been content within your family circle?"

Constance shook her head. "She was always trying to create discord between us," she said, bitterness making her voice rough. "She drove my brother Edward away, and tried to cause me to turn against my older sisters. She told me once, when I came home from school for the summer, that it was only through her agency that I had not been forced to stay there, because my older sisters did not want me at home: she said that they had called me a tiresome girl. When I taxed Elizabeth and Mary Ann with this they both denied making any such comment. And she is always praising her own children, and setting them above us. She and father make such a pet and a fuss over Saville, and William gets scarcely a word or glance. Often, at night, we visit each other's rooms, and he tells me how upset he is at the treatment he receives."

"Yes, you are both fortunate that you have rooms of your own, and do not need to share. On the top floor, so far removed from the business of the house. It must be very quiet."

"And that is another thing!" cried Constance, the dull red flush back in her face. "We—the children of father's first marriage—must sleep with the servants, while father and my stepmother and their children sleep on the first floor. Indeed, I believe my stepmother thinks me a servant. It is always 'Constance, fetch this' or 'Constance, do that'; and if anything in the household goes wrong I am immediately blamed."

"But my dear Miss Kent, you must admit that you can be somewhat provoking."

"If I act in a provoking manner, sir, it is because I have been sorely provoked."

"Is that why you and William ran away to Bath three years ago? That took considerable courage: you, a girl of thirteen, and your brother, a mere lad of eleven!"

Constance tossed her head back and looked straight at Mr. Hobbes. "I have never lacked resolve, sir."

"That is quite obvious. There are not many thirteen-year-old girls who would disguise themselves as a boy—even going so far as to cut off their hair—in order to make the endeavour more likely to succeed. You hid the clothing, and disposed of your hair, in the disused closet in the shrubbery, did you not? A useful place for secreting something."

The girl eyed him with some suspicion. Until this moment she had been carried away by the passion of her feelings, the sense of injustice, but only now did it occur to her to wonder precisely how Mr. Hobbes knew so much about her and her family. As if in answer to her unspoken question, her companion said in a cheerful tone, "I have had my eye on you for some time, Miss Kent; ever since the Bath incident, as a matter of fact. It brought you to my notice, and since then I have taken an interest in your affairs; from a distance, you might say. It seemed to me, however, that the time was ripe for me to make your acquaintance personally." Mr. Hobbes glanced up at the sky. "Dear me, Miss Kent, it looks as if the rain will recommence at any moment. What a dreary Spring it has been, to be sure. Summer, however, looks a good deal more promising. I would suggest that you hurry along to the village, before you are soaked through."

"Are you not continuing on to Beckington?" asked Constance, somewhat confused. "I had thought you had business there."

"No, not in Beckington itself. My work takes me to many places. But I would like to speak with you again, if I may. I have enjoyed our conversation. It has been most illuminating."

Constance gazed at the stranger. She could not imagine that her father or stepmother would approve of her meeting with a strange man, alone in the countryside; but she did not like to suggest that he come to their house. The thought of the questions she would be asked, the disapproving words and looks, the punishment which was sure to result, made her shake her head. Again, Mr. Hobbes seemed to read her thoughts, for he said in a light voice, "I do not propose that I pay a social call, Miss Kent. I would much prefer to speak with you *tête à tête*, as the French would say, without the formality of tea and cakes, or the interruptions of family and servants. I suggest that when you have occasion to walk to Beckington, you take this path instead of the road, and I am sure our ways will cross again. Good day to you." And with a polite tip of his hat he turned and walked back the way they had come, leaving Constance on the wet and muddy path, her face a white mask of confusion and apprehension oddly mixed with pleasure.

She said nothing at home of her encounter with Mr. Hobbes, even to William, her one confidant in the family. She was scolded for the state into which she had got her dress, after which her stepmother sighed and added, "But I have come to expect this from you, Constance. If I ask you particularly not to do a thing, you deliberately go out of your way to do it. Perhaps, in future, I should ask you to take care to get your clothes as dirty as possible, and you will return with your dress spotless, to spite me."

"What does it matter to you?" asked the girl, with a toss of her head. "It is Mrs. Holley who does the laundry, not you."

"Impertinent girl! I should think I do not do laundry. The mistress of the house does not look after such matters like a common washerwoman. And in my condition"—again her hand went to her belly, in the gesture which Constance found so intimate, so repugnant—"it is not advisable that I do anything of a strenuous nature. You should have more respect for my state."

"Yes, I should," replied Constance, and her stepmother looked at her in some surprise. "After all," the girl continued, "you have spent the better part of your marriage to my father in this *state*, as you call it, so we should all of us be used to it, at the very least." And she turned and left the room before her indignant stepmother could formulate a reply.

Constance recounted this incident to Mr. Hobbes four days later, when she once again made the walk to Beckington. Mindful of his words, she had taken the path rather than the road, and had been surprised, but secretly pleased, to see him ahead of her. She hurried to catch him up, and as they walked she told him of what her stepmother had said. Mr. Hobbes shook his head as if in sympathy with her.

"Your stepmother does indeed seem abundantly blessed in this regard, Miss Kent. And your father, too: such a passion for life, one might say. Four children survived from the first marriage, and soon to be four from the second. Something of which a man might well be proud. As I said upon our first meeting, it was fortuitous indeed that he found such an admirable partner, and under his own roof, too." Constance said nothing, and Mr. Hobbes glanced sideways at her. "Yet not, perhaps, so very fortuitous," he added in his light, pleasant voice, for all the world as if he were discussing the weather, or the crops. "For, of course, your father had ample time and opportunity to assess your stepmother's suitability for the role of the second Mrs. Kent, long before she was called on to assume it."

Constance stopped. She had previously been looking at the ground beneath her feet, but now her gaze was fixed on her companion, her dark, deep-set eyes standing out even more than was normal in a face grown more pale than usual. Mr. Hobbes stopped too, and turned to face her.

"Of course, I am not telling you anything which you did not already know, or at least guess, an intelligent, observant girl like yourself."

"Yes." The word was spoken in such a low voice that it was almost inaudible. "Yes, you are correct. I knew . . . "

"Certainly you knew, Miss Kent. How could you not? The evidence was there before your eyes."

She swayed for a moment, but Mr. Hobbes was confident that she would not faint. He knew her far too well to suppose her capable of such behaviour, and had a good idea of what she was thinking. She would be going back, in her mind, over the events of the past; events which she had seen but the full import of which had not made themselves felt until this moment. She recalled her then governess taking fright during a thunderstorm and rushing to her father, who pulled her down onto his lap and made to kiss her before the governess half-whispered "Not in front of the child." She thought of her bedroom in their last house, whose only entrance lay through the governess's room, and of the door between the two chambers which was kept locked at night. She remembered her father being away from the house for several nights, and the governess begging Constance to share her bed, "Because I am lonely." At the thought of whose place she had taken, while her mother lay a few feet away, she cried aloud, a strangled sound of disgust mingled with anguish.

Through all this Mr. Hobbes stood quietly, a slight smile on his lips, his burning dark eyes the only outward sign of his own thoughts. When she cried out he nodded his head once, as if in acknowledgement of something completed.

"You see, Miss Kent? You knew the truth all along; you simply did not realise its full import until now. I must make allowance for the fact that you are still a child in many ways."

"I am not a child, I am not!" she cried out, hands clenched in anger, eyes blazing, her face suffused with a dull, ugly red. "Do not call me that!"

"You sound like a child when you speak thus," Mr. Hobbes said, his voice sharp. "If you wish to be thought of as an adult, you must speak and act as one."

"I want to be an adult," she said in a low voice. "I have wanted it since I can remember."

"And why is that?"

"Because I used to pray to be good, and could not be, and decided that I would be good when I was a grown-up, because grown-ups never do bad things."

"Ah, but they do, Miss Kent. Grown-ups do bad things as a matter of course, because they can. Who is there to send a grown-up to her room when she is bad, or deprive her of food, or tear up her garden? Grown-ups do bad things because they have little fear, if they are at all clever, of being punished for them."

"Like father and my stepmother?" She continued without stopping, the words tumbling over themselves. "They were bad, weren't they, when my poor mother was alive, convincing those around us that she was a madwoman, slighting her, laughing at her, and all the time they were . . . they were"—she hardly knew how to phrase it—"acting the part of husband and wife, and then as soon as my mother was dead they married, and they have not been punished at all; at all! Instead we are being punished, William and Mary Ann and Elizabeth and I, treated as little better than servants, kept like prisoners in the house—Mary Ann and Elizabeth are not even allowed suitors!—while she goes on having children who take our places, who are loved as we are not, set above us, his first family. Saville is not yet four, but father tells William that this toddling child will be a better man than he ever will, and makes William push him in his pram, while I am expected to read him stories and dandle him on my knee and coo and fuss over him, until I want to . . . "

"Yes, Miss Kent? And what is it that you want to do?"

"I want to hurt them. I want to kill her. I have thought of it; thought of putting poison in her tea."

She was staring straight at her companion, awaiting his reaction to her words; but if she expected shock, disapproval, censure she did not see it. His look was thoughtful, if anything, and he tilted his head to one side, as if to observe her better.

"I see. Certainly a very forthright declaration, but no less than I would have expected from you. Still, I confess myself surprised at your words."

Constance closed her eyes for a moment and shook her head, as if to clear it. A strange desire to laugh aloud came over her, but she fought it down, realising in some dim fashion that madness lay that way. Instead she said—and she was startled by how calm, how ordinary her voice sounded—"Only surprised, Mr. Hobbes? You are a very strange man indeed."

"Oh no, Miss Kent, not strange; simply one who has a great deal of experience in the ways of the world and its inhabitants.

When I say that I am surprised at your words, I mean that I am surprised because they indicate that you do not appear fully to have thought the matter through in logical fashion."

"In what way?" When he did not answer, she stamped her foot. "In what way have I not fully thought this matter through? For the past three days I have thought of little else."

"Then your thinking has not taken you far enough, Miss Kent. Do not consider your words, so much as the idea of which they are but an expression."

"I said that I want to hurt them; that I want to kill her, poison her. That will hurt them, surely?"

"Oh yes, it will; but your thinking seems to stop at the deed itself. Let your mind take you beyond that event."

Constance furrowed her brow, trying to think, consider. She could see herself placing the poison in her stepmother's teacup, but what poison to use, and how she would get it, were matters she had not reckoned with. Still, that was not what Mr. Hobbes meant. He had told her to look beyond the actual deed, into the hours and days and weeks to come, and for several moments she tried to think of what he could mean. She saw the doctor being summoned, her father bewildered, shocked; she saw her older sisters and William trying to display the requisite grief; she saw the younger children, confused and frightened—no, there was nothing there. She went further forward and saw the family, dressed in black, filing into the church, her father bowed and old, her sisters quiet and still, William wide-eyed, the young ones squirming in the arms of servants. Still nothing.

And then, like the swirling shapes in a kaleidoscope suddenly resolving themselves into a pattern, she saw what she did *not* see: her stepmother. She was gone, dead and gone, past caring, past hurt, past everything. The one person in the world she most wanted to hurt would be beyond her reach forever.

She drew in a deep breath and looked steadily at Mr. Hobbes. "She will not be there." Her words were flat, like those of a schoolchild reciting a lesson learned by rote. "My stepmother. I will hurt her the once, and then no more. It will be too short a pang."

Mr. Hobbes clasped his hands together; for a moment she thought he was going to applaud. "Miss Kent, Miss Kent, I see I was not mistaken in you. You have, in those few words, penetrated to the very heart of the matter."

"Have I?"

"Indeed you have. And here I must mention an entirely different matter. I think it possible that you have had some difficulty, recently, in saying your prayers. Am I correct?"

Constance appeared confused more by the sudden change in topic than Mr. Hobbes's knowledge of this fact. "Yes, sir. It has been more than a year since I have said my prayers. The words— I found they did not come readily, and when they did they were empty words, so I ceased."

"I see. And is it for this reason that you are considering making an excuse so that you do not have to attend church service the day after tomorrow?"

"Yes. I find it difficult to play the hypocrite, merely for the sake of appearance."

"You are to be applauded for your resolution, Miss Kent. Would that more people were like you! The result, I suspect, would be empty churches, and not a few empty pulpits, if truth were known. However, I urge you to reconsider, and at least attend Matins this Sunday."

"Why? Shall you be there?"

Mr. Hobbes laughed, as at some rich private joke. "No, Miss Kent, I shall not be in attendance. It is some time since I took an interest in such things, but I believe that 24 June is the Holy Day of St. John the Baptist, and that you will find some edification during the service. But I am afraid that I must now leave you once more. When I am with you I quite forget the many other matters which require my attention! We shall meet again soon, however. That I promise. In the meantime you will, I think, have much on which to ponder." Another tip of the hat, and Mr. Hobbes had turned on his heel and left her.

She was barely able, later, to recall any details of what she said or did in Beckington. The village and its inhabitants seemed as unsubstantial as ghosts; or perhaps she herself was the ghost, drifting amongst the living. Their mundane talk of the poor weather and the lateness of the harvest set her teeth on edge, and polite enquiries as to her stepmother's health made her want to scream and lash out at the speaker. She completed her business as quickly as possible, glad to escape, to be alone with the thoughts which chased themselves round and round her head, clamouring for attention, thoughts which had been given form and shape by Mr. Hobbes's honeypoison words.

She entered the grounds of the house through the side gate, hoping to escape the notice of her family. The good-natured Newfoundland dog which her father kept as a guard raised its head to look at her, but seeing who it was put its head back down on its paws without making a noise, and went back to dozing. She could hear subdued sounds from the knife-house to her left, and the voice of Holcombe the gardener, his words inaudible, but there was no one in sight.

She paused and looked to her left, where a cluster of bushes hid the disused servants' privy in which she had hidden the clothing she wore when she and William ran away three years earlier. She closed her eyes and thought of that night: she and William creeping through the silent house, alert to every possibility of detection; her fear that her younger brother's clothing would not fit, and bring a premature end to their plan; William's faltering attempts to cut her hair, his sudden burst of tears at his inability to complete the task, her own hand snatching the scissors from his and cutting feverishly at her long hair, sending the tresses down the privy after her dress and underclothes; their flight through the dark night; their unmasking at Bath, and the ignominious return to the house; her stepmother's face as, cradling the infant Saville to her breast as if to keep the child from being tainted by contact with his half-siblings, she had watched from the hallway, stern and silent, disgust and anger written on her face.

Constance opened her eyes once more. All was still and silent; she was unobserved. What had Mr. Hobbes said of the privy? "A useful place for secreting something." She stepped through the yard towards it, the grass wet under her feet, the bushes crowding round it heavy with rain. It was seldom used, even by the outdoor servants; it could once more serve as a place of concealment.

Deep in thought, Constance walked through the yard and entered the house by the kitchen. She hoped to slip to her room unnoticed, but as she started up the main stairs the door of the drawing-room burst open, and Saville emerged at a run.

"Constance, Constance, mama says you are to play with me now you are home. Oh"—the boy had made to hug her, but drew back when he felt the dampness of her skirts—"you are all wet! And dirty!"

"I hope you have not soaked your dress through again, Constance," called her stepmother from the drawing-room, her voice angry. "You make more work than the younger children put together. Really, at your age you should know better. But I am not surprised."

Constance drew in a sharp breath, almost a hiss, and glared at Saville. "Sneak," she whispered through clenched teeth. "Horrid little monster."

The boy's face crumpled. "Am not!" he cried. "I am not a monster! Mama, mama, Constance says I am a horrid monster, and I am not!" He burst into tears and ran to the door of the drawing-room, where his mother had appeared, looking pale and tired. He hugged himself to her dress, and his muffled sobs filled the hall as she stroked his head with one hand, the other pressed to the small of her back.

"Constance, I am ashamed of you; but that is hardly new. Your every action seems intent on bringing shame upon yourself, if not this entire household. You are indeed your mother's daughter; she was entirely the same. And now to say such things about Saville, who is a mere child!" At the sound of his name the child, whose sobs had been diminishing, redoubled his crying. His mother placed an arm protectively around him. "He is not a monster at all; he is mother's darling angel, are you not, Saville? He brings your father and me far more happiness than you ever shall, Miss Constance; and yet you call him a monster! If you wish to see a monster, then I suggest you look in the glass, where you shall see a monster of spite and selfishness. Come, Saville, come and sit with Mama; we shall leave Miss Constance to her sulks." And with Saville still clinging to her skirt, her stepmother turned and entered the drawing-room, shutting the door firmly behind her.

Constance stood stock-still in the hallway, her breath coming in hard little gasps, two spots of colour high on her otherwise pale cheeks. Then, with the suddenness of a curtain coming down on a stage, she took a deep breath and her features relaxed into something which hinted at a smile.

"Thank you," she whispered to the closed door. "Thank you, dear *mother*, for your kind words. They were helpful indeed." And she turned and walked slowly up the two flights of stairs to her narrow room on the second floor, where she lay on the bed and closed her eyes. She did not, however, sleep.

On Sunday the family went to church; her father, stepmother, and Miss Gough the nursemaid, with little Eveline, in the phaeton, the rest of the family and the servants on foot. Mindful of Mr. Hobbes's words, Constance went with the others, only her dragging feet betraying her reluctance. The opening responses were as sawdust in her mouth, the Venite a cacophony of meaningless words, and it was all she could do to keep herself still as the first lesson, from Judges 13, was read out. It was not long, however, before her restlessness was entirely stilled, and she sat as a statue, her face a pale mask, the words she had just heard echoing in her ears like a peal of thunder:

For, lo, thou shalt conceive, and bear a son; and no razor shall come on his head.

She was surprised that she did not cry out. As it was, she expected all eyes to turn on her, accusatory fingers pointing her out, marking her, driving her from the church. But no one took any heed of her, and throughout the remainder of the service she moved and spoke by rote only, those few words continuously running through her mind to the exclusion of all else. During the walk home she tried to separate herself from the rest of the family, lagging behind the others, but to her disgust Saville came running back to her, and it was all she could to not slap away the small, soft white hand which groped for hers. Instead she gritted her teeth and steeled herself against his chatter, glad when they arrived home and she could disengage herself from him and hurry to the privacy of her room, where she could be alone, but not lonely. No; she had too many thoughts in her head, too much to plan, to be lonely.

She saw Mr. Hobbes once more, the following day. In the space of a week he had assumed the position of confidant once held by William, and she poured out to her companion the thoughts and plans which she could not divulge to her brother. Mr. Hobbes listened in silence, his mouth set in the easy smile which she had come to know so well, for all the world as if she were talking of a village social event, contributing a well chosen word here and there but otherwise letting the girl talk on uninterrupted. In truth, there was little he felt he could say, other than to guide her gently, on one or two occasions where she faltered, in the correct direction.

When they parted he said in his pleasant voice, "I must say how very gratified I am to have made your acquaintance, Miss Kent. I have quite enjoyed these past days. In some ways it is a shame that my time here is nearly at an end."

"You are not going?" asked Constance in some dismay. "So soon!"

"I am afraid so, Miss Kent. My work here is almost complete, and as I have intimated upon other occasions, I have many matters which require my attention. But do not fear; you shall see me again. I will come to you when it is time, of that you may rest assured. Indeed, I would not be absent at such a moment for all the world."

ಐ ಚ

She knows now that it is time. Mr. Hobbes does not need to tell her. Indeed, he says nothing as she rises from her bed, her nightdress of pure white clinging to her, and reaches under the mattress for the razor. She holds it for a moment in hands which do not tremble, noting how small it is. No matter; its destination is small enough. It will do.

She slips from her room, Mr. Hobbes behind her, and she does not need to look at him to know that he is smiling, always smiling. The rich, thick carpets on the first floor absorb her footsteps, and she moves silent as a cat, but she has confidence that she will not be discovered or betrayed. She continues to the ground floor and enters the drawing-room, where she opens the shutters covering the centre window. Only then does she return to the first floor, where she softly opens the door of the nursery, being careful to do it just so in order that it will not creak. For all her silence, though, Miss Gough must sense something. Perhaps the nursemaid realises dimly, in some region of her dream-haunted sleep, that a course is being set in motion which will change forever the lives of many people. If she does sense this, however, it is not strong enough a feeling to wake her. She merely stirs restlessly in her painted French bed—nicer, larger than Constance's, for all that Miss Gough is a servant—in the corner of their nursery, while in their cane cots, little Eveline and Saville sleep peacefully.

Constance passes by Eveline and gazes down at Saville's sleeping form for a moment, the razor a weight in the pocket of her nightgown. Her breathing is steady, her pale face set, as she watches him. It is not too late, she knows; she can still turn back, return to her room, replace the razor in her father's cupboard, blame the open shutters on the carelessness of a servant. If she leaves the room now, no one will ever know.

She hears a hiss of indrawn breath behind her; Mr. Hobbes. She has almost forgotten his presence. He leans forward, his face almost in hers, and she smells for a moment something foul, rotten as he whispers "You must do it now, Miss Kent. You wish to hurt them—to hurt *her*—and this is the only way adequately to punish them, for what they did to your mother, what they will continue to do to you. Or are you going to prove yourself, at the last, to be a mere weak girl, content to let them triumph?"

She draws herself upright as if stung. Her hand reaches out, as if to touch the boy's golden curls; then she reaches down the bed and moves the sleeping child, oh so gently, removing the blanket from beneath him. She wraps the blanket round him and raises him from the cot, and even though he is a heavy lad she manages it easily. She has brought a thick pad of cloth with her, thinking to use it to muffle the child's noise should he cry out, and now she places this over his mouth, holding it firmly in place. She does not recall smoothing down the sheet and counterpane after—although later she knows she must have done—and moves to the door, closing it silently behind her.

She is at the drawing-room once more, moving assuredly through the dimness towards the open shutters. At some point she puts on the galoshes which she has left tucked inside the door, but she does not remember this later, either. Perhaps Mr. Hobbes helped her; she does not know. He is still there, in the dark with her, as she raises the centre window and climbs out, the sleeping child seeming no weight at all. She rounds the house, feeling the wetness of the grass dragging against her thin nightgown, but it does not stop her nor even slow her down as she approaches the stable yard from the back and passes through it like a ghost.

The Newfoundland dog raises its head but, recognising her, does not bark. She pushes her way into the patch of yard where the closet nestles amidst rank grass and bushes, and enters it. There is that smell once more, as in the nursery, of something foul, but she pays it no heed as she fumbles for the candle and matches which she has previously hidden. There is a brief burst of light, harsh on her eyes after the darkness, and she blinks before touching the match to the candle's wick. Once the flame has taken hold she places the candle on the seat of the closet.

And now all is ready, and it is time, and she hears once more a hiss, as of anticipation, as she withdraws the razor from the pocket of her gown. She places the child so that he is lying on the seat beside the candle, and the cloth falls from his face, but the eyes are not open, and he makes no movement. She gazes steadily at him for a moment. The candle seems to flare up, and the inside of the closet is suffused with a red glow; or perhaps the light is coming from inside her. She cannot tell. She takes a deep breath, and then her arm moves, quick, strong, true, and at last the boy moves, his head falling back in a hideous parody of a grin.

She thinks the blood will never come, and a panicked thought occurs to her, that the boy is not dead, so she stabs him in the chest, once, twice, the razor gleaming in the light of the candle. But now the blood is there, rich and red, falling like small flowers which burst open when they touch the floor. The body is still wrapped in the blanket, and Constance pushes it through the hole in the seat, the blanket settling round Saville's form like a shroud. The candle, which has burned low, winks once, and then burns out. *Finis.*

When she leaves the closet all is dark and still. Mr. Hobbes has gone, and she understands now what his business was, and that it is at an end. She goes back into the house the way she came and enters her room, where she realises she is still holding the razor. She cleans it and then examines her nightgown, which has two spots of blood on it, so she washes it carefully in the basin— how pleased her stepmother would be, to see her thus having a care for her clothes—and changes into another, and then climbs into her narrow bed once more, where she joins the rest of the household in peaceful and uninterrupted sleep. It is a sleep from which the others will soon emerge, unaware for a few blessed hours that life has turned from fairy tale to nightmare.

There is no happily ever after.

ᛒᛯ   ᛢᛞ

> I vowed a deadly vengeance, renounced all belief in religion and devoted myself to the Evil Spirit, invoking his aid in my scheme of revenge. . . . From that time I became a demon always seeking to do evil . . .
>
> Constance Kent, in a letter to
> Sir John Eardley Wilmot, 1865

> She said that she had felt herself under the influence of the devil before she committed the murder . . .
>
> Charles Bucknill, alienist, after visiting
> Constance Kent in prison, 1865

STORY NOTES

"The Appointed Time"

First published in *Supernatural Tales 9* (2005)

This story was originally written as a submission to an anthology of stories about haunted bookstores, hence the central idea. I've long been an admirer of the writings of Charles Dickens, and while *Bleak House* is not my favourite of his works, I've always had a weakness for the chapter entitled "The Appointed Time", which contains one of fiction's few scenes of spontaneous human combustion. I could not, alas, figure out a way to work that particular incident into my story; but on re-reading the chapter I was struck with how eerie it is, even before that incident occurs. The initial idea was to use only one or two quotes from Dickens, but as I saw how the chapter progressed, and how it mirrored and echoed the story that was forming in my head, I couldn't resist using just a little bit more. After all, if you're going to borrow the words of another writer, borrow from the best.

ಚ ಚ

"Endless Night"

First published in *Exotic Gothic 2* (Ash-Tree Press, 2008)

When Danel Olson began putting together *Exotic Gothic 2*, he knew that he wanted at least one story from each continent; and knowing of my interest in Arctic and Antarctic exploration, he asked me if I could write something set in the world's most desolate continent. Right from the start I knew that the story would be set during the "golden age" of Antarctic exploration—

the days of Shackleton and Mawson and Amundsen and Scott—
and gradually the idea of an outsider being introduced into a
close-knit group began to work its way around in my head. The
character of Emily is based on my maternal grandmother, Glenna
Grant, a lovely and gracious lady who died in the spring of 2008,
not long after I had written the opening scene in this story; it
made going back to resume the tale a poignant experience.

ஐ   ௐ

"The Palace"

First published in *At Ease with the Dead*
(Ash-Tree Press, 2007)

For several years in the early- to mid-1980s I worked in the
Vancouver hotel industry, mostly on the front desk, and for
eighteen months I worked the graveyard shift. Vancouver was,
in those days, a fairly quiet provincial backwater; how else to
explain a 469-room major airport hotel operating at night with
only three staff members and a security guard? I'd long wanted
to set a story in that environment, and came up with the idea of
moving my hotel close to what's now known as the Downtown
Eastside of Vancouver, an appalling piece of urban blight and
wrecked lives in one of the world's most beautiful and prosperous
cities. One of Canada's worst serial killers operated, unchecked,
in the area for several years, and I drew on details of that case—as
well as details in the case of Peter Sutcliffe, England's "Yorkshire
Ripper"—for my story.

ஐ   ௐ

"Out and Back"

Original to this collection.

My cousin-by-marriage, Sean Lavery, knows of my taste for the
outré, and is always sending me links to weird and wonderful
websites that he thinks I'll enjoy. Some time back he sent me a
link to a site which featured pictures of bizarre playgrounds—
mostly in Eastern Bloc countries—which would, to be frank,

give most children (and many adults) nightmares. Linking to this were other sites featuring photographs of abandoned places and things, and my imagination was fired by pictures taken at Chippewa Lake Park in Medina, Ohio, which opened in 1878 and was abandoned in 1978, with the buildings and rides left to rot where they stood. I've always had a fondness for amusement parks, ever since I was a child visiting Vancouver's Pacific National Exhibition with my father and my brother: an annual trip which was one of the red-letter days on my calendar. The photographs of Chippewa Lake Park were equal parts eerie and sad, for anyone who has ever thrilled to the sights and sounds of a midway, and the story sprang, almost fully-formed, into my head; one of the few times that's happened. Anyone interested in seeing the images of Chippewa Lake Park that inspired the story should visit *http://www.defunctparks.com/parks/OH/ChippewaLake/ chippewa-lake.htm*

℞ ℟

"The Wide, Wide Sea"

First published in *Exotic Gothic* (Ash-Tree Press, 2007)

Several years ago, the Canadian news magazine *Maclean's* ran an article about a new book celebrating the beauty of the Canadian prairies, accompanying it with a photograph, spread across two pages, showing the immensity of the landscape: if I recall it correctly, there was a tiny wooden house and then nothing, as far as the eye could see, apart from grass and wheat and rolling hills. The article mentioned that in the early days of Prairie settlement, some of the women who made the trek across the Atlantic to start a new life in Canada were so overwhelmed by the vastness and emptiness of the Prairies that they literally ran mad with terror; accustomed to life in a small village, surrounded by the familiar and the comforting, they could not cope with their new life, one in which they were an insignificant dot in a pitiless landscape. This image stayed in my head for some time, until Danel Olson asked me if I had a story in me that would be suitable for *Exotic Gothic*. In thinking over what constituted, in my mind, a Gothic tale, I thought of this image from the *Maclean's* article; and thus was "The Wide, Wide Sea" born.

ೞ ೲ

"The Brink of Eternity"

First published in *Poe* (Solaris, 2009)

This story was written for Ellen Datlow's anthology *Poe*, published to celebrate the bicentenary of Poe's birth in 2009. The guidelines were simple: write a story based on a theme found in the works of Poe. Eschewing the obvious—I didn't want to bury anyone alive—I went back to two early Poe stories that are favourites of mine, "MS. Found in a Bottle" and "A Descent into the Maelström". In reading about the stories I was reminded of the "hollow earth" theory of John Cleves Symmes, and Poe's support of it. I have something of a fondness for scientific beliefs that could charitably be called "eccentric", and the idea of combining Poe, Symmes, the hollow earth, and Arctic exploration was well-nigh irresistible. Read no further, if you haven't yet read the story: while many of the people, places, and incidents mentioned in the tale did exist, all quotes—with the exception of two excerpts from Symmes's pamphlet—are from my own imagination.

ೞ ೲ

"Tourist Trap"

First published in *Shadows and Silence* (Ash-Tree Press, 2004)

This is the second supernatural tale I ever wrote, and if it strikes anyone as being faintly reminiscent of the work of the great Terry Lamsley, then they're quite right. While "Tourist Trap" wasn't written until 2000, its genesis came in 1996, when I was typesetting the Ash-Tree Press edition of Terry's collection *Under the Crust*. Many of his stories featured ordinary people stumbling across extraordinary—and unsettling—things in seemingly placid surroundings, and I began thinking of a very ordinary woman who takes what should be a very ordinary trip, and who encounters something that's anything but ordinary. For those who are interested in the writing process, I should mention that the story originally featured another 800 or so words, explaining a good deal about the strange events occurring in the tale. On reflection, however, I realised they explained far too much, and took them out before the story was published; my first lesson, as a writer, that I have to learn to trust the reader.

ಬ ಲ

"Northwest Passage"

First published in *Acquainted with the Night*
(Ash-Tree Press, 2004)

This story is set only a few miles from where I now live, and the cabin where most of the action takes place is one that I know very well. The seeds of the tale were sown during a stay there more than twenty years ago, when my father, looking at the hillside above the cabin, remarked suddenly, "I always feel like there's something up there watching me." I had no idea, at the time, that I would ever be a writer; but this statement stayed with me, until in the summer of 2004 Christopher asked if I'd have a story for our next anthology. I immediately thought of my father's comment, and over the next few weeks began assembling the story, which I sat down and wrote in three days. Its success, once it was let loose on the world, took me completely aback; I had written a story that I was pleased with, and the fact that others thought highly of it too was my first indication that I might have a career as a writer.

ಬ ಲ

"The Hiding Place"

First published in *Strange Tales II*
(Tartarus Press, 2007)

This little story came to me suddenly, in an afternoon, sparked by the idea of a little girl trying to find a safe place to hide, one where she wouldn't be found. Unusually for me, the end came first, and then it was a matter of filling in the blanks, and suggesting how and why she finds this particular hiding place.

ℰ℧ ℭℨ

"After"

Original to this collection.

In the summer of 2008 I read Kate Summerscale's *The Suspicions of Mr. Whicher*, a book-length account of the Kent murder case which shocked England in the summer of 1860. I was familiar with many of the details of the case, which inspired writers such as Wilkie Collins, Mary Elizabeth Braddon, and Charles Dickens, but was fascinated by the wealth of original documents which Summerscale quoted in her book. What I found most fascinating were Constance Kent's comments, in at least two places, that she felt herself possessed; and from those two references the entire story sprang, fully formed. The fact that the Sunday preceding the murder was, in reality, the Feast Day of St. John the Baptist has not, to my knowledge, been commented on by anyone else who has written about the case; I stumbled across the information while doing some research for the story, and even though it was a hot Saturday in July, with the temperature pushing 100° F., I confess I shivered as the full implication of this fact sank in.

ACKNOWLEDGEMENTS

WRITING IS, for the most part, a solitary pursuit. The initial stages of writing a story are (for me, at least) internal, as I wrestle the work into shape; after that it's me, the keyboard, and a screen which I hope starts to fill up with words. Not until I have a story in what I feel is its final form am I willing to share it with anyone, beyond a cursory "It's going well" or "I'm pleased with how it's shaping up."

Writers, however, don't live in a vacuum. Those nearest and dearest are ready with encouragement; editors provide advice and guidance; readers are there with feedback. I write the stories; but a good many people have, over the years, contributed to these tales in one way or another. Three of the stories in the collection benefited immensely from the fine editing of Ellen Datlow and Danel Olson, and my thanks also go to editors John Betancourt, David Longhorn, and Rosalie Parker. Jim Frenkel provided excellent advice and encouragement at a critical moment, while Sean Lavery was instrumental in inspiring one of these stories, via one of the weird and wonderful website links he sends along. Steve Duffy, Jim Rockhill, and Jason Zerrillo have been the best friends a writer could hope for, willing to comment on stories, lend an ear, and be there to talk to. Thank you to Sean Wallace, for making this volume a reality, and to Michael Dirda, for encouraging me to think of myself as a writer, for his friendship, and for writing the kind words that preface this collection.

Last, but certainly not least, my thanks to the people who have known me longest and been unfailing in their support and love over many years. My brother John Hacock and my parents Bill and Heather Hacock have been a constant source of inspiration and encouragement, and have always been certain I had a book in me, even when I doubted it myself. My son Tim is one of my best critics, always eager to hear my latest story when it's hot off the presses; few responses can be more gratifying to a writer than an eleven-year-old sitting silent and wide-eyed while you read, then giving you a bear hug and a heartfelt "That was awesome, Mom; I'm so proud of you." Finally, love and gratitude to my husband Christopher: my best editor, my best adviser, and my best friend. I could not have written this book without him.

This edition of 2,000 trade hardcover copies was printed
by Thomson-Shore, Inc.
on 55# Natures Book Natural
for Prime Books in October 2009.

ALFRED BAUMANN LIBRARY
WEST PATERSON, NJ
Northwest Passages

36591000918298

F ROD
Roden, Barbara.
Northwest passages /
$24.95

DATE DUE

JUN 1 2010	

GAYLORD   PRINTED IN U.S.A.